I0735051

MARY CRAWFORD

Love Claimed

HIDDEN BEAUTY NOVEL 6

COPYRIGHT

© 2016 All rights reserved. No portion of this book may be reproduced in any form or by any electronic or mechanical means including information storage and retrieval systems – except in the case of brief quotations in articles or reviews – without permission in writing from its publisher, Mary Crawford and Diversity Ink Press.

This novel is a work of fiction. Names, characters, businesses, places, events and incidents are either the products of the author's imagination or used in a fictitious manner. Any resemblance to actual persons, living or dead, or actual events is purely coincidental.

All brand names and product names used in this book are trademarks, registered trademarks, or trade names of their respective holders. I'm not associated with any product or vendor in this book.

Published on May 27, 2016, by Diversity Ink Press and Mary Crawford.

ISBN: 978-1-945637-45-2 (Diversity Ink Press)

Cover by Covers Unlimited

HIDDEN BEAUTY SERIES

Until the Stars Fall from the Sky
So the Heart Can Dance
Joy and Tiers
Love Naturally
Love Seasoned
Love Claimed
If You Knew Me (and other silent musings) (novella)
Jude's Song
The Price of Freedom (novella)
Paths Not Taken
Dreams Change (novella)
Heart Wish
Tempting Fate
The Letter
The Power of Will

HIDDEN HEARTS SERIES

Identity of the Heart
Sheltered Hearts
Hearts of Jade
Port in the Storm (novella)
Love is More Than Skin Deep
Tough
Rectify
Pieces (a crossover novel)
Hearts Set Free
Freedom (a crossover novel)
The Long Road to Love (novella)
Love and Injustice (Protection Unit)
Out of Thin Air (Protection Unit)
Soul Scars (Protection Unit)

OTHER WORKS:
The Power of Dictation
Use Your Voice
Vision of the Heart
#AmWriting: A Collection of Letters to Benefit The Wayne
Foundation

DEDICATION

To the people who find the strength to get up and fight their own personal demons every day and win.

Special recognition to those people who still get up and fight after they've been knocked down more times than they can count.

We support you in your battle.

Chapter One

Donda

"Mom, do you realize I'm a sophomore in high school? You don't have to drop me off at basketball camp every morning like I'm a kindergartner. I can take the bus like my friends. You're embarrassing me."

Gabriel's words twist deep in my soul. There is still a part of me that sees him as I did the first day I dropped him off at preschool even though he towers over me. I know he's right. He is a much better child than I deserve, given the upheaval he's been through in his life and the role model I've been for him.

Gabriel's attention is focused on something outside his window so I take a few moments to study my child. It's amazing how much he changes every day. Although people tell me he is the spitting image of me, I just don't see it. I hope he's not. I'm just a tenuous collection of hopes and dreams held together with a few should'ves, could'ves and really-wished-I-hadn'ts. When I look at my son, I see a wonderful mix of my brother and my dad. He has the razor-sharp methodical, curious intellect of my brother. There's nothing that Gabriel can't conquer. He's a spectacular athlete, a National Honor Roll Student and a magnificently creative artist. Although my dad died when I was young, I still remember his quick smile and offbeat sense of humor. I remember standing still by his side as he would struggle to frame the perfect picture or waiting with him as the sun went down so we would have the perfect lighting to capture a drop of rain on a rose petal in my grandma's garden. Gabriel has that same sort of mix of humor and intensity. It's heartbreaking that my dad didn't live long enough to see his grandson grow up. Sometimes, when I like to mentally torture myself, I ponder how my life might have been different if my dad had never died. As fun as it is to think about my dad being around to see Gabriel grow up, the rest of it's just too painful to consider.

As the traffic in front of me slows down for a passing train, I lick my thumb and wipe a smudge of paint off of his face.

"Mom, that's disgusting! Stop it," Gabriel insists, batting my hand away.

"How late did you stay up working on the storyboard for your comic book? You've got paint all over yourself again."

"Mom, newsflash: you've got as much paint on you as I've got on me."

"It's my job, and unlike you, I don't really have anyone to impress today. I told you to get plenty of sleep. Your coach said he doesn't take very many sophomores to play on the varsity team."

"*Relax.* I'll either make it or I won't. Mindy and I

have been practicing an insane amount. That girl is like a drill sergeant if she sets her mind to something. I don't think I've ever thrown so many free throws in my life. I can make them in my sleep now."

"That's good because your coach is a stickler for those —"

Gabriel interrupts me, "Mom, I know you said you aren't trying to impress anybody but, have you noticed that same Beemer follows us to basketball camp every day? I think he's into you."

"How do you know it's the same one? They all look alike."

"For one thing, he has a bumper sticker that says, 'Sarcasm is my closest friend.' I noticed it a while back and I thought it was funny. Secondly, he looks like us. That's uncommon around here, so it kind of stands out."

"I suppose it would. The Willamette Valley is not well known for its racial diversity, especially the small towns. How do you know he isn't just checking out this cool car Denny fixed up? Why do you think he's checking me out?"

"Mom, I'm a guy. I can pretty much tell when people are checking out cars. He wasn't scoping out the car, he was looking at you."

I shake my head at him as I laugh. "Just when I thought you were coping well with the stress of basketball camp, now I find that you're just delusional. Perhaps I should cut back on your workouts, I think they're getting to you. You seem to have lost your ability to think reasonably."

Gabriel turns and grins. "Go ahead, laugh, but the next time we stop at a stop sign, I want you to look over and see if he's looking at you. I bet his eyes are glued to you. If I win, you have to take me to the art store to get more paint, deal?"

"Let's evaluate that risk, shall we?" I tease with a wide grin. "You spend most of your time lost in your computer, drawing or playing basketball. I don't think you have much time to observe the world around you. I think the risk that you're right is pretty low. Most days, I look like some reject from those 'People of Walmart' websites. If, by some off chance, he looked at me on the first day, the likelihood he would ever take a second glance is slim. Given all of those factors, I highly doubt he'll be scoping me out today."

Gabriel's smirks at me. "We'll see. I've got a whole list of new colors I want to get. This will be *epic*."

I chuckle. "I'll take that as the compliment I'm sure you meant it to be instead of a smart-aleck remark."

Gabriel rolls his eyes at me. "I totally meant it as a compliment, Mom. Don't you speak teenager by now?" Gabriel sticks his headphones in and starts to read. His latest obsession is reading books on the art of drawing. We've been scouring secondhand stores across the state to try to find old tomes for him to read. It's been quite an adventure to find books. It's not exactly a popular genre.

As we drive, I think about the last time someone was really attracted to me. To say I've gone through a bit of a dry spell is the understatement of the century. Strictly speaking, my whole life has been one big dry spell. My relationship with Gabriel's dad was a huge mistake.

The only good thing that came out of that relationship was Gabriel. Ricky had it all on paper; he seemed wonderful. He was everything I thought I needed in a guy. He looked stable. He had lots of money to flash around and he made all sorts of promises about how he would be the perfect guy. For a while, he was. He took me out to dinner and to concerts. He never forgot my birthday or our anniversary. The guy was good. He celebrated our one week anniversary together and every month thereafter. He was kind and thoughtful to my dog. Heck, he even bought him presents.

On the surface, it all seemed very stable, but what I didn't realize was that it was all built on marbles. I don't know why I didn't see it all coming apart. If anyone should've seen it, it should have been me. After all, I'm my own alphabet soup of disorders. I have a history of eating disorders, alcoholism, drug addiction, and I'm a survivor of incest. You might've thought I would have been the first one to recognize I had a drug dealer living right under my roof. Yet, somehow I wasn't. I guess I wanted things to work out for Gabriel so much that I overlooked the signs. Eventually, I ended up like every other single mom with a deadbeat dad in the picture — only Gabriel's deadbeat dad ended up going to prison and dying there in a gang fight. I have been unwilling, or unable to trust my judgment since then. Sure, I go out and have a little discrete fun every once in a while, but it's not as often as anyone thinks and it's not nearly as wild as people believe. I can't really blame people though because when you have a past like mine, it's easy to jump to conclusions, even if they are unfair.

I'm still lost in my inner musings when Gabriel taps

me on the knee. "Mom, don't freak out, but he's right beside us."

Instinctively, I whip my head around to look at him.

Gabriel releases a horrified gasp as he slinks down in his seat. "*Mom*," he chastises. "I told you to play it cool — not act like Grandpa at an antique car show. This guy doesn't need to know you're checking him out. That's just rude. Do you even remember how to be a playa'? The game isn't supposed to be visible — at least not at the beginning." I don't even have to be looking at Gabriel to know he's rolling his eyes in total exasperation.

I glance over at my son and I wonder once again how it's possible he's giving me dating advice. It seems like just the other day I was bringing him home from the hospital. Where is the child who cuddled with me while we watched Disney movies or the little boy who needed me to blow on his ouchies before I put a Band-Aid on them? Where is the curious young man who wanted me to read him one hundred and one bedtime stories? I barely recognize this child — the one who once needed me — when I look at my tall, handsome young man who seems to have all the answers.

The sad thing is he's probably spot on. I've completely lost any finesse I once had with guys. I can't even flirt in the produce aisle anymore. I used to have a little something, but the most action I see these days is from the romance novels Madison throws in my direction.

"Right … so how am I supposed to tell if he's looking at me if I can't look at him?" I ask, as I stare straight ahead at the stoplight.

Gabriel sighs heavily as he patiently explains, "Mom, I didn't say you *couldn't* look at him I just didn't want you to gawk like a tourist. A little chill factor would go a long way. You don't give away your game up front."

"Okay, okay I get it. No taking inventory. No ranking him or giving him stars…"

"Mom, I think you're losing focus here, the only goal here was to see if he was looking at you. That's it, no big deal. Think you're ready to handle that?"

I raise my eyebrow at him. "Child-o-Mine, I've been flirting longer than you've been alive, I think I can handle a sideways glance and a few come-hither looks."

"*Eww*. Keep your come-hither looks to yourself and just leave it at sideways glances, okay? You don't want to scare the guy off." Gabriel shudders.

I take a deep breath. It's remarkably disconcerting to see who my matchmaking son thinks is appropriate for me. The last time he tried this maneuver, he was five and thought the sixty-year-old mailman would be a good husband for me — despite the fact that the mailman was already married and had grandkids. I trust that Gabriel's taste is at least marginally better by now.

I risk a brief look over at the car next to me. Gabriel wasn't kidding about the BMW. It's deep charcoal gray — it's not a loud car — but it's still quietly powerful in a solid, sedate kind of way. It's imposing nonetheless. In the past, I have gone for much flashier guys in much flashier cars, but the result was predictable.

For a minute, I thought that I had gotten away with peeking at the neighboring car without being spotted. However, it quickly becomes apparent that I've made a grave miscalculation when the driver catches my eye and gives me a little salute.

Either my son watches me much more carefully than I give him credit for or I wax poetically about men far more frequently than I realize because the man in the car next to me looks like something I could've ordered off a fantasy wish list. His Royal Hotness is apparently old enough to know what he wants in life and how to get there. He obviously takes care of that gorgeous body. When he smiles at me, I literally feel the ground move.

CHAPTER TWO

JAXSON

EVERY MORNING, I LAUGH at my foolishness as I drive clear across town to get coffee at a little obscure coffee shop in the middle of nowhere. Don't get me wrong, the coffee is delicious — but let's be real. I don't go there for the coffee. I go there because every day for the past three weeks, I've been able to see this gorgeous, intriguing woman. I know I'm acting like some lovelorn teenager, but there's just something about the way she carries herself that holds my attention. She is truly striking. Most women are trying so hard these days to attract attention they forget to be real. From what I can tell from Ms. Bold — as I've nicknamed her, being real doesn't seem to bother her. Most of the time, she wears her hair straight, but I've noticed that on Wednesday and Friday mornings, she lets it curl naturally and ties it back with a headband.

A lot of people get frustrated when we get caught by the long freight train on our commute. Ms. Bold just cranks up Michael Jackson or George Michael on the radio and dances in her seat. I can't tell if she really likes this music or if she's just doing it to annoy her son. I'm pretty sure that the kid with her is her child because he is her mini-me right down to her dimples. It seems incongruous that she has a child that age.

This is interesting. It looks like my days of silently observing her are over. I'd wondered how long it would take her to notice that I've been studying her like a lab animal for weeks. I'm feeling a bit like a creepy stalker out of some film noir, but how exactly do you go about meeting someone you've only seen at the railway crossing on your way to the coffee shop? Technically, I could look up her plates, but that would be crossing a few too many ethical boundaries for me.

I check my watch and when I look back up, she's still watching me. This is both fascinating and frustrating, because from this distance, I can't really read the full expression on her face. Just from watching her expressive body language, I suspect her eyes could tell more stories than I can fathom.

I hear an odd sound behind me, and my eyes travel up to my rearview mirror. I force myself to relax once my brain comprehends what I'm seeing. I take a deep breath and exhale. I know bracing myself will only make it worse. I'd give anything to still have my Mustang convertible right about now. At least if I had my convertible, I would be able to warn the other car. I feel absolutely helpless because I know what's going to happen and I can't stop it. Vaguely, I wonder if I left my bag in the back or in my locker. I know better than to do a mental countdown, but my brain does it anyway. All my brain can process is the loud crunching and grinding of metal.

Astonishingly, it appears that my car is completely clear of the wreck and any blowback. I hit the trunk release and run around my car to grab my go-bag. Much to my relief, it's in the trunk where it belongs. I stop by the passenger's side of the cherry red convertible first. The teenage boy is trying to undo his seatbelt but his hands are shaking from adrenaline. I reach over and unfasten it for him. He looks up at me with eyes wide with fear. "Please check on my mom, she looks really hurt."

"I'll get there. I'm going to give you a super quick check on my way over there. You doing okay? Can you see me and hear me? You got any bleeding or bones sticking out anywhere?" I ask. "What's your name? My name is Jaxson. Most folks just call me Jax."

"Dude, no disrespect man, but my mom is *hurt*. I'm fine. We can do all this social stuff later."

"Okay, I'm just checking in with you, that's all. Your mom is next. I promise, I'll take good care of her."

I run around to the other side of the car and unbuckle Ms. Bold's seatbelt. I shout over to the other side of the car, "Son, what's your mom's name?"

"Donda. Donda Whitaker," the kid answers grimly.

I gently shake her shoulder as I prompt, "Donda, are you with us?" As she lifts her head, I notice a serious gash along her hairline. Inexplicably, the other thing I notice is that her eyelashes are impossibly long. I know it has nothing to do with my medical assessment of her, but it's impossible to ignore her beautiful face even though there is blood dripping down her forehead.

Donda blinks slowly. "Hey, aren't you supposed to

be in the other car? Did the Earth really move when I looked at you?"

I can't hide my smile behind the illusion of a professional demeanor when she says that. It's exactly the way I felt when I first saw her and there wasn't even a motor vehicle accident involved.

"I can't address that situation one way or the other but, I can tell you that the Earth moved in part because it had help from a rather large vehicle. I'm just here to help you until the ambulance arrives. I already called for them from my car."

Donda tries to tilt her head up and look around for the other vehicle. "Relax, you have a laceration on your head and you have to wait until someone has cleared you for neck injuries. Don't move around like that, you could do yourself some serious harm. You need to stay still for as long as possible. The only reason we're allowed to move you is if your car is in danger of catching on fire."

Both mother and son look at me with great alarm as they ask, "Is it going to?"

"I don't believe so, but you'll need to go to the hospital. You need some stitches in that knee. Your cut is pretty deep. They'll probably want to do some tests to see how hard the blow was to your head. You'll probably need an MRI or CT scan to rule out internal bleeding."

"Gabriel's basketball tryouts are today. He's supposed to find out whether he makes varsity. This sets him up for college. If he gets on the varsity team as a sophomore, a lot more colleges will look at him seriously for sports scholarships. I have to give him the best chance I possibly can; I need to get him to his practice. He can't be like me. I'm still trying to finish my degree one piddly course at the time. I don't want him to be like me … he just can't be like me."

The boy looks at me with pleading eyes as he responds to his mom, "Mom, I got you covered, okay? If it doesn't happen this year, I've got two more. If basketball doesn't happen, I've got decent grades. If my grades aren't enough, I've got art stuff. We're good. I'll just call Uncle Tyler. He can pick me up from here. You know him; he'll probably take me all the way to practice with lights and sirens on. Go to the hospital and I'll go to practice. I'll meet you back at the hospital when I'm through."

The paramedics arrive and put Donda on a backboard and ask me, "Shepherd, anything we need to be aware of?"

"Negative. I didn't have a chance to get a full set of vitals; I just did a cursory search for acute injuries. Patient was mostly alert and conscious. Although she was a little confused at the start."

"Shepherd? Your name is Shepherd? I thought you said your name was Jaxson?" Gabriel challenges. "What the heck are they talking about? What were you supposed to be examining my mom for?"

"My name *is* Shepherd," I respond. "My name is Dr. Jaxson Shepherd."

"That sucks. I was beginning to like you," responds Gabriel in a dejected voice. "Unfortunately, that means you're toast. My mom hates anyone in the medical field even worse than she hates the guy that used to be my dad. It's been nice knowing you, Jax. Thanks for trying to help us. I've gotta call my uncle and get to basketball practice now."

I have to admit that's a first. I've never been dismissed because I'm a doctor. Usually, people decide I'm their newest, closest friend if they think I'll give them free or discounted care. Never have I been completely written off because of what I do. This will be a very interesting challenge.

CHAPTER THREE

DONDA

MADISON LOOKS AT ME skeptically as I climb the ladder. I can't say I blame her as I wince in pain. "Should you be doing that? Oh, that's right, you don't know because you left the hospital early," she remarks pointedly.

"Of course I did," I snap. "They were just going to suggest I take pain meds and you know my history with all that stuff."

"I *do* know your history." Madison studies me. "That's why I'm concerned. You don't like to ask for help and you can get yourself in trouble that way. That knee doesn't look great. You and I both are stubborn, even when it hurts us. Will you at least let Trevor look at it and make sure it's not infected? He's used to evaluating his pressure sores on his stump — so he might know what's going on with it."

"Geez, you're as much of a mother hen as Gabriel. You would think I had major surgery instead of just a bump," I protest, as I gingerly step back off the ladder.

"Go sell your BS to somebody who's buying. It took

both Tyler and Trevor to pull the metal away from your tire and tow your car back to Denny to get it repaired. That jerk took your entire back quarter panel out. You're lucky you guys weren't hurt worse."

I groan as I respond, "Don't remind me how bad the damages are. I still have to haggle with the insurance company. They're not thrilled with how much we are claiming the car is worth because Denny is not a certified restorer."

Madison smirks. "Can't you sic Jeff on them? What good is it to have a little brother who is a prosecutor if you can't use him as a lethal weapon?"

"Believe me, that's my next step if I can't get them to see things my way soon. If they don't come around, I'll pull out the big guns and call William. William likes me since I helped him redecorate Isabel's reading and craft room for their anniversary. A call from a former Supreme Court Justice might help move a few papers around if they continue to drag their feet."

"Somehow, I don't think you'll need to do that. You're persuasive when you set your mind to something. Speaking of that, how is it going with the bank? Any progress?"

I flop down on Gabriel's favorite beanbag chair and then regret my choice to sit in the low chair as my knee twists awkwardly. "Unfortunately, no. I had to miss my meeting with the bank manager because of the stupid car accident but I don't think it would've made any difference. It sucks big-time when a lifetime of bad choices comes back to bite you in the butt. Let me tell you, bulimia is terrible for your budget and it takes forever for that stuff to go away. Not to mention that my ex used my credit cards to take out cash advances to make drug deals. Even though it's been years, my credit still sucks. If he wasn't already dead, I think I would kill the son-of-a-gun." I pause to think. "You know… on second thought, he wouldn't have been worth the effort.

"I'm sorry, Donda; I wish there was a way to wipe the slate clean and erase all the bad things. You deserve the right to claim your life back from your past."

"It would be nice if it was my turn, wouldn't it? You and Tara got a chance to start over. It always seems like my luck isn't so good." I sigh.

"I don't know, as nearly as I can tell, things seem to be looking up for you guys. From your perspective, they may seem like baby steps but they seem big to me."

"I suppose you're right," I concede.

"Look at all the things that have gone right recently. Gabriel not only made varsity, but he is a starter. That doesn't happen often to a kid his age. I don't know if you know this, but the coach told the sports reporter that Gabriel was one player he keeps an eye on to make national news. Rod is close-mouthed about his beat, but he wanted to let me know about it because it's so unusual for the coach to say anything like that."

"Really? I didn't know."

"It's true. The coach is big on treating his players equally and not promoting one over the other for media coverage."

"You know, it's weird, Gabriel doesn't say much about how it's going on the team. If I ask him how his practices go, I'm likely to get a one-word response like, 'Good.' or 'Long.' Sometimes I wonder where my chatty youngster went. I remember the child who used to tell me all about every collection he's ever had from baseball cards to random seashells. I miss that kid."

"I think every parent goes through that. Even with as young as Lydia Rose is, I already miss some of her baby-ness."

"Do yourself a favor and catch as much as you can on video, I'm sorry I didn't make more videos when Gabriel was a baby. Now that he is a teenager, he won't even let me take his picture."

"Don't worry. Moses, my former cameraman at the news station, already warned me about that. Lydia will be one of the most filmed babies on the planet. Mindy has taken it upon herself to document every state of Lydia's development whether she wants it or not."

I snicker. "Becca's every bit as bright as her sister, she's just not quite as noisy about it. I overheard her tell Mindy, 'Do you think you're Jane Goodall or something? Lydia is not like a chimpanzee. You don't need to make a movie out of everything she does. This isn't National Geographic'."

"Dare I ask you what Mindy's response was?" Madison asks with a laugh.

"That was the funniest part. Mouse got serious and replied, 'No, I think most of her shows were actually for Public Television'."

"Yeah, that is a conversation your brother's children would have for sure. Mindy is not your typical babysitter by any means."

My phone beeps and I almost drop the phone in my rush to answer it. I hope it's the insurance company but much to my surprise, it's a client. I have to catch my breath when I read the text.

When Madison sees my expression, she grabs a bottle of water out of my refrigerator and hands it to me. "Are you okay?"

"I'm fine. But I'm still processing this — I'm not sure if this is good news or bad," I confess.

"What is '*this*'?"

"This gets a little confusing. A while ago, I did a Portland Trail Blazers mural for Kelly Marino from Channel 12, you know the entertainment reporter? She had me do one for her husband's man-cave as a surprise. Apparently her mother-in-law loved it so much that she wants me to decorate her new Bed and Breakfast she's opening. Kelly just asked me if it would be okay if she covers the remodel as a feature story for the TV station. I don't even know what I think about that. I don't even have Claim Your Space officially off the ground yet. I don't know if I'm ready for this."

"It sounds like it would be a great opportunity to get your name out to the public. A home improvement business needs all the word-of-mouth it can get. With a business that's as visual as yours, the chance to put it on TV in the Portland Metro TV market is huge. If you didn't have to pay for that marketing, it would be even better. Congratulations, Donda!"

"I hear what you're saying, but I hope I'm ready. Doing these wall murals for friends and family is one thing, but doing them for the public — that's a whole other thing. What if I really suck and people just aren't saying anything?"

Madison raises an eyebrow. "Do I really strike you as a person who would keep my opinion to myself if I wasn't pleased with your work?"

I think about that for a moment. "No, not really. You had the tile guy come back four times to fix your counters."

"How many rooms in my new house have you done?"

"Four," I answer with a shrug.

"I think you've lost count, my friend. You did both bathrooms, Lydia's nursery, her play room, my office, the kitchen, and then you did Trevor's man-cave. If you had done a bad job, you would've never made it out of the first bathroom."

"I guess I did underestimate how much work I have done for you. Did I bill you for it all?"

"I don't know. You'll have to ask Trevor — my Mr. Forensic Accountant wouldn't let me near the computer when I was sleep deprived after Lydia was born so, he's been handling all the bills."

"I don't think I could give up my independence again. After Gabriel's dad screwed me over, I'm not ever going to let another guy take over my finances."

"That's totally understandable, if I were in your shoes, I would be reluctant to trust anybody too."

My phone beeps again as Kelly asks me about her offer.

I hold my phone up in front of Madison. "What do

you think I should do about this?"

Madison shrugs. "Donda, you're one of the most talented people I know. It really comes down to how much faith you have in yourself. What do you want to do?"

With shaky, sweaty hands that rival anything I had while I was actively using drugs, I carefully type the words, **"Yes, I'd love to accept the job. It would be a pleasure to work with you. Sincerely, Donda Whitaker — Claim Your Space."**

Chapter Four

Jaxson

That was a brutal shift. I wish people would pay attention to the instructions from the doctor after they have surgery. I had to repair sutures on three people today. Why is it so hard for people to be immobile when they are asked to stay still or wear a brace? Don't they understand that they could do permanent damage to themselves by not following instructions? Even though we are orthopedic doctors, we cannot fix everything. I can't wait until this rotation is over and I can have some semblance of a normal schedule. As the new resident, I get yanked in for every oddball shift ever invented.

I have had far too much coffee to go to sleep at this point — not to mention it's in the middle of the afternoon on a Saturday. I guess it would probably be a good idea to work off some energy before I try to sleep. I grab a basketball from the trunk of my car and lace up my sneakers and go to the local park to shoot a few hoops.

I've missed my sixth free throw in a row when a

voice behind me says, "Your left elbow is flaring out." Right before I toss the next one, I tuck my elbow in and the ball drops in without even touching the net.

I turn to the voice and I'm surprised to find that it belongs to a teenager. "Hey, that was a good catch on the body mechanics, I didn't even notice I was doing that. How did you notice?" I ask.

The kid looks at me closely before answering, "Hi, Doc. It really wasn't a big deal. I guess I notice stuff like that because I draw tons of people every day for my comic book characters and something looked off to me."

"Gage, right?" I ask, as I take a second look at the gangly kid.

"Close, it's Gabriel. Thanks for your help the other day," he responds, sticking his hand out for me to shake.

"How's your mom? Did the MRI show any damage to her knee?" I shake his hand.

"As if my mom would stick around a hospital long enough to get an MRI," Gabriel mutters under his breath.

"She didn't get any follow-up care? I thought we sent her in an ambulance?" I ask. I know I'm tired, but I'm not *that* tired. I have been watching his mom for a few weeks. She's hard to forget.

"You did, but she's my mom and the minute her butt hit the gurney at the hospital, she was checking herself out. My Aunt Heather couldn't even make it there before she was calling herself a taxi to get home. I was going to meet her there after basketball tryouts, but she was already home," he explains with a look of frustration.

I try to school my expression so I don't upset him

because as I remember it, her knee looked pretty messed up at the scene of the accident. "How is it doing now?" I inquire.

His scowl says a million words. "*Officially*, I don't really know because she doesn't say much. *But*, as an athlete, I think she did some serious damage — maybe a torn ACL. She seems like she's having some trouble putting weight on it. She'd never admit that. She's making a big show out of pretending everything is fine, but she's my mom and I totally know she's not fine."

"Why doesn't she get it taken care of? The accident wasn't her fault. Insurance should cover it."

A mutinous expression crosses Gabriel's face. "Hear what I'm saying, Doc. My mom doesn't like doctors — and when I say that, I mean she *really* doesn't like doctors. Usually when people dislike doctors that much, they have a solid reason. Reasons I can't tell you because she's my *mom*. Got it?"

My mind just spins with the potential implications of what he is trying to tell me without telling me. I have to hand it to him, not everyone would try to be so discreet. "I appreciate the fact that you're trying to protect your mom. Loyalty means a lot."

"What am I supposed to do? It's just *us*. If I don't watch out for her, who is going to? It's not fair for people to judge my mom for things that happened to her a long time ago. She's worked hard to pull her life back together. It's not her fault that her life has been plagued by one asshole after another."

"What about your dad?" I ask.

"He's *not* in the picture," Gabriel explains. "He's

never been in the picture."

"It's not fair for your mom to exclude him from your life — a boy needs his father."

"Forget it," Gabriel hisses as he picks up his basketball and sweatshirt and walks away. He stops and turns around before continuing, "You know what? For a second, I let myself believe you might be different from all the other jerks my mom has had around, but I should've known better. Everybody's the same. My bad. Have a nice life, Doc. Maybe you won't make the same mistake the next time you meet someone who outclasses you — even if they don't make a fraction of what you make. For the record, my mom has been a single mom almost since the day I was born because she was suckered by a guy like you. My dad was killed in prison. Still want to talk to me about what a good influence my dad would be? Think I'll pass. My mom is doing just fine." He chucks his water bottle at the trashcan and stalks away.

The anger in his voice alerts me to how far out of line my words were. After a stunned moment of indecision, I jog after him and place my hand on his shoulder. "Stop, please," I command.

He shrugs my hand off his shoulder, but stops and turns around.

"That was a faulty assumption for me to make. I come with my own baggage and I shouldn't unload it on you. I was married when I was in college and my ex-wife kept my daughter from me. She got all wrapped up in drugs and played custody games with me. Instead of taking care of Jasmine, she left her in the car so she could get high and Jasmine died. I was home that day. I could've watched her. I don't know if I'll ever get over that. I'm sorry if I took that out on you."

"Doc, I'm sorry. Drugs suck. They're the reason my dad was killed in prison, the reason my mom won't stay in the hospital long enough to get a stupid x-ray on her knee and they're the reason I'll never see you again. You seem like a cool enough dude. I hope you find what you're looking for. I'm sorry drugs ruined your life too."

Before I can process everything he just told me, Gabriel stalks away again.

Crap! Why can't I ever walk away from a puzzle? Nothing bothers me more than unfinished business.

I jog to catch up with him again. "Gabriel, wait. Our conversation wasn't done."

"Trust me. It's done," he answers cryptically. "It's too bad too. I wanted to like you."

I rub my throbbing left eye, trying to stave off the migraine that's been threatening to emerge for the last seven hours. "Look, I've worked the better part of sixteen hours and I'm exhausted. Can we stop talking in code and just pretend we didn't? What are you talking about?"

"I'm no snitch," Gabriel answers defiantly.

"This conversation never happened," I vow.

"I'm only doing this because I'm worried about my mom. I think her knee is janky. She needs help."

"Fair enough. What does that have to do with whether I'll be around?"

Gabriel sighs deeply. "I'm afraid that once you know the whole story about my mom, you'll never see her through the same eyes again. It'll be like looking at your ex-wife every day. That's not fair to you or to my mom."

Gabriel's words are like a punch to my gut. "Your mom's a drug addict?" The words spill out of my mouth before I can stop them.

I wish life had a rewind button. Gabriel looks so disappointed in me. I wish I could reach out and give him a hug.

"For what it's worth, my mom has her ten year chip and two more — but it sounds like you've already decided about her. I don't know why I'm wasting my time trying to explain the eff'n crap that my mom's been through — and before you lecture me about my language, there is no other way to put it. My step-grandfather is in jail for sexually abusing her when she was a kid and my other granddad died when she was a little girl. My mom can't look at a single bite of food without mentally calculating the number of calories in every speck. She still managed to stay out of the hospital even though my grandma almost died of cancer a couple of years ago. Many people look at my mom and see a pathetic loser, but I look at her and see the strongest woman I've ever met. If you've got a different opinion, you can just keep it to yourself. I gotta go." He scoops the basketball off the asphalt.

"Gabriel," I call after him, "Can I at least have your cell phone number?"

"What's the point, Dr. Shepherd? Are you ever going to see *me* or are you only going to see the son of a drug addict?"

Since I can't answer the question with any degree

of certainty, I remain silent and watch the remarkable young man walk away and think about the full extent of what I may have just allowed to slip through my fingers.

CHAPTER FIVE

DONDA

I LEAN ON THE big industrial cart at the hardware store as Gabriel helps me load paint. The size and scale of Mrs. Pennington's job is overwhelming. It seemed like a good idea in theory, but as my little garage fills up with building supplies, I'm starting to wonder if I've bitten off more than I can chew. The fact that my knee feels like it's on fire doesn't help anything. Gabriel brings over a five gallon bucket of joint compound and slams it onto the cart as he comments, "Do you ever think it might be nice to have a guy around the house?"

His question catches me off guard. It's just been the two of us for as long as I can remember and Gabriel usually relishes his role as my guardian and protector from all things bad. Still, my first coherent thought is *only every other darn day*.

"Sure, especially when I have to clean out the gutters every fall, why?" I answer sarcastically.

"No, Mom, seriously. Don't you get tired of doing it all yourself?"

I look around for a place to sit and there really isn't one so, I respond, "It sounds like we need to have a conversation that's a little more serious than is appropriate for the sheetrock aisle. What do you say we go out for breakfast?"

"I can't. The coach called for an extra practice because half the guys missed their free throws at the last game," Gabriel answers glumly.

"Another extra practice? Isn't that the fourth one this week? When does the coach expect you guys to study?"

Gabriel shrugs. "It's a good thing I am a fast reader. Don't worry, Mom, I'm keeping my grades up. I know the stats on athletic injuries. I don't have all my eggs in one basket. Speaking of injuries, have you gone to the doctor to get your knee checked out? It's not getting better. I can tell."

"If I can't get the swelling to go down by next week, I'll see what I can do."

"Mom, if you don't go soon, I'll have to take time off from school to drive you to the doctor. You know I will, right?" Gabriel threatens.

"No, don't do that!" I argue. "You've got AP classes now. If you take time off, it might mess up your prep."

"If you don't want me to take you, go with one of the Girlfriend Posse or something. Just get it checked out. There has to be something they can do that has nothing to do with pain medication."

"Gabriel, it's not your job to worry about me so much. You've got school, sports and presumably some semblance of a social life." I throw my hands up in the air. Sometimes, he forgets which one of us is the parent.

"Mom, if you won't worry about yourself, one of us has to. You were an athlete — you know your injury is serious. If you don't take care of it, it'll be permanent. You can't look around at our friends and family and say it's worth the risk of a permanent disability."

"I hate it when you're right. I can't even argue with you. It's been so long since I've been to the doctor, I don't even know who to go see."

"You could check with Aunt Kiera I'm sure she knows a few orthopedic doctors. Call her … please?"

"Since you so effectively twisted my arm, I promise I'll call," I reply.

"This century?" my son counters.

"Yes, smart-aleck, I will call next week."

"I'm not sure if you guys are amazing or absolutely crazy. I can't believe the whole Girlfriend Posse showed up to take me to the doctor."

Heather laughs. "Didn't we warn you at the beginning that this is what we do?"

"I suppose you did, but I didn't think you were serious," I respond, as I look around and see the whole group there, including my mom.

"After beating lung cancer, nobody knows better than I do how scary it is to go to the doctor by yourself. We wanted to make sure you didn't have to face this alone."

"I think it's safe to say I'm not alone." I snicker, as I look at the crowd of five women around me.

"Don't look at me," Madison responds as she picks up a toy off the floor for Lydia. "I'm just here as an excuse to get out of the house. I have a serious case of Sesame Street brain."

At that moment, baby Charlie belches loudly and Kiera blushes. "No comment."

"I think I can only have one of you with me, the doctor might object to the whole gang. Who wants to volunteer to face the music with me?"

Madison reaches out to catch Lydia who tripped over Kiera's diaper bag. "Normally, I would volunteer myself because I take impeccable notes. However, my hands are full of noisy baby at the moment. It should be Tara because, as a dancer, she knows the most about rehabbing the knee."

I nod. "That makes perfect sense. Tara, do you want to go back with me?"

"That's fine. I've seen enough of those plastic 3-D models. I could probably walk the doctors through their paces. I'll be your fact checker."

⸺⸺◆⸺⸺

I always forget what a spooky chick Tara is until she studies me closely and advises, "Donda, stop focusing on the feel of the paper on the back of your legs, this is not like before. You are an adult and in control of this visit."

"I will never figure out how in the world you do that. I wasn't even sure why I feel like I'm sitting on a pile of fiber glass, but you're exactly right. Every time I set foot in a doctor's office, it's like every ounce of power I've ever had is taken away from me. Someone is always telling me everything about me is wrong: I'm too skinny, I don't try hard enough, I'm weak, and everything that's ever happened to me must somehow be my fault. Intellectually, I know that's probably not what they're saying, but that's what it always feels like."

"That's not what you're here for today. What you are here for today is to figure out ways to make your knee feel better. To do that, we need to figure out what's wrong. Your only task today is to allow the doctor to examine your knee and to be open to hearing the doctor's recommendations about a treatment plan. That's it. You don't even have to decide today whether you're going to follow her advice. You just need to hear what that advice is and ask questions, if you have any. No one will make you do anything you don't want to do," Tara advises softly.

"I love how you make me not sound like I'm a crazy person for failing to get help sooner," I blurt self-consciously.

"Donda, there was a time in my life when I was much less functional. You didn't know me then. I could barely stand to make eye contact with anyone and avoided touching people or leaving my apartment. That was the way I dealt with conflict in my life. Obviously, I did not choose the healthiest path at first."

"Tara, I know you've told me this before, but I can't wrap my brain around that image of you. Look at you. You've got your dance school, you go on tour with Aidan

O'Brien who, oh by the way, happens to be your hot rock star *husband* and to top it all off, you're stunningly gorgeous. Is there anything you can't do?"

Tara flashes me a tight smile before she responds, "There's a lot I can't do. If you don't believe me, just ask the Girlfriend Posse. I can't cook to save my life, anything to do with filing taxes confuses me beyond all recognition, and don't ask me to play video games beyond the difficulty level of Pac-Man."

"No, I'm talking about the serious stuff. Do you ever feel like you can't cope, like your past is going to swallow you?"

"Not as often as I once did. Every once in a while, it sneaks up on me. If someone crowds me in an elevator or I hear someone with a particular tone of voice say something that sounds like my attacker, I'll have a flashback that brings me to my knees. Sometimes, it's a smell or a general sense of foreboding that makes me feel like I need to run from my life. Fortunately, Aidan knows to watch for that stuff. If I'm not sleeping or eating right, he'll be the first to notice my distress — sometimes even before I do. I'll be so caught up in the minutia of my life I don't notice that my patterns have changed, but he will. If it happens, I need to stop and deal with what's going on."

"How?" I practically breathe the question with my soul. "How do you even start to let someone get that close to you?"

Tara reaches over and grips my hands with hers as she responds with intensity in her eyes, "One breath at a time. There are no shortcuts, no magic pills; it just takes one brave breath at a time. Inch by inch, person by person, relationship by relationship and your little world gets built."

"I'm not sure I'm strong enough for that," I admit, wiping away tears.

"I think you are. If you look around, your world building has already begun. You've already got five amazing women in your inner circle ready to fight with you."

———•———

"Mom, I thought the doctor told you to stay off of that knee for a while," Gabriel chastises when he sees me try to pick up a book of wallpaper samples.

"She told me I need to strengthen my quadriceps," I argue defensively.

"Mom!" Gabriel rolls his eyes. "You know she meant for you to do that under the care of the physical therapist in a supervised setting, preferably in hydrotherapy while taking some Advil or something. Pre-patellar bursitis isn't anything to mess around with."

"Have you been spying on me or something?"

"Nope," he answers smugly, "you forgot that behind Little Bit, I'm Aunt Tara's favorite of all the nieces and nephews."

"You know, she's not so little anymore. Mindy skipped another grade this year. She's in the eighth grade now," I remark.

"That's nice, Mom. She's so smart. I'm surprised she hasn't gotten her doctorate by now. Stop trying to change the subject. Go! Do you want to lie on the couch or in your bed?" he asks in a tone which suggests that he won't allow me to weasel my way out of resting. I'd argue with him except my knee is absolutely killing me.

"I guess I'll sit up on the couch because I need to work on the bid for the Pennington job."

"Great, I'll bring your books over. Do you want the Coleman & Sons too?"

"No, she ruled them out on her last consult."

"I'm carb loading today. Do you want some whole-wheat pasta?" Gabriel offers as he plumps the pillows on the couch and put an ice pack on the coffee table.

I stumble as I try to maneuver in the small space with my crutches Gabriel handed me to use. "Are you sure these are any safer? I was doing just fine hopping around on one leg," I assert.

"Yeah, just fine until you lose your balance and fall with all your weight on your bad leg," Gabriel points out as he takes the crutches away from me after I sit down on the couch. "Boy, you sure are grumpy when people try to help you. I'd hate to see what you're like if you dislike someone."

CHAPTER SIX

JAXSON

I no more than put my foot into the hydrotherapy tub when my cell phone goes off. *Crap*! I think these muscle spasms in my back are going to be a permanent thing. I knew better than to help Mr. Huxley into bed by myself. The man has to weigh five hundred pounds on a skinny day. Since it's the ring tone of the answering service, I know I need to answer it. I grab the towel I left sitting at the edge of the tub and dry my foot off as I grab my cell phone and dial into the service.

My favorite operator is on call and I can tell she's amused as she gives me the message, "Jax, this falls into my too-weird-to-be-anything-but-true file. Out of respect for you, I'm not even going to put it on the bulletin board," she snickers before continuing, "but this is strange, even by your standards."

"Lorena, come on let me have it; it's been a long day," I reply as I do some neck rolls to loosen up the perpetually tight knots in my back.

"Promise me you'll cut the kid some slack, he sounds like my little brother did after he wrecked the car," she replies.

"Lorena —" I threaten.

"Okay, one Gabriel Enrique Whitaker called for you at 3:27 PM."

"Oh no, I hope everything's all right with his mom. Did he say what he wanted?" I press.

"No, he indicated that the nature of his call was personal — but not 'that kind' of personal. He also said to tell you it was rather urgent that you call him back as soon as you could. When I pressed him for more details, he told me he couldn't comment. I've sent the phone number to your contacts if you want to call him back."

"What did you tell him I'd do?" I ask, as I mull over the ramifications of the phone call in my head.

"That was the strange thing. I didn't get a chance to tell him much of anything. He hung up after I told him I would page you. I wasn't able to give him a timeframe or anything."

"Thank you, Lorena," I respond as I disconnect the phone call.

I'm not sure which potential patient I'm most worried about, Gabriel or Donda. They both carry their own brand of complications, but strangely enough, I'm looking forward to the prospect of contacting either one of them — or both. The circumstances are highly unusual — but I guess the only way I'll figure it out is to call Gabriel back.

I head back to my office and gingerly lower my body into the antique leather office chair that used to belong to my grandfather who was an optometrist back in the day. After I punch the number into my cellphone, I wait for it to ring and try to play a mental game with myself and guess what the issue might be before Gabriel answers. I suppose I should really dock myself points for wildly wrong guesses.

"'Lo," comes a low growl from the other end of the phone.

"Gabriel?" I clarify, making sure I have the right person. "This is Dr. Shepherd. What can I help you with?"

"Hi, Doc. Thanks for calling me back. I'm sorry I was kind of rude," he greets.

"Not a problem, it's not like you don't have some good points," I answer, still curious as to the reason for today's call. "You had to hustle a bit to get a hold of my answering service so what's going on? Is it your mom?"

"No, she went to the doctor, and she's actually getting help now. She's got bursitis or something going on. That's sort of why I called. I know that you know your stuff about cars and my family is out of town celebrating my grandma's wedding anniversary… um… I guess I should ask you if you're busy first," he asks in a rush.

"No, not really. I'm good," I declare in a bold-face-lie. What's a few more hours without sleep?

"Thank God. Can you meet me at Lancaster and Center about seven?"

"You want me to meet you in Salem? Why?" I ask. I didn't get the feeling that the kid was going to shake me down for money when we first met, but now I'm not so sure.

"Like I said, there's nobody here because everybody went to Grandma and Grandpa's party and I've been watching Grandpa's car auction sites since my mom's accident because we're looking for a rear corner panel for her car. Anyway, I've been planning to surprise my mom. She's all worried because I'm sixteen now but she doesn't have money for my car because she's putting it into her new business. She has no idea how well my comic books and YouTube channel have been doing. She doesn't follow my stuff much. I've shown her my YouTube channel and everything, but she doesn't know I have sponsors and followers. They ran a fifteen-second spot of mine on the Cartoon Network about three months ago. I didn't tell anybody because I didn't believe they were going to pay me any bank for it, but they did. So, I found a car on the auction site. If it's everything the guy says it is, it's a good deal. I don't want to check it out by myself — even though I've got cash."

"Gabriel, I don't want to freak you out but you just gave me a ton of scary information. If I would've been a bad guy, I could've used all that stuff against you," I caution.

"Jax, if you had been a bad guy, I would've never told you any of that stuff. I would've never called you in the first place. I'm pretty good at this, I've been watching after my mom for a really long time. By the time you followed us for the third day in a row, Uncle Tyler had already run your plates."

Instinctively, I whistle between my teeth. "Oh-kay," drawing the word out. "Interesting approach, impressive, a little creepy… but still impressive. Gotta hand it to you, if your mom was my sister, I'd want somebody like you watching out for her."

"Thanks, but I didn't really go into full-out-creeper-mode. If I would've put my Uncle Trevor on the case and he would have done a forensic autopsy of your bank accounts — *that* would've crossed the line into creepy."

I let out a disbelieving laugh. "Yes … yes, it would. I would've had nothing to hide. I'm a broke college grad with thousands and thousands of dollars worth of student debt. I'll probably be retired before I pay all of my loans off."

"That's why I'm busting my butt to get all the scholarships I can. I don't want to worry my mom. She's afraid I'll be like her and not finish my college degree. I keep telling her I have two or three routes to college, but she's afraid to believe me. She's sure I'm going to end up in community college like she did. I told her that my pre-SAT scores alone are high enough to give me a full ride scholarship to state college. I would like to go to one of the Ivy leagues if I can. I have to wait until next year to take the official SAT because my mom wants me to make sure I've taken as many AP classes as I can get under my belt before I take the real deal."

"If you're making all these long-range plans with her, why aren't you including her in your scheme to get a car?"

"I don't know; she's weird about that. I don't know if it's because her dad died or because she's in competition with my Uncle Jeff over everything or maybe she misses my dad and just won't tell me. I've tried to figure it out but I can't. The whole family is so close there's nobody I can ask without hurting somebody's feelings. If I ask my grandma, then I'm poking around somebody's old ghosts. If I ask my Uncle Jeff, it highlights the fact that they don't always get along so well."

"Didn't you say your Uncle Tyrone is a cop or something?"

"Uncle Tyrone? That's funny … it's Uncle Tyler. Yes, Uncle Tyler is an officer with the Sheriffs Department. My mom doesn't want him to teach me to drive because she's afraid that he'll teach me evasive driving stuff from the police academy. She thinks if I learn to drive from him, I'll be a less safe driver. That logic doesn't make any sense, but I can't talk her out of it."

"What about the other uncle, the one who's an accountant? Doesn't she think he would be safe?"

"Probably not. Uncle Trevor served with Uncle Tyler in the Army. In case you haven't guessed, my mom is a little bit of a worrywart when it comes to me."

"Let me get this straight. What you're asking me to do is go car shopping with you without your mother's knowledge or permission when your mother worries about every little microscopic detail and is probably predisposed to dislike me anyway because: a.) I am a man and b.) I am a doctor — a profession she loathes above all others? Have I summed that up about right?"

Gabriel gives a hoot of laughter from the other end

of the phone. "Yep, that about sums it up, except you forgot the part where you're so broke you can't even afford to buy a nice dinner. That ought to charm her immensely as well."

I chuckle. "By all means, let's not forget to add that to my sterling resume. You never know when a woman is absolutely dying to date somebody who is completely dead broke."

"At least you're upfront about it. I can't tell you the number of creeps who approach my mom online. Most of them pretend to be rich when they probably don't have enough money in their pockets to buy a Happy Meal. I got so tired of screening out the scum for her, I built a filter into her web browser to filter out the words oil, Baron and gold. You wouldn't believe how many instant messages that weeds out. If I filter those out, plus the ones that send her unsolicited penis pictures, it saves her three hundred messages a week."

"Really? What in the world is your mom wearing in her profile picture?"

"Would you believe it's just a blue suit that my grandma got her for Easter? It was nothing revealing, gross or sexy — that's the sick part. If my mom knew all the stuff that goes on behind the scenes, she would probably completely freak. She put nanny software on my computer when I was eleven, but she didn't realize that I was already programming my computer with more powerful stuff than she was using. So, I took that stuff off and strengthened it and put it back on to make the computer a safer place for her to use. She was so afraid my pedo-freak step-grandfather could contact her via social media from prison she wouldn't even go online. So, I fixed it."

I resist the urge to look at my watch. I learned in medical school if someone is freely telling you a story, take the time to listen to everything they're telling you and all the things they're not. Something tells me that Gabriel doesn't have a lot of people in his life he feels comfortable unloading to. He has taken on a ton of responsibility for a kid his age. I'm trying to remember what I was like at sixteen. Sure, I worried about my mom and sister — what big brother doesn't? Though realistically, my biggest challenge was trying to come up with money to go to the movies and buy CDs with my friends. I can't imagine the pressure of trying to figure out how to protect my mom from sexual predators online.

"Tell me again why you need me to go with you to this car sale? You've done more research on this guy than the FBI. It sounds like you probably know all there is to know about the car, car safety and finances. Why do you need me?"

"You're one of the few people ever to take me seriously even though I'm only sixteen. Usually, when people see my height, they just believe all I'm capable of doing is playing sports. It turns out I'm good at them. I have talent because of genetics but also because I study the mathematics of making shots. There's a reason I hide behind computers. If I'm behind the keyboard, people don't know I'm young. They treat me as if I'm an adult. If they want to think that, I don't do much to change their minds, but I don't want to commit a crime."

"Basically, what you're telling me is that I'm your shill bidder?"

"Geez! It sucks that you and my mom probably won't get along," Gabriel exclaims. "Do you know how few people know what shill means, never mind how to use it in a sentence?"

I chuckle, as I respond, "Your mom has dated some real winners in the past, huh?"

"There was a guy she dated for four months who couldn't seem to remember my name. He called me Lil Buddy. He called my mom Sugar Cup — you wanna talk about creepy? *That* guy was creepy. So, are you in? I just want to see if this car is anything like the guy described in the pictures. I probably won't even buy it tonight. My grandpa always tells me that if I see a good deal, I need to act while the iron is hot. I think I need to check this one out to see if it's real," Gabriel explains.

"I guess I can go with you to look. I wouldn't feel comfortable buying it without your mom being involved in the decision. Buying your first car is a huge deal. A lot of people plan for stuff like this for months and months. It's a rite of passage. Your mom won't have too many of those left before you go to college, let's not take that away from her."

"I see your point," Gabriel allows. "Let's get all the legwork done ahead of time so that my mom doesn't have to stress out about it. She's already wigged out about having to fix her own car; I don't want her to have to worry about a new car too. If we have all of that figured out, it would be much better."

"I'll see you in about forty-five minutes. I hope this

move doesn't completely backfire. Your mom could completely hate me for this. You know that, right?"

I can hear Gabriel sigh as he considers my statement, but he gives a dry laugh as he advises, "Look at it this way, she is already not going to be your biggest fan, so you don't have far to fall."

⸻ ●●● ⸻

As I sit in my car, absentmindedly drumming my fingers to Michael Jackson's *The Way You Make Me Feel*, the song is a poignant reminder about the complete injustice of life. Because of the impact of drugs in our lives, I'm taking a complete stranger's child shopping for his first car instead of my own. There is a message in there somewhere, but I'm too tired to figure it out. Never did I think that I'd be doing this for somebody other than Jasmine. I always figured that I would help her get her learning permit and be the one to take her to an empty parking lot somewhere and teach her where the gas pedal is and how to use her parking brake. Knowing my mom, she would've probably had a neighborhood block party complete with Michael Jackson music playing in the background on all sorts of eighties boomboxes so she could take pictures of the occasion and document it for the whole world to see. Given the opportunity, Yvette Shepherd would invite anyone and everyone to see the whole event unfold on VHS tape over, and over, and over again as many times as you would sit and watch it. I'm crushed every day that my mom was robbed of the opportunity to watch her granddaughter grow up. I still remember how excited she was at just the thought of being able to be involved in her life. Mom was already planning to teach her Brownie troop how to make crochet friendship bracelets. Sadly, my daughter died before she could even learn to tie a knot.

Before I can sink even further into my morose thoughts, I see a tall figure screech to a halt on a skateboard next to me. He knocks on my window and says in a winded voice, "Sorry I'm a little late, I miscalculated and got off a couple of stops too early. As nearly as I can tell from Google maps, I think the guy has the car about three blocks from here. If you don't mind my skateboard, I can hop in your car and we can drive or we can just walk from here."

"Up to you — the seller might decide you can pay more if he get's a look at mine." I reason.

"Good point, Doc. I think he's close. Would it be okay to hoof it from here?"

"Let's go before I remember how tired I am," I tease.

"Oh come on, you look in great shape for an old man. How old are you anyway?" Gabriel asks me giving me the once over.

"Old enough to know better than to tell you how old I am," I answer with a smirk. "Besides, didn't your Uncle Tyler tell you when he ran my background check?"

"Unfortunately he wouldn't tell me anything other than you have a remarkably clean criminal background check except for your fondness for getting parking tickets — but my Uncle Tyler can totally relate to that. He has the same issue. He told me not to worry because it shows you're a busy man with too many places to be," Gabriel explains.

"I'm a busy man. I swear they put those parking meters around all the places where residents have to go to meetings. The senior residents know, so they keep us in meetings for precisely three minutes longer than the meters run just so they can see the look of terror on our faces when we run out to make sure that our meters are still good. I think they like to see us turn green with nausea."

I swerve to get around a kid on a bike as Gabriel asks another question, "Aren't you a little old to be going to college?"

"I guess I'll tell you the story. It sounds as if you won't be satisfied until you know the whole thing. Although, I rarely go around telling the long saga to the entire world."

"You sound like my mom when she tells people about her whole life story. It takes about a week and half for her to tell somebody the whole thing," Gabriel says with a laugh.

"I'll let your mom decide what she wants to share with me, okay? Anyway, in answer to your question, I will be thirty-seven," I answer.

"That's even a couple years older than I was going to guess. How long have you been in college, anyway?"

"Aren't you a wise ass?" I reply with a scowl. "You're right though; it seems like forever. My undergraduate career was interrupted by life a couple of times. I started late and then I had to deal with Jasmine's death. So, life happened and here I am just now in my residency program."

Suddenly Gabriel stops and points. "Look, there it

is! Doesn't it look great?"

I look over at the gleaming Volvo sitting in the driveway. It looks great all right, almost too great. "What year is this supposed to be again?" I ask.

"The guy said it's a 2010. It barely has any miles on the odometer. It has way less than the other cars I was looking at."

I can think of a bunch of reasons, but I don't share my suspicions with him yet. The guy's garage door is open so Gabriel goes to catch his attention. While he does that, I lie down in the driveway and slide my head under the frame of the car as I take a look underneath. That tells me everything I need to know. I quickly stand back up and take a look at the back license plate number.

The guy comes out of his garage wearing a Hawaiian shirt and a barbecue apron, looking every bit the guy next door. I have to decide how I'll give Gabriel a heads-up without having a chance to talk to him privately first. Thinking quickly, I extend my hand and say, "Hello, it's nice to meet you. My name is Null Shill."

At first, Gabriel gives me a puzzled, blank-faced expression but then comprehension dawns; he nods tightly as disappointment settles over his face. He turns to the gentleman. "I didn't bring the ad with me, can you remind me about your car?"

"Oh, this beauty? She was my wife's car. She hardly ever drove it. Pretty much only to her nail appointments and to church. We were together forty-seven years, God bless her soul. Now I have no use for her car so I need to sell it. You know, my wife can't drive her car from the pearly gates. So, I'd like to see it go to a better home," he explains with the saddest puppy dog eyes I've ever seen.

"Where is your car registered?"

"It's got Oregon plates," he responds, pointing to pristine plates.

"Ever been registered anywhere else?" I ask.

"Nope, me and my missus, we didn't travel much. We were kinda homebodies. We would just go down to the bingo hall at the lodge once a week for the steak dinner — you know the money goes to charity."

"I'm sorry, Sir, could I get a bottle of water from you?" Gabriel requests. "I took my allergy medicine a little while ago and I tried to take it dry. It feels stuck in my throat."

"Sure, you want the fizzy stuff or plain?" he offers.

"Plain is fine, thanks," Gabriel swallows hard.

"Be back in a jiffy."

As soon as he's out of earshot and back inside the garage, Gabriel turns and hisses, "What gives, *Null*?"

I escort him over to the side of the car blocked from view of the house and squat down. I motion him to look under it. "See the rust and paint blisters? That tells me that this car has been around salt on the road a bunch. The water marks on the hubs tells me it's been standing in flood water a while," I whisper quietly. "It's hard to tell exactly when the damage was done, it could be from Super Storm Sandy for all we know. Oregon does not use rock salt on the roads, so it's not likely a local car, despite what the tags say."

"Crap, I thought it was a tight deal too," complains Gabriel with a sigh.

I pat him on the shoulder. "I know; somewhere out there is the perfect car for you, but I don't think this is it."

"Wait, are you trying to talk him out of buying my car? There's nothing wrong with my car!" the guy lies as he pulls a small cooler behind him and parks it at my feet. "I was being nice and bringing your son drinks and everything."

"That was very kind of you. However, you might have better luck selling your vehicle if you were honest with people about where it came from and what its true value is. It's obvious that this vehicle has sustained some water damage and been exposed to salt on the road. It didn't happen in Oregon," I answer, pointing to the underside of the car.

"Oh, I get it now. You guys are all the same. You're some sorta hustlers trying to trick me out of my car. People like you are all the same. I don't want your money anyway — it's probably from pimping or drugs," the guy huffs indignantly.

Gabriel is studying pictures on his phone. Finally he looks up at the gentleman and says, "If you're going to use stock pictures for the inside of your car, you might want to at least use images from the right model and year. The sad thing is that I wanted to believe you were one of the good guys and planned to help me get my first car. I didn't realize you were just a jerk."

"Watch your back, Boy, I've got guns to put holes in people like you. All your kind is good for is target practice —"

Instinctively, I put my arm around Gabriel and steer

him back toward the car. After I remind him to put his seatbelt on, he finally asks me in a low shaky voice, "Why does that still happen? This is 2016. We've had a black president for nearly two terms. I thought this garbage was supposed to be over. You're a doctor and I was going to pay him cash, not from drug money, but from money I earned illustrating my own comic book series from an internet site I designed — starting from when I was about eight years old. Exactly how successful do we have to be before people start looking beyond the color of our skin and judging us for the people who we really are?"

"I don't know, Gabriel," I answer thoughtfully. "I don't think people who are prone to that much vitriol and prejudice are going to listen to logic and persuasion. The two just don't seem to go together."

"That was just whacked and a whole lot scary. I know I'll be watching over my shoulder when I take the bus home tonight," Gabriel remarks, as he shivers.

"That's precisely why you're not taking the bus. Tonight, you're getting door to door escort service because there are a bunch of crazy freaks in the world."

CHAPTER SEVEN

DONDA

"Where's that son of mine?" I mumble to myself as I'm precariously perched on the top of the ladder, trying to remove the battery from the screeching smoke alarm. Much to my dismay, removing the battery doesn't stop the thoroughly annoying sound. It's then I remember that I elected to install the upgraded model in this house to help protect Gabriel in the event of the catastrophic. Right now, I'm thoroughly regretting my decision. Of course, I *know* how to disengage the hard-wired kind. I just don't have my tools on me and I barely made it up the ladder this time.

My frustration is about to reach a boiling point. Gabriel didn't tell me he was going anywhere. The last I knew, he was studying for tests. He's been so busy with basketball practice, I'm afraid his grades may suffer. I know I'm being paranoid, but everything is hanging in the balance with Gabriel's future. I haven't been able to save anything for his college fund. It's almost as if he has to shoulder all the responsibility himself. I know that it's not fair, but it seems to be our reality right now. Instantly, I feel bad begrudging his ability to get out of the house to do something fun. He could've gone down the street to get some ice cream for all I know. I'm probably just overreacting, but it's still frustrating that he's not here to help me.

Even as I have that thought, I kick myself for my own selfishness. Gabriel is always helping me — he does everything from helping me grocery shop every week, cooking on the nights I have class at the community college to more traditional 'guy' tasks like mowing the lawn. He has even stepped up to do a sizable chunk of work involved with my new business, Claim Your Space.

My heart races with instinctual fear as I see headlights shine through the front window. I grip the ladder a little tighter as my knees wobble. I try to hold very still as I see the deadbolt turn.

I can't hear a thing over the screeching of the smoke alarm, but I can see my son throw up his arms in frustration as he sees me up on the ladder. He shakes his head in dismay. I can read his lips. "Mom, I can't believe you."

Just when I think I can't be more humiliated, someone steps out from behind Gabriel. Turns out it's not just any someone, it's Beemer Guy. Of course, I look like a refugee from skid row while the man looks like he could've just walked off of some editorial fashion shoot somewhere. He looks flat-out drool-worthy. As gorgeous as he is, nothing explains what he's doing with my son.

Before I can ponder the answer to that, my knee buckles again and pain shoots from my mid-shin all the way up through my hip. Vaguely, I think to myself that it's going to hurt when I pass out from the pain and fall all the way to the ground. That's probably why my doctor told me not to climb ladders; but it's too late now to talk my stubborn butt out of doing what I just did. I try to hold on as I sway wildly. Unfortunately, I'm not even able to call out to Gabriel for help because he's busy running out of the living room toward the garage.

Just as I crumble toward the ground, I land in a set of phenomenally solid arms and against a chest that would make a bodybuilder proud.

My knee screams in protest at the abrupt movement and I wince in pain. My rescuer leans down and whispers against my temple, "Take a moment and try to breathe through it. I know it hurts, but it will pass."

That voice. Deep, like James Earl Jones and oh-so-sexy. It's soothing to my core; it makes me want to forget all of my troubles, including that annoying torture device disguised as a must-have safety feature. What does it do — set itself off until all the homeowners move out of their homes permanently?

When the alarm is finally extinguished, it is almost eerily silent. Although my ears are still ringing, I can now hear the water dripping in the kitchen sink. I absentmindedly wonder how Gabriel managed to turn the alarm off without having to disconnect it from the wiring in the house, yet it's difficult to puzzle through the problem effectively when I'm distracted by the feeling of being in Beemer Guy's arms.

Suddenly, I'm a little embarrassed. I am not a small woman. I am tall and athletic. I run — well, I used to run.

Now I don't do squat — it's really frustrating. I'm sure I'm going to start putting on weight here in a New-York-minute. I definitely don't need to put on any extra weight. However, whether I weigh one hundred and twenty-five pounds or I'm pushing one hundred and sixty, it's not easy to hold onto my long lanky frame. Finally I find my voice. "Um, don't you think you should put me down? There's a couch in the den."

"I can put you down, I suppose; but you feel just a little too comfortable in my arms. Perhaps I consider this a perk of rescuing damsels in distress."

I bristle a little at his comment. "Do I really look like some hopeless bimbo who needs rescuing?" I huff indignantly.

Beemer Guy's eyes widen slightly. "Why do I get the feeling there is no good answer to that question?"

I'm so focused on the conversation I don't even realize that he has carried me through our house to the den. He gently deposits me on the couch and quickly arranges pillows under my knee. I'm impressed when he is able to put it at the perfect angle and he takes the time to make sure that my ankle is supported. He unzips the side of my workout pants and examines my knee. Part of me is taken aback by his forthright manner but another part is just relieved not to have to make one more decision in my life.

The scowl on his face is intense as he gently examines my knee. "Have you been staying off of this? Your swelling is quite marked. Is your therapy progressing well? Have you been completing your at-home exercises?"

"Who died and made you a doctor?" I snap, embarrassed that he has caught me not following through with my rehab like I should.

"Actually, I did go to Oregon Health Sciences University with some help of an endowment. Technically I suppose somewhere along the line someone died," he quips.

"Gabriel Enrique Whitaker, what in the blazes are you up to?" I bellow, incensed at my son for allowing this interloper to invade our privacy.

He comes down the stairs holding his iPad with his ever-present earbuds in his ears. He looks into the den with trepidation and asks, "Need something?"

"Gabriel Whitaker, what is the commonly accepted practice in this household if you bring guests over?" I inquire sternly.

"I'm supposed to introduce them to you by name and I'm supposed to use your formal name and not just call you Mom," he repeats the mantra as if he's answered my question a dozen times.

"Why is that?" I prompt.

"So you know who my friends are and can keep me safe?" he recites my often-repeated safety rules.

"Gabriel, do I *know* this person?" I demand sharply.

"Not exactly, but you know of him. Uncle Tyler knows all about him and he's probably told Uncle Jeff. Uncle Jeff probably told everybody else, just to keep you safe. You know how they are," Gabriel explains with a shrug.

"Gabriel, I don't even know him and you left me

alone in the room with him — why would you do that?"

"I don't know; you guys seemed to have great chemistry. I figured I'd leave you guys alone so you could see what would develop. You said he was cute and had a nice smile. I thought that sounded like a pretty good beginning at least — usually you don't even notice that much."

"Gabriel, that's ludicrous. I don't know this guy from Adam. He could be a serial killer for all I know."

"Mom, I was careful. I know he's not a serial killer. You should give him a chance. He's a really good guy. He's nice and super smart. I mean, Mom — the guy knows how to use the word 'shill' correctly in a sentence. Shouldn't he at least get bonus points for that?"

I try to draw Gabriel over to the side of the couch so I can have a more private conversation with him. Beemer Guy seems to notice because he picks up his cellphone and says, "I received a message from my answering service and I need to check it, so I'm going to go outside for a moment; I'll be right back."

I smile weakly at him as I look down at my leg all propped up on the pillows and joke, "Take your time, I don't think I'm going anywhere."

Once he's outside, I turn to Gabriel and unload, "All right, no messing around here, exactly how long have you known he was a doctor? I mean, I assume you know his full name and credit history. I'm going to also guess you know exactly where he's from and you probably know his Internet browsing habits and his favorite kind of deodorant by now?"

Gabriel puts his hands up and protest. "Geez,

Mom, I was just trying to protect you. You were oblivious to the fact that anybody was even following us. I thought Uncle Tyler gave you a class in self-protection. I had Uncle Tyler run his plates just to make sure he wasn't some creeper stalking you. It turns out he's a doctor who goes on a coffee break. He also happens to think you're smoking hot. Lucky for you, he's single, if you're interested. I'm not telling you what to do here … but mom, if you're smart — be interested. The dude is totally cool. He treats me like a regular human being and doesn't try to talk down to me and he isn't creeped out that I'm smart and artistic."

"If he's so great, why is he still single?" I challenge, brushing my bangs out of my eyes.

"I don't know if this is a conversation you should be having with me. It's probably something you need to talk about with him. Just my opinion, but people who are smart and complex often have tangled backgrounds. Before you decide to write him off, maybe you should listen to his story too. Don't just judge him by what he does for a job."

"Gabriel, do you think I'd be shallow enough I'd decide not to talk to somebody just because of what they do for a job?" I ask, slightly amazed at my son's perception of me.

"Can you honestly tell me you wouldn't?" Gabriel challenges.

"That's pretty harsh," I complain, stung by his words.

"I don't mean to be, Mom. I just want you to give this guy a chance."

Chapter Eight

Jaxson

As I PACE UP and down the sidewalk in front of Donda's house, I'm mentally kicking myself. If there's a laundry list of terrible ways to handle things, I've ticked off every single option. Now I have to figure out a way to untangle the mess I've made. Unfortunately, I don't have a lot of time to do that. Sometimes, being a doctor can leave you with inconvenient timing issues when you try to match them up with real life.

Giving my lower back one last stretch before I stand up and head to the front door, I try to organize my thoughts into some coherent order before I approach what I suspect will be a tense situation.

I don't even have time to fully ring the doorbell before the door is yanked open and Gabriel asks me, "Were you planning to stand out there all day? My mom wants to talk to you."

I can't contain my low, wry laugh. "I imagine she does. I'd be shocked if she didn't."

By force of habit, I pull up an ottoman beside

Donda so she doesn't have to strain her neck to see me. "Sorry about that, it was the hospital. I've been called in on an emergency, so I don't have long to talk. I want to take a moment to formally introduce myself, since I've forgotten to do so in all the excitement both times we've had encounters. My name is Jaxson Shepherd and I'm honored to meet you and your son."

"Jackson, like Michael Jackson?" Donda asks, "I think you look more like Michael Jordan."

"Sadly, I don't have Michael Jordan's talent. I haven't played ball since college and even though I was on the team, my most prominent role was as a benchwarmer. My mom was a huge Michael Jackson fan, but I spell mine with an x."

"My son tells me you're a doctor, but I'm not supposed to be upset," she remarks with a hint of dark humor.

"Listen, I'm not going to tell you what to be upset about," I reply, "Quite frankly, at the moment, my job isn't doing it for me either. I'd much rather be able to fix us both something nice to eat and talk about anything and everything interesting, but I don't have the luxury. I've got to go help repair someone's leg. He had an unfortunate accident with a piece of farming equipment."

"What are you doing standing around, talking to me then? Go!" Donda instructs, waving me away.

"I wish it were that simple, but it'll take them nearly an hour to extract him and twenty minutes to transport. I've still got enough time to make introductions and hopefully to persuade you to go out to dinner with me.

Unfortunately, I'm on call this weekend, but would next Tuesday work?"

"Would Tuesday work for what?" she asks with confusion in her voice.

"I know it's been a while since I've done this, but I thought I just asked you out for dinner."

"I suppose you did. It's been a long time since I've been asked, I guess. It's just my luck I finally found someone to ask me out on a real date and I can't even go dancing," she mutters to herself.

"Your knee won't be injured forever, so I can give you a rain check. Do you think you'll be able to handle dinner?"

"Do you mind if we do it here and have a teenager present? I learned my lesson the hard way trying to go to Mom's anniversary party. I think I should be a little more of a homebody for a little while."

"No problem, is there anything you absolutely hate to eat?"

"I'm just not fond of frou-frou food and stuff that crawls around on my plate," she answers, grimacing.

"What a coincidence, neither am I. This should work out great. I'll see you on Tuesday and I will be bearing edible gifts."

"Wait," she calls after me, "You never explained why you decided to follow me all those weeks."

"Donda, there is no short answer. That conversation is going to take longer than I have at the moment. Can we talk about it when I see you next week?" I suggest.

Donda rolls her eyes and me. "It must be a guy thing. Gabriel does the same thing with his graphic novels. Don't you guys know I have absolutely no patience to wait for the answer?"

"There is nothing I'd like better than to stick around to tell you the whole story, but unfortunately duty calls, so I'll see you next week. Promise me you'll take care of yourself, okay?"

As I'm waiting for my order of barbecue ribs to be ready, this young flirty thing comes up and notices the I.D. badge clipped to my belt loop. I can see the dollar signs appear in her eyeballs like a cartoon character as soon as she realizes I'm a doctor. Her game sharpens exponentially as I go from being merely a random cute guy to a potential paycheck in the bank. I laugh silently as I contemplate what a joke that is. It will be so long before I'm actually operating in the black if we were to get together, we would probably have grandchildren before she would have the spare cash to buy one of those fancy purses she has strewn so carelessly at her feet. My sister, Jordan, is an executive assistant to one of those big name designers in New York, so I have some vague idea about the value of the satchel the woman is carrying her wallet around in.

To my shock, she reaches up and pulls down on my tie until my head is within her reach. She strokes her hands across the top of my head and exclaims, "Mmm, this is so sexy! Who cuts your hair? I volunteer to do it. I think it's so romantic to do that."

Instinctively, I stand up, practically dragging her off her impossibly high heels as I challenge, "Do I know you?"

"No, but I wish you did. My name is Vivian, and I've been waiting my whole life for a guy like you,"

"Have you really? You don't even know anything about me," I state blandly, walking away to check on my order.

"Honey, I don't have to know anything about you — other than you're hot, you're a doctor and you're black. You know what they say about black men in bed …" she trails off suggestively.

It's all I can do to not roll my eyes in disgust. She acts like I haven't heard that stereotype a million times since before I hit puberty.

She rushes to stand between me and my order as she tries to stuff her phone number in the pocket of my scrubs.

I've been here often enough the manager just reaches around her and hands me my order as he declares, "You better hurry Jax, you don't want to get a ticket."

By the time I make it back to my car, I feel like I need a shower in more ways than one. At first, I found it frustrating Donda wasn't interested in me because I'm a doctor, but I realize the alternative scenario could be so much worse. Shaking my head, I realize it's the second time this week someone has made gross assumptions about me which simply aren't true. I am really batting a thousand. I hope the rest of my day turns out better.

As I get on the freeway and turn up my stereo, I let

the music wash over me. I wonder if Donda really likes Michael Jackson and George Michael or if she listens to it to bother Gabriel. Although come to think of it, Gabriel didn't look too bothered by the whole exchange. I'm thrilled to learn Donda loves to dance. Dancing is a great way to burn off stress from working such long hours. I don't claim to be great at it, but I do have a great deal of fun. If she can put up with me, I'm game.

I glance down at the clock radio and realize I'm only about five minutes from her house. I don't remember falling victim to my nerves in forever. I think I was probably in the seventh grade and picking up Janata Green for our class roller-skating party the last time I felt this mixed up and out of sorts.

I ponder the wisdom of calling my mom for advice, but I soon think better of it because I knew if I let her know anything about Donda, I would never hear the end of it. She would be planning weddings for our grandchildren by the time I finished having a simple conversation with her about how nervous I am before our first date. It hardly seems worth the effort for some dating tips. I'm on my own for this one. As I look down at the way I'm dressed, I conclude it probably is a good thing my mom isn't around to see me. If she was, I would get an ear full. I wanted an opportunity to go home and change my clothes, but it simply didn't happen. My Chief wanted me to go observe a complicated compound fracture repair. The poor kid was a mess after he slammed his skateboard into a granite sign. It took a while to stabilize and set the fracture because there were so many small pieces which had to be put together like a puzzle. When the plastic surgeon was brought in to make sure the nerves were attached correctly, they had me stay even longer to watch him make the nerve repair. I got out of surgery far later than I'd planned. I'm showing up for a date in generic blue scrubs — not terribly impressive, especially for someone who doesn't particularly care for doctors. It's not my brightest move, but I had to decide whether it was better to be even later than I had planned or to take the time to dress up. I figured it would be better to be almost close to being on time than to be dressed like a fashion model, but still jeans and a sweater would've been preferable.

I'm surprised when Gabriel opens the door and secrets me inside as if I'm not supposed to be there. He pulls me into the alcove and whispers urgently, "Doc, proceed with caution. Mom had a bad day. Apparently, physical therapy was murder today and her knee is killing her. She's not feeling much joy right about now. If she bites your head off, try not to take it personally. I just try to stay out of her line of fire when she's like this. I swear, my mom is usually pretty chill."

I can't disguise my grin as I respond, "It's all right; I deal with surly patients all day. I'm used to it."

"This isn't like her at all. I wish I could make her feel better."

"It will get better, knee injuries just take some time."

"Why are the two of you over there whispering like school girls? I thought we were going to eat," Donda shouts from inside the house.

"Coming!" I answer, as I round the corner with my arms loaded with bags of food. "I hope you guys are hungry. I might've gone a little overboard, but when I go into Adam's Smokehouse I can't seem to stop myself. I want to order everything on the menu because everything smells so delicious."

"I love that place," Donda responds. "Did you happen to get any barbecue chicken? It is the bomb. He puts herbs under the skin and it's to-die-for."

Gabriel peeks into the bags. "Is this the place where the beef ribs are the size of Fred Flintstone's?"

Donda sighs with contentment. "You got it in one. I guess I gotta hand it to you, Beemer Guy, you've got good taste in food."

"Beemer Guy?" I question with a grin. "I guess I don't have much room to talk, my nickname for you before I met you was Ms. Bold."

Donda gives me a look of surprise. "My nickname was kinda obvious, but what's up with yours?"

"I dunno, it's just something about the way you always carry yourself. You always seem to be confident about the way you present yourself in life."

"You can tell all this from ten-seconds at the stop sign?" she answers with a chuckle.

"Don't forget the four and a half minutes every day we seemed to always be caught by the train. Most people would be cranky and throw a fit every time they get caught but you use it to throw yourself a little mini concert and I think that is the best attitude ever. You never seem to worry about whether people saw your joy in the moment and I love it. I started calling you 'Miss Bold' because I appreciate your approach to life."

Donda groans. "I can't believe you paid so much

attention to me. Most mornings, I look like I got dressed in the leftovers Goodwill rejected. On the mornings after I go to my night class, I don't even have time to do my hair because I'm too tired. This is so embarrassing."

"You look absolutely gorgeous. It doesn't matter whether you do your hair or not. You don't put on layers and layers of artificial garbage. I find you adorably sexy. I don't want to have to find the real you. I love that you don't pretend to be something you're not. Don't get me wrong, I love it when women dress up to the nines to go out, but you don't have to put on all that stuff every day to impress me. I like seeing the real you."

Donda openly scoffs at me. "Come on, you're a guy. You can't possibly know anything about this. Where do you come off telling me how to dress or not to dress? I have to say, I resent it. You have no idea what we go through or the judgments we face every day. If we decide to dress up, we're sluts, if we decide not to dress up, we don't care enough about ourselves enough to even try. There's no way we win. It's just a really weird place to be. You don't know how hard it is to even get up and open the front door to step out of the house. It takes major courage."

"I didn't mean to offend you. I know it's tough. I have a little sister. Jordan has told me more than most because she works in the fashion industry. She's an assistant to one of those high-level designers who works on fashion row in New York. She has more grizzly tales than most about what it takes to be on the top in an industry which judges you by every move you make and by every ounce of fat on your body. Women can be really mean to each other. Honestly, I was trying to tell you I find you absolutely captivating and a refreshing change from what I usually see. I think you're absolutely stunning and you've done a remarkable job as a mother. I think that's beautiful too."

Donda is stunned into silence for a moment. "I didn't get a chance to ask you about Gabriel because of your work situation, but how is it that you had so much time to spend with my son the other day?"

"The answer is both quite simple and very complex. The simple answer is your son asked me for help. He reached out to me for some expertise and I could provide it to him. The other answer is a little more complex."

"Doc, it's okay, you can tell her about the car. I told her about what we did," Gabriel supplies helpfully.

"I guess you already have the simple answer as to why I was hanging out with Gabriel. He wanted me to help him evaluate the quality of the car he was looking to buy. He figured since I own a BMW, I might be able to help him evaluate the Volvo he was looking at. I'm not an appraiser by any means, but I had some helpful knowledge for him," I explain.

"I guess the part of this I still don't understand is why he would turn to you of all people. He doesn't know you from Adam. Why wouldn't he turn to one of the family members?"

"Mom, don't take my decision out on him. I didn't want to bug anybody from the family because everybody was so busy with Grandma and Grandpa's anniversary party," Gabriel explains, as he tries to save me from the awkward moment. "Besides, I wanted to see how we got along. I didn't want it to be a repeat of the guy who never even bothered to learn my name after he dated you for four or five months."

Donda smirks. "He was quite a prize, wasn't he? I'm not even sure he managed to learn my name either."

Gabriel suddenly stands up and grabs his backpack. "Mom, I need to give Tori my biology notes and we have a test coming up. Can I go run them over to her house? We should work on our speech for English class anyway."

"Don't be out too late, it's a school night. Tori's mom doesn't like her to have company later than eight thirty. Take your cellphone," she instructs.

"Later, Mom. Have a good time. Don't eat all the good food — I'm sure I'll be starving when I get home," Gabriel predicts, as he heads out the door.

"Your son is one great kid."

"True enough. I can't say I'm thrilled about the two of you conspiring behind my back."

"You raise a fair point. I overstepped my bounds. I apologize," I admit, as I bring Donda a plate of food. "I stopped and got some organic lemonade because it just seems lemonade goes with ribs. Ribs always remind me of summer barbecues."

"You know, what's funny. I haven't remembered this in years, but my dad — my real one, Don — he was a firefighter and he believed kids should have a healthy respect for fire. He would allow me to help him light the barbecue — with lots of help of course. My dad, he was the life of the party, so he always had people over for some reason or another, and a few weeks before he died, he decided I was grown up enough to light the barbecue on my own. I remember how mature I felt to have received such an honor."

"It's so great you have wonderful memories of your dad. I don't have any memories of my dad. He was long gone before I had any conscious memory of him. Most of my fond memories have to do with my grandparents. My grand-pop was an optometrist. My mom says when I was little, I used to go with him after hours when he used to write in patient files and clean all the equipment. She says I used to pretend to be a doctor; I don't remember any of this but she has a vivid memory of it and a couple of blurry Polaroids to prove her point."

"The fact that you were raised by a single mom gives someone like me real hope. I always wonder how much Gabriel misses in his life by just having me. Every once in a while, I'll panic and go on a dating flurry. You can tell by his comments how well that turns out for us sometimes. It's hard to know how to juggle it all. I don't want bad influences in his life, but I don't want him to have no one besides me in his life either."

"I know you don't know me well, but I've spent time with your son and a couple of things are clear. Obviously he does not lack for positive role models in his life. He was openly talking to me — let me correct that — bragging about his cousins and his aunts and uncles and his grandparents. Most importantly, he told me, without any prompting, that you were the strongest woman he's ever known and if I had a different opinion of you, I could basically take my opinion and shove it. I don't think you have to worry about your son thinking any less of you or your family because his dad isn't around."

"I worry that he feels like he has to be my protector all the time. I hate that he feels that way. I wish I was stronger. I'd give anything to take back all those years when I was weak and fought to hold it together," Donda confesses as she wipes away a tear with the back of her hand. "Who am I kidding? I'm still struggling to hold it together every day. I think Gabriel senses this and that's why he works so hard to fight my battles for me."

"There could be some of that involved, but it also could be because he's a naturally mature kid. When Jordan was in college, she worked as a nanny for six-year-old twins. I swear the one kid, Zoe, is going to grow up to be an environmental activist. The first time my sister took them to the zoo, Zoe had a complete meltdown. She wanted to let every animal out of its enclosure. She sat down on the ground and refused to move because the zoo employees were being mean to the animals. On the other hand, Oliver's only missions were to feed a giraffe and play on the giant slide. He couldn't care less about social injustice or anything else except playing outside and getting dirty. They are just two very different children. Even if you would've had the stereotypically perfect family, complete with white picket fences and the ideal relationship, there's no guarantee Gabriel wouldn't still have the same kind of personality prone to shoulder responsibilities. The only difference is he would have two people to look after instead of just one."

The corner of Donda's mouth quirks up as she looks at me with a twinkle in her eyes. "You're awfully good at this pep talk stuff. It's tempting to keep you around. I could use more of that in my life. Do they teach you that in medical school?"

"No, actually they don't. They tried to drum it out of me in medical school. This is a skill I learned straight from the knee of Yvette Shepherd. My mom gives the best pep talks on the whole planet. It's really a sight to see. My basketball coach in high school called her a secret weapon. He would bring her in at halftime to rally us to give us a shot at coming from behind. You'd be surprised how often it worked. My mom is incredibly inspiring. I'd love for you to get a chance to meet her," I remark, but then I flush as I realize how presumptuous that sounds.

Donda picks up on my embarrassment and she laughs. "Don't you think it's a little too early in our relationship for me to be meeting your mother since this is only our first date? I don't even know if you're allergic to my cat."

"I didn't mean it that way, but it's never a bad time to meet my mom. Although, she can be a bit overwhelming and persistent. You might find your refrigerator suddenly full of homemade preserves and chess pie at random times, but in my book, that's not necessarily a bad thing."

"You're kidding! My mom makes chess pie too. She says it used to be one of my dad's favorites. When I look at people and tell them about chess pie, they look at me like I'm nuts. It's not a common pie around here like it is in the South. How did your family end up here?"

"I mentioned my grandfather was an optometrist. For a while, I guess he was hoping to go to ophthalmology school. He decided that he wanted to be part of the Casey Eye Institute up at OHSU, but before he could start classes, my uncle got sick and my grandpa decided he couldn't take on any more expenses. We moved from Georgia to Oregon and he set up a practice in Hillsboro. He ran it there until he sold his practice in ninety-four."

"What does he do with his time now?" Donda asks softly.

"Sadly, both of my grandparents died within a couple of weeks of each other in 2010, but I will never forget what outstanding people they were."

"It's amazing how much impact some people have on our lives. You know, my mom had a cancer scare recently; I don't know what I'd do without her. The whole thing scared me to death. It really brought home the fact that if something were to happen, Gabriel would be all alone in the world," Donda admits with a sad shrug. "It's hard for me to believe he's sixteen years old and I'm still doing this alone. I never, in my wildest dreams, thought I'd still be single after all these years. I feel like a gigantic, pathetic loser. Do you know he is giving me dating advice? How sad is that?"

"This, I have to hear," I respond with a chuckle. "What is your son's sage dating advice?"

"I'm still not sure you guys aren't in total collusion with this — but his unsolicited dating advice maintains I should totally put aside all of my preconceptions about dating and life and I should give you a chance to prove yourself because you are a 'totally cool dude'. Presumably, for reasons I can't figure out, your coolness factor has something to do with your shared fondness for obscure words. I haven't quite figured out how it calculates into your coolness factor but, apparently it raises it exponentially high."

"Are you going to follow your — admittedly bright — son's advice?"

Donda gives me a mischievous grin. "I suppose so, as near as I can tell, there isn't really a downside. You're very easy on the eyes, you have above average taste in food, my son apparently thinks you're the best thing since Oreo cookies and you're a fun conversationalist. The only thing more I could wish for is for you to be a world-class kisser, and for the sake of argument, I'll assume that you are."

"I can't have that. You know I'm a logical doctor, I like to have things shown to me by empirical proof." I stand up from the ottoman and lean over her.

Her eyes widen and she licks her lips. "Is that so?"

"Yes, I don't like to rely on assumptions," I whisper before I brush my lips across hers in a soft kiss.

Donda raises her hands and captures my face between them as she pulls me closer, deepening the kiss. She lets out a sigh before she announces, "That was better than I imagined; you better go before I forget I'm supposed to be resting this stupid knee. I know we planned a rain check for dancing; can we expand it to include other things as well? I have quite a wish list."

At first, I'm surprised by her forthrightness, but then again, I didn't nickname her Ms. Bold for nothing. Collecting my wildly galloping thoughts, I smile. "Sure, I'm adaptable. I will call you when I know what my schedule is for next week. They haven't updated the surgery rotation yet. I had a great time tonight, I hope you know Gabriel is not the only truly awesome Whitaker in this family."

CHAPTER NINE

DONDA

I'M READY TO TOSS my stupid laptop across the room. It is impossible to work this way. I don't know how my sister-in-law, Kiera does it every single day. I needed to get to work on this project two weeks ago. What a joke! I needed to be much further along six weeks ago. Mrs. Pennington felt sorry for me and gave me a break, but her schedule marches along even if I can't.

It's not that my friends and family haven't made a valiant effort, because they have. My mom has taken time away from her floral shop to help Mrs. Pennington choose colors and themes for her bed-and-breakfast and Denny, my new step-dad has even volunteered to go over and do some minor repair, take off old wallpaper and remove the old floor coverings. Even Madison tried to help. It's fair to say that Madison does not have her sister Heather's sense of style or color. Heather owns Joy and Tiers bakery and makes the most amazing cakes with an incredible sense of color and design; unfortunately, it seems Madison did not inherent that ability. However, as a journalist, she has been helpful in helping me source the most economically sound suppliers with the best business records. What all my friends and family *cannot* help me do is plan and paint all the decorative murals on the walls. I need to do that part by myself. Even though Gabriel has tried to help me by making 3-D renderings of every single room by programming them into the computer so I can make sketches from them to scale, it's not the same thing as being able to stand in the room and visualize my work. I guess I'm a bit of a dinosaur that way but I can't really translate what I see on the screen to the paper without being able to stand in the room and look at it myself.

Unfortunately, I'm just not able to safely navigate the stairs yet. I've been working on trying to climb stairs in physical therapy, but it's just too painful. I am so frustrated with my progress in physical therapy I could just scream. I am an athlete; I should be able to do far better than I'm doing. Why can't I get this one part of my body to behave?

As I think about it, my brain goes to very dangerous places. Places I haven't been in years. You know, those places which tell you that you've been down to seventy-five pounds and got there all by yourself without any help from anyone else. Maybe you could do that again and show everyone how much control you have. Or the places in the dark recesses of your brain that tell you that maybe it wouldn't be so bad to ask the doctor for some strong pain medicine. If you had drugs, you could climb the stairs and get the job done so you could feel like you're worth something again.

I shake my head to clear my destructive thoughts and pull out my phone. I frantically try to remember if Jaxson said he had surgery this afternoon. Taking the risk that I might sound stupid, I decide to go ahead and text Jaxson; consequences of sliding backwards are just too high. During our many late-night phone conversations, he keeps telling me that if I need anything to let him know. I hope he means it, because today, I really need someone. I suppose I could reach out to my family again, but I feel like all they ever do is rebuild me, as if I am some never-ending game of Jenga or something. Sure, it's fun the first few times you do it, but after you've repaired the damage over and over again, it stops being fun and starts being a tedious chore. I feel like my family has reached that point with me. I don't want to face the disappointment in their eyes one more time. Oddly, I'm more comfortable reaching out to Jaxson, so I hope he wasn't kidding about being there.

With shaking hands, I pick up my cell phone and send Jaxson a simple text message. "If you have a sec — need to talk. Rough day."

I put my phone back in my armband and hobble back over to the kitchen counter to get an ice cold drink of water; I am surprised how much I wish it was something else. It's odd because I haven't had a craving for alcohol for several years; I can't believe I'm letting the stress get to me this much, but for some reason it is. After I take a long drink, I set my glass in the kitchen sink and head over to the curio case that used to be my grandmother's. I pull out the sobriety chips I display there. For a moment, I let the weight of them settle in my hands. Ironically, they feel heavier than they actually are; perhaps it's because of the struggle I went through to earn them. They are worth much more than the materials from which they are made. I feel a wave of guilt wash over me as I think about all I would give up if I were to give in to those urges. With new resolve, I decide this is not the first time I felt this way, and it certainly will not be the last. I didn't earn the chips for nothing. I know what I need to do. I've just been feeling complacent in my recovery.

I gingerly walk over to the sideboard and pick up my purse and keys, but as I do so, my phone rings from my carrier on my arm. Since I am alone in the house, the sound startles me and I about fall over as I jump several inches off the ground at the unexpected noise.

After I catch my breath, I answer the phone, "Hello, this is Donda from Claim Your Space."

"Donda, this is Jax. Is everything okay? I got your message. I've got about ten minutes now, but I should be off in a few hours. My whole evening is yours," he offers.

"Oh, I was just being stupid. I am having a tough time right now because I'm feeling really claustrophobic. I'm used to being able to be up and around helping other people do things like grocery shop and get the laundry. Now that the shoe is on the other foot so to speak, I'm not sure how to cope. It's wearing on me and makes me feel very trapped. I just need to get out of the house. I don't know if you can relate to this, but I need to talk to somebody to get some balance back in my life. Gabriel is at a sports retreat over break and even if he wasn't, I'm not in any great state of mind to talk to him anyway. I'm not feeling very parental right now," I trail off fearing I sound like I have completely lost it. He's going to think I'm a total basket case now, I just know it.

After a minute goes by without getting a response

from Jaxson, I figure I have completely blown it, so I say, "I don't know what I was thinking. I really shouldn't bother you at work, I'm sorry. I'll just deal with it on my own."

"Donda, that's not it at all. I was just sending an email to a colleague to make sure that my evening rounds are covered so I can spend the evening with you. The only other thing I had planned for this evening was an evening session with the hydrotherapy tubs to treat a nagging back injury. I don't suppose you would like to join me? I know it's not the most conventional of dates, but it's quiet and private and we both could use some relaxation."

"You would do that for me?" I ask incredulously.

"Of course I would. Sharing your pain, physical or otherwise, is good between friends. It's the sign of a healthy relationship, right?"

"I always heard it was the ability to clean up puke without puking yourself, but that's just me," I answer with a chuckle.

"Trust me, as a doctor, I'm not underestimating the value of that skill either. But tonight, I think I'd rather just listen," Jaxson responds, humor clear in his voice. "I don't get off until five thirty, but I should be able to make it to your house by about six fifteen. Does that work for you?"

I swallow hard. "Yeah, I think it does. I'll see you then. By the way, Jaxson, I appreciate this, more than you know."

As soon as I swipe my phone to end the call, I sink back into the cushions of the couch and start to shake; I've either done the smartest thing I've done in a while, or I've done the most absolutely insane thing under the sun.

Eventually, I pick up my phone and dial Tara's number.

When she picks up, I unceremoniously engage in random word vomit as I confide, "Tara, I hope you're not busy at the moment, but I could really use a big favor. I don't want the whole Girlfriend Posse, but if you have a little bit of time, I could use a friend."

"Actually, I'd like to get out of here. It drives me crazy to sit around and watch everyone dance and not be able to teach the kids to dance," admits Tara.

"Why aren't you dancing?" I ask, puzzled.

Tara is quiet for a moment before she finally breathes deeply and answers in a shaky voice, "Aidan and I weren't really planning on telling very many people because the family is so close, but since you asked directly – we are trying to get pregnant and it's not going so well. I don't know if it's because of my past sexual trauma or because I waited so long to try but we've had to resort to infertility treatments. Right now my ovaries are super stimulated on hormones and feel like they're about the size of softballs, so my doctor doesn't want me to be active and around flying feet and elbows."

I flinch as she paints a verbal picture of the situation. It's one I'm glad I'm not faced with at the moment. "I don't blame you, that sounds extremely painful," I concede. "Are you sure you're up to helping me? I'm not the kind of girl who considers shopping a relaxing hobby, and I didn't think you were either."

"You know, it's funny. Hanging out with Heather and

your mother has somehow changed my mind. I think I've moved over to the dark side of consumerism. Count me in. What's on the agenda for today?" Tara asks.

"Would you believe I need to buy a bathing suit?" I reply.

"Man, don't make it hard or anything! A bathing suit in December — that'll be a piece of cake," Tara teases dryly.

"I told you, I don't really do this stuff. If I get new clothes, my mom usually buys them for me because she and her girlfriends like this kind of stuff. If I call her up and tell her I need a bathing suit, she'll have a million and one questions I don't want to answer at this point. I'm not even sure I haven't entered the cuckoo's nest. I don't know what I'm doing, and I don't know why I'm doing it. If I tell you what I'm doing, you'll think I'm crazy. Since you're one of my least judgmental friends and with that weird mental ability thing you have going on, you probably already know. I guess I don't have to worry about you forming snap judgments, you are probably the safest person to tell," I clumsily explain. "Listen to me, I'm babbling like a teenage girl trying to explain to her dad why a guy got caught in my room. I haven't even done anything except kiss the guy and holy smokes… he's totally amazing, I haven't had a kiss like that in years."

Tara snickers as she interrupts me to clarify, "Donda, are you in this much of a dither because you like somebody or you *don't* like somebody?"

"I like him, maybe a little too much," I confess glumly. "We have a date this afternoon."

"So what's the problem?" Confusion tinges Tara's

voice.

"Aside from the fact that my son seems to think Jax invented the sun and hung it all by himself?" I ask pointedly. "I guess there's not one until reality sets in and Dr. Shepherd figures out I'm one screwed up puppy and probably not worth his time. My son is going to be doubly heartbroken and I'll have to fix not only my broken heart but Gabriel's as well. This has disaster written all over it."

"Donda, before you start writing a post-apocalyptic script for your relationship, have you stopped to consider that perhaps it won't end that way?"

"Why? Do you know something from those special Spidey-senses of yours that tell you something different?" I pounce on her words. I know her reputation, and she is rarely wrong in her predictions.

Tara waits a second or so. "You know I can't answer that for you. I wish I could. It's not fair to you or Jaxson for me to put expectations in your head based on my gift. What I can do is encourage you not to view it through your most negative filter. Look at all the positive relationships around you. Things can work out and they often do."

"Tara, you know I'm the most impatient person on the whole planet. I don't know if I can wait for things to just work out. In my whole life, very little has worked out for me. It is hard for me to trust that miraculously, all at once everything in my life will fall together in one big happy puzzle. If you were me, would you trust that?" I ask with an edge in my voice. Intellectually, I know Tara is not the enemy, but I'm frustrated. I feel like I have done nothing but fight and fight and fight until I have nothing left for the battles which matter.

After a long beat of tense silence, Tara comments, "I don't know if I told you this before but sometimes, I still have to go and visit my sexual assault survivor group for some support. If you need some help, don't be afraid to ask. That's what strong people do to stay strong. You don't stay strong by yourself, you stay strong by admitting things are tough."

⎯⎯⎯⎯➤•➤⎯⎯⎯

As I sit in the basement of the Community Center, the sense of déjà vu is overwhelming; it's almost as if I've made no progress in twelve years. I haven't wanted to run this badly since the first day I did this. My throat is dry and my skin is crawling with dried sweat from the adrenaline that is flowing through my veins. I know I need to stay. A large part of me argues that I've been clean for all these years, why do I need to be here with people who've not obtained my level of success? The other part of me who fought tooth and nail to get clean knows the public nature of the program is part of what makes it successful. People need to know that the struggle continues even twelve years on.

Very soon, I am snapped out of my internal struggle as the leader of the group not so subtly looks directly at me and waits. I know that it's completely my choice to speak or not, but if I don't share my story, why did I bother to come all this way to seek out a meeting? I shakily stand up and walk over to the podium and lean heavily on it as I softly speak, "Hello, my name is Donda, I have multiple substance abuse addictions and I have been sober twelve years, three months and nine days."

There is a light smattering of applause at my introduction, and selfishly, I wish I could stop right there and relish in my success, but I know that there's more to the story that I came here to share. For my safety and the well being of my son, I must go on. I take a deep breath and continue, "The tragic part of that is I have a sixteen-year-old son. He pays the price for my bad decisions every day and I can't take those decisions back and give him the life he should've had. I'm here this morning because a couple of months ago I was in a car accident and I hurt my knee. At first, I tried to pretend that it wasn't injured all that severely. You know, that whole thing — if you pretend it's not there, it's not really there? Unfortunately, it just kept getting worse. Finally my son threatened to skip school to take me to the doctor if I didn't go on my own."

A lady from the crowd mutters, "God bless our stubborn kids."

"I went to the doctor on my own and did the responsible thing. I told the doctor about my history of substance abuse. I am so afraid of going back to the person I was back then I'm not even taking my anti-inflammatories unless I absolutely have to. I'll be honest with you, the frustration and the pain are so unbearable, and I feel urges to escape my reality. I haven't craved a drink in years — not like this. You all know what I mean. I sometimes watch a television commercial and something will look enticing. I love coffee and Kahlúa was one of my favorite drinks. Around Christmas, when they show all of the coffee-flavored alcohol, I will sometimes get nostalgic over what it used to taste like, but this time it's different. This time, I feel like I want the feeling that went with being high and drunk. That scared me. I can't afford to go back to the old me. I almost lost my son the first time I went down this road; I can't do it again. This time, Gabriel is almost eighteen years old, if I lost him again, he would be gone forever," I explain.

By the time I reach the end of my speech, I'm exhausted physically and mentally. I wobble a little as I almost completely lose my balance and fall flat on my face in front of the crowd. I know what they probably think, but I have worked really hard to maintain my sobriety and I haven't touched a drop.

The leader must be able to read my frustrated expression because he slides the chair under me and says, "Easy, don't put any more stress on that knee than you need to. It's not easy for any of us to admit when we need help, but I'm really happy that you came to a meeting before you had a back slide instead of after. We can help be your safety net; we'll get you hooked up with a sponsor and help you work through this. You can succeed; I know you can. Look how strong you've been. You just need to work the program. You are going to be at some meetings, right? Don't try to white knuckle your way through a crisis. That's what we're here for."

⸺ ● ⸺

I'm just putting my earrings in when Tara lets herself in my front door. She studies me for a moment before she assesses, "You seem much more at peace now."

I grin at her. "I took your ever-so-subtle advice, thank you. Is it all right if we take your car? Denny finally found the right part for mine, so he's working on it."

Tara spins her key chain on her finger. "Lucky for you, I brought the Scooby Doo van instead of the clown car. I think you would've had a hard time collapsing yourself into my Baja."

"True that!" I confirm. "The last time I was short enough to fit into a VW bug, I think I was about nine. The thing that cracks me up though is that Aidan makes enough money to buy a fleet of car lots and he still drives that ratty old van. I think the only things holding that van together are Rustoleum and wire coat hangers."

"I know," agrees Tara with a laugh. "I understand where he's coming from though. It was his touring vehicle when he first became a musician, and it's got nostalgic value for him. I told him he could keep it until the baby comes. After we have a child, he's agreed that he's not ever going to transport the baby in the Scooby Doo van."

I narrow my gaze at Tara. "Did you also agree to give up the Clown Car?"

Tara flushes . "The funny thing about that is, Aidan won't let me give that one up either. He says he's going to build a mini-museum next to the school to house both vehicles because eventually they'll have historic value to fans."

"Tara, I hate to break it to you, but your husband is a dork, he's a sweet dork — but he's a dork," I announce, as I pat her on the shoulder sympathetically.

"Tell me something I don't know. The man will be a monster when we have a kid. I can see him keeping every scrap of paper that the little tyke brings home. Lord help us if we have a daughter like Becca or Lydia. He'll be tied up in knots so tight, he won't know which end is up," Tara smirks.

"I don't know if a boy would be much better. I can see Aidan being one of those guys that teaches your son to rock climb when he's ten months old like on the YouTube videos that are making the rounds. You know the little babies with the helmets in the harnesses?"

Tara's brows furrow as she thinks about it. "Oh my, two adrenaline seeking O'Brien boys — that's a dangerous thought right there. He'll probably want me to teach him martial arts too. Wow, maybe I should think this baby thing through a little more."

"I know it's hard to believe, but it's all scary and it seems like you'll never figure it all out, but somehow it all comes together and your kid is the perfect kid for you," I assure her. "Nobody knows it all up front, but somehow we just all learn on the job. You'll be great at it — I see how you are with all of your little students. If you can teach them all of those complicated dance maneuvers, potty training will be a breeze."

"I wasn't even thinking about that stuff. That's even more daunting. Let's focus on you for a while before I get so scared I can't leave the house," Tara suggests. "Why do you need a bathing suit?"

"Maybe because the last one I bought was a maternity suit? Seriously, if I go swimming, it's usually at a river in an old tank top and cut off jeans," I sheepishly confess.

"That would pose a problem. I'm curious why you chose it as a date possibility," Tara questions.

"I didn't really choose it so much as it was chosen for me. I told Jaxson that I needed to get out of the house tonight and he told me he's having problems with his back and is planning a session in the therapy pools and wanted to know if I wanted to join him. I said yes before I had a chance to thoroughly think it through. For some reason, that seems to be something I do a lot when I'm around him. The man seriously short-circuits my brain."

Tara breaks out laughing. "That cute, is he?"

"Girl, you have no idea. My hormones are rushing around so fast I forget my own name when he's around. I seriously have to censor myself because I never know what's gonna come flying out of my mouth when he's in the same room with me. Actually, scratch that, he doesn't even have to be in the same room with me. I just have to be thinking about him. Trust me, this makes for some very strange phone conversations. I totally have to make sure Gabriel isn't anywhere within earshot so I don't make a fool out of myself. Jaxson thinks what I say is pretty funny. I'm not sure what Gabriel would think if he heard his mom acting like a junior high school girl with a major-league crush. I tell you, Tara, it's embarrassing. You'd never guess I'm old enough to have a child who'll graduate from high school in a couple of years."

"Knowing Gabriel, he would probably be relieved that you're having fun, letting your hair down, and being normal for once. I know that he worries about you and what's going to happen to you when he goes away to college."

I just shake my head. "Good grief, is there anything my child doesn't worry about? I've got three years before he goes away to college. I haven't withered up and died yet. It is possible that some man somewhere may find me attractive and I won't die an old spinster."

"Who says we can't help the process along — you have incredible abs, let's say we show them off. How do you feel about bikinis?"

"Need I remind you that this body is pushing forty and I haven't been able to properly exercise in months?"

"Please!" Tara rolls her eyes. "I know you. You're still doing your abdominal crunches during every commercial break like clockwork — bikini it is."

CHAPTER TEN

JAXSON

THE UNIVERSE IS SMILING on me today. My last appointment was a no call, no show. Since it was scheduled to be a procedure, there was some padding in the schedule. For once, I have some time to shower, shave and look presentable before our date. The irony is that this time we're not going to do anything fancy or go anywhere. In fact, she's not even going to see me in street clothes for more than a few minutes. But I'll take the positives where I can get them. I take the time to stop by the deli and get us some snacks to eat and a variety of juices and teas to drink. The weird thing is aside from not crawling off the plate, I don't know what Donda likes to eat. I pick up a variety of stuff and hope I've managed to choose wisely somewhere along the way.

As soon as Donda opens the door, I notice that she looks really tired. I can't help but wonder what her pain level has been like. I know from our previous interactions that I need to leave Dr. Shepherd behind and just show up tonight as Jax. I need to remind myself she has a very competent medical team taking care of her and she doesn't need me to be her doctor. It's difficult to not go into evaluation mode when I can see clearly that something is not right.

Leaning down, I kiss her tenderly before I whisper, "Rough day?"

She melts into me as she nods tearfully. "You have no idea."

Enveloping her into a hug, I just hold her for a few minutes. I wish I had the ability to absorb her pain. Unfortunately, all I can do is be there. When she pulls away, I ask, "Something going on with Gabriel?"

"Thank goodness things are pretty perfect on that front. He's doing really well. If I didn't know better, I would swear he's got a crush on the coach's daughter. She is the scorekeeper for camp and apparently she is a video game developer as well. According to him, she has 'mad skills', which apparently is among the highest form of compliments. By all appearances, he has met his soulmate in geek-dom and all is well in the world."

"Has he had 'the talk' with anyone — maybe a doctor or somebody?" I hint.

Donda gives me a sour look as she sarcastically responds, "Hey, Einstein, I had to drop out of school because I got pregnant. What do you think? Of course I've had this conversation with him. I even buy him condoms and keep them stocked for him, no questions asked. What kind of mom do you think I am?"

"No judgment here, I just —" I stammer. "Wait, that came out totally wrong. You would be surprised by how many parents just assume their kids will know this stuff. When I was in medical school, I did some rotations that just blew my mind. I didn't mean to sound at all judgmental. I don't have any room to talk. Had my daughter lived, she'd be getting ready to graduate from high school. I was barely out of high school myself when I got my girlfriend pregnant. I'm hardly the upstanding citizen you likely envision. Maybe if I'd been a little more responsible, my wife, who was impossibly young, wouldn't have been so stressed out that she felt the need to turn to drugs — I'll never know. Jasmine was so smart, she could speak in English and in Spanish — heck, she was even learning to talk in French. What were her mom and dad learning to do back then? I was learning to bag groceries like a champ at Albertson's. My wife was learning to skim drugs off the top of the orders she was delivering for the neighborhood drug dealer. The sad thing is that I never even knew this because I was so busy trying to be the super dad everybody wanted me to be, I forgot to pay attention to the world around me. I buried my child before I was twenty-one years old."

Donda hides her head in my chest and sobs. After she regains some composure, she sighs deeply, as she walks over to the kitchen counter and grabs a paper towel to wipe her face. "You might as well take a seat. Honestly, after I tell you this, you may never want to see me again. This may be the shortest date in history. I want to tell you in advance I'm sorry, so very sorry that drugs ever touched your life. I can't ever make up for whatever role I played in that. Make no mistake, I did play a role even if I didn't mean to and there isn't an excuse for that, period. It isn't fair! I was such a screw up and my son is here and thriving while your beautiful child is gone."

"Donda, stop —" I try to interrupt. I never intended for her to lay the blame at her feet. There's plenty of blame to go around, but none of it should be hers.

"No, Jax, listen to me," she pleads. "I knew what Kevin Buckhold was doing to me was wrong. I also knew he was hurting my mom. I felt helpless to stop him. I knew that it was really screwing up my life, but I didn't reach out to any of the people who could've helped. I was seeing doctors and therapists. I was in and out of treatment programs and not once was I honest with any of them about what was going on because I was afraid of the power the jerk had over me. He told me that if I told anyone, he would kill my little brother. I believed him. I wasn't strong enough to stop the monster — even though I was an all-star athlete. The irony of that still haunts me today. I had coaches fawning over my every move, but I couldn't raise my voice loud enough to make the slime-ball stop raping me and beating my mother."

Donda's stark words are almost too much for me to bear; I move closer to gather her up into a hug but she stops me and says, "No, I need to get the whole story out. You will probably hate me by the time I'm done."

"No, I don't think that's possible," I argue.

Her voice shakes. "You don't know that, I have so much more to tell you that's ugly, dark and disgusting — things I don't even think my family knows. Things you probably *should* despise me for."

I have to shove my hands in my pockets to stop myself from reaching out to hold her. Every instinct I have tells me to gather her up and hold her as tightly as I can, but she specifically asked me not to. It goes against every protective and care-taking instinct I have as a man and a human being to sit there and watch her suffer as she wades through her memories like shredded photographs in shards of glass.

"You don't have to do this —" I try again.

Donda holds up her hand to stop me. "I do," she insists firmly. "Whether I intended for you to be or not, you were a victim of my bad choices and I need to make amends and tell you I'm sorry."

"Donda, you were just a mixed up kid," I growl.

"Yeah, but I *knew* right from wrong. My mom had done a better job than that raising me. I started punishing myself for what my jerk-wad of a stepfather had done to me. It was a way I could control my world. The one thing I could control was the amount of food I put in my body. It made perfect sense, I was an athlete, I had to watch what I ate. At first, no one noticed. I gradually ate less and less. I skipped meals at school. First, it was my snacks and then, I conveniently had projects to do at lunch. Eventually, I scheduled extra practices at dinner. I would ritualistically count my calories. Soon, I started counting my bites. Toward the very end, I was counting the number of chews. I had come to believe saliva had invisible calories. I was afraid that if I chewed too much, I would put on weight. I was unbelievably ill. I almost died. My lowest weight was 75 pounds. My mom doesn't even know I was that skinny, she knows I was 82 pounds because I was hospitalized at that weight — when my organs shut down and I was put on a deathwatch. My family was told to pick out a coffin for me — a child size coffin."

Donda buries her head in the crook of her elbow and sobs for a moment. The sheer isolation of that move is too much for me. I don't care what she asked me to do; I'll do what I need to do. I walk over, pick her up, carry her over to the couch and set her beside me. I tuck her next to me as I place my arm around her shoulders. She wiggles for a second to make herself comfortable, and she whispers, "Thank you."

I silently heave a huge sigh of relief. I don't know what it means, but it must mean something that she's allowed me to give her some comfort during this highly charged, emotional time. I gently stroke her upper arm. "Obviously, you started doing better, what was the catalyst?"

"My little brother," Donda answers as she takes the paper towel and blows her nose. "You haven't met him yet, but Gabriel is a lot like him. Jeff is very serious. When Gabriel was little, I had a major relapse and everything came crashing down. My little brother had to step in and rescue me. I wasn't having too many periods of consciousness during that time because I was really critically ill, but during one of those times I remember Jeff grabbing my hand and looking me straight in the eyes and telling me very firmly, 'You have to get better, the battle is too big to fight alone.'"

"Do you know what he meant?" I question, drawn in by the story.

Donda shakes her head no. "I don't. Those words haunt me to this day. I still have no idea what that sick son of a bleep did to him. Mostly, the lack of communication was my fault because I couldn't seem to think about my former step-dad without getting red-hot angry. The whole topic is like handling defective fireworks. Sometimes, I still get furious at my mom for ever bringing the Jerk-Wad into our household, I'm angry with her for not protecting us better, I'm sorry she was ever a victim, I resent Jeff for being able to handle it better than I was and seeming to come through it virtually unscathed.

I almost hate him for the fact that he nobly gave up his scholarships to go to medical school so he could raise Gabriel for a couple years while I took time off from life to get my act together. Geez, he was like nineteen or twenty years old and here he was taking care of my kid for me because I couldn't do it myself. Gabriel was so little back then, even though he was a toddler, he would sleep in this big old dresser drawer that Jeff had in his room. You know, the ones that go under the bed?"

I nod and swallow hard.

Donda takes a deep breath and fiddles with the string on her sweatshirt for a bit before she continues, "I know he's my little brother, but it took me a few years to stop hating him for having his life so perfectly together that the judge thought that he would be a better parent than me when he just graduated from high school. He was barely grown when he started the process, but the judge could see that even he was a better parental figure than me. That's how screwed up I was. I felt like the whole world knew I was a giant fraud. My kid brother knew more about being a parent than I did when it was my own kid. The crazy thing was, he was insanely good at it — that pissed me off even more. I know I should have felt grateful Jeff stepped up to be Gabriel's guardian; Ricky and I were not in any position to take care of him and if he hadn't, we might have lost Gabriel completely, but at the time I was too angry to get that."

"I'm sure it must've been hard to understand everybody's motives."

Donda barely acknowledges my comment as she continues, "I still can't believe that I fell into all the stereotypical bad relationship traps that all those fancy therapists warned me about for years. I had been doing better right after Gabriel was born and I was pretty stable for once in my life, but Ricky kept trying to talk me into coming back. He promised me he had changed and he was clean. He showed me papers that proved that he'd gone through rehab while I was in the eating disorders clinic. We would finally be the happy family he had always promised we would be. It was going to be perfect. I would get to go to college and he'd be the provider with a real job. He showed me his pay stubs from an electronics store. He finally had a legit job. Everything seemed on the up and up. For a while, it seemed true. We were happy. We did family stuff and he never missed an anniversary or a birthday or a play date with Gabriel; he even treated my dog like a prince. He was a model boyfriend; I was shopping for wedding dresses and venues. I was sure I had broken the 'bad man' curse. This guy was nothing like my evil step-dad. He was perfect, after all. He supported my recovery; he didn't let me injure myself by not eating or eating too much."

"A real Prince Charming," I sarcastically mutter under my breath.

Donda flashes me a ghost of a smile before she remarks, "You have no idea. What I didn't realize, because it was happening slowly right in front of me, was he was helping me substitute one vice for another. I was an athlete and I was never much of a drinker, but Ricky said it was a family tradition and that I would offend his family if I didn't try some. So, whenever we were with his family, I would always drink a little so I wouldn't let them down. Gradually, those drinks became bigger and bigger. Then, there were cutbacks at Ricky's job and he lost his job. I had to pick up another shift at my job. Of course, that meant I had to drop out of school again. I was working as an early morning waitress, then going to work as a hotel maid in the midmorning and then going home to take a quick nap and then working the other part of my shift at the restaurant. I was basically working about sixteen hours a day between the three shifts. I was so exhausted, I couldn't even see straight.

Of course, Ricky had a solution for that. He told me he had gone to a Naturopathic doctor and gotten some special medication to help regulate energy. He gave me some stuff."

"I'm guessing there was no doctor involved?"

"You got that right," she answers grimly. "Only Dr. Feel Good."

"What did he end up giving you?"

"I never knew exactly, but I believe in the beginning, it was something like Ritalin and then he would have to give me something to counteract that so I could sleep. Often he mixed pills mixed with alcohol. On the weekends or other times that I wasn't working, we would go out with 'friends' and he would make me special drinks. I have no idea to this day what he put in those. I know I would wake up the next morning higher than a kite. It didn't act like Rohypnol exactly, but I didn't have much memory of what happened."

"That must've been terrifying."

"Yeah, it was. I went from having control over everything I put in my body to having absolutely none." Donda shivers at the memory.

"I still don't understand how any of this is your fault," I reply.

"Come on, Jax, I was out of it and under the influence, but I wasn't stupid. I knew they weren't some fancy herbs from a doctor; I knew they had to be bad news. I didn't call the police on my fiancé. I pretended everything was fine even though I knew deep down they were so not fine — just like I did with my step-dad. I had learned nothing. For all I know, my fiancé could've been the drug dealer who was supplying the drugs to the neighborhood drug dealer that your wife was working for."

"Or, she could've been dealing with one of thousands of others. Donda, you could've made some better choices, sure — but you had the deck stacked against you from the very beginning. You did the best you could under the circumstances you had. You have lots of years sober, right?"

Donda nods. "Twelve years, three months."

"That's pretty phenomenal. You need to celebrate that. I see a lot of patients that don't manage to stay sober twelve days, let alone twelve years. You should acknowledge that you've been incredibly successful. It's true. Your life didn't go according to plan, but given the blows you've sustained in your personal life, you're an incredible survivor. There are a lot of people who would have waved the white flag and completely surrendered. They would've been knocked out and never gotten up off the mat, but you keep getting up and starting over. I'm so proud of you. You have an amazing son who thinks the world of you and is bound and determined to make you proud of him. He totally adores you and credits you for his success."

"I'm so lucky. I don't know how I was so blessed with such an amazing child. If Jeff hadn't been there to step up when I relapsed, I would have lost him."

"You didn't lose him. You pulled yourself together and you've done an amazing job with him."

"Thank you, but it's hard not to feel responsible."

"Donda, I guess I could loosely hold the drug culture responsible, but you aren't accountable for the whole drug culture. You were a victim every bit as much as Jasmine and Marquette. Substance abuse is ugly no matter how you look at it. There are no winners, really. Even the people who think they're winners eventually lose."

"No kidding. Ricky was killed over drugs in prison. I guess he got what was coming to him; I'm only sad that Gabriel won't get a chance to confront his father. He'll just have to take my word for it. Right now, that's okay with him, but I don't know that it always will be."

"I know the feeling, but it is what it is. Gabriel will have to accept the answers as they are and not how he wishes they were, but you've gone through the same things so you'll be able to help him."

"How did you get so smart?" Donda asks, as she cuddles back up against my chest.

I kiss the top of her head. "Life has been a tough teacher, but sometimes the rewards are worth it. Are you ready to go on our date?"

CHAPTER ELEVEN

DONDA

RAW. I FEEL RAW, there is just no other word for it. I feel like I've been put through the meat grinder. I'm exposed on every level. I'm a little shocked at myself. I've somehow told Jaxson things I haven't ever told anyone else. I'm not even sure how it got to that point. Maybe it's because I know that he knows what it feels like to have life betray you and hurt you to the point where you may never come back from the edge. Perhaps it's because he took time to listen and not judge.

I can't remember the last time I've had a chance to tell my story without terrible repercussions. Instead, he surrounds me with warm words and cozy hugs. I take a deep breath as it occurs to me that for the first time in years, I'm truly happy.

I study myself in the changing mirror in the little dressing room beside the therapy tubs. For the first time in a long time, I can actually take a deep breath. As I step into my swimsuit bottoms, I grin like a loon when I see the whimsical little flower the nail technician put on each of my big toes this afternoon. Tara was so funny; she told me that as long as she was going to spend an hour talking me back from the edge of panic, we might as well be sitting in a pedicure chair. She spent a couple hours giving me the confidence to go on this date. I'm so glad she did, because talking through the past has given me a whole new perspective. I've been keeping it buried for so long that I haven't really taken it out to look at it through the eyes of an adult. It's funny how we look at things differently through the years. Gabriel is only a couple years younger than I was when I went through all my issues with Ricky. That is such a scary thought for me. Gabriel is so much more mature than I ever was. I was such a gullible person. Fortunately, my son seems to have a little more common sense than most kids his age, so I hope he never falls into any of the same traps.

I adjust the swimsuit straps on my bathing suit's top and give myself the once over in the mirror as I put lip gloss on. I love to do funky things with my hair and makeup; I've always been this way. I even used to make Jeff stand in for my dolls and cast him as a living fashion model. Finally, he wised up and played the hairdresser instead of the fashion victim. Even to this day, I don't pay all that much attention to my clothes, although, even I have to admit Tara did a pretty amazing job with this suit. I don't look like the mother of a teenager.

I am startled by the sound of a little bell and Jaxson's deep voice. "Are you ready? I think the tubs are filled."

Pulling in a deep breath and sucking in my stomach, I try to summon my courage as I open the curtain and step out. I can't remember the last time I put myself on display for anyone who really mattered. Going out dancing to a dance with a bunch of strangers in a club doesn't really count in my book. I really want Jaxson to be impressed by what he sees. I have learned enough about him over the past few months to know he is far too polite to give any indication to the contrary if he is not impressed by what he sees — but I would really be ecstatic if I could turn him on a little too. It makes me feel like a hypocrite. I spend a lot of time teaching Gabriel not to judge girls by the way they look, but here I am hoping Jaxson finds me desirable. I shrug as I give my hair one last fluff and lick my lips out of force of habit and nerves.

I am not sure which one of us is the most surprised when I open the curtain. He's standing in front of me in a perfectly ordinary set of board shorts. I pay them almost no notice as the thing that draws most of my attention is his broad muscular chest with a smattering of dark chest hair with tight curls. My fingers itch to run through it and feel the texture and I want to trace the defined muscles. This desire is confusing. Usually, I do my best to not touch anyone. I guess it's a holdover from my phobias about food. I got some really weird ideas about what things contained calories when I became so anorexic. I first started controlling my diet for athletic reasons like monitoring salts and carbs, but then it quickly swung out of control, I'd binge and purge and then severely restrict my diet. That progressed to believing saliva had calories. Eventually, I came to believe sweat and skin cells were bad as well. At my sickest, I couldn't touch or hug anyone for fear I would gain weight. The fact that I'm at all tempted to touch Jaxson is a little mind blowing, to say the least.

Finally, I remember to let out the breath I've been subconsciously holding. I gather my nerves and raise my eyes to meet his gaze. I'm trying to be bold and unaffected, as if his opinion doesn't matter to me, but nothing could be further from the truth.

At this point, I feel as brittle as a dry fall leaf in the wind. I feel about as vulnerable too. Anything could happen at this point. I want to silently kick myself. You would think with all the counseling I've had over the years, I wouldn't feel this insecure, but I still do. It doesn't matter how strong I get on the outside, I'm still that young girl whose stepfather told her she was worthless crap who was so ugly that no man would ever want her. I hear the voice echoing in my head every time I stand before someone.

It doesn't matter how many times I remind myself of all the compliments I hear about my looks or how beautiful I am, the voice I hear loudest is the one who used to whisper foul, awful things to me as he did unspeakable things to my body. I don't know what it'll take for that voice to go away. Clearly, I can't gain enough control over my body, and losing control through drugs and alcohol is not the answer, and it seems that although counseling is helpful, it does not silence the thoughts completely — because at this moment, I feel anything but beautiful.

Tears gather on my lashes before I can hide them. It's just my luck that Jaxson is studying my every move. "Angel? What's wrong?" he asks softly.

"Don't call me that!" I exclaim bitterly. "My name

is Donda — not Angel, not Sweetheart, not Honey, not Lovely, not Sugar Buns or anything else. I'm sorry it has to be this way, but it just does."

I'm so embarrassed, I want the floor to open up and swallow me. I haven't had a visceral reaction like that in years; I thought I had those under control. I have to concentrate on breathing deeply in through my nose and out of my mouth over and over. Much to Jaxson's credit, he doesn't try to rush my progress, he's merely standing very still as he observes me with a look of deep concern on his face. I can almost feel him willing me to share his strength and resolve.

Finally, I'm able to catch my breath and start to repair my injured psyche. I duck back into the dressing room and grab a bottle of water. As I quickly return to the therapy room, I catch Jaxson off guard and see a look of profound sadness on his face. I know he probably never intended for me to see that unguarded expression. It breaks my heart. I feel terrible that I'm the cause of his pain. It's bad enough I have to endure the ongoing consequences of incest; it's beyond any definition of fairness that the effects of my step dad's abuse linger years later like ripples in a pond. It's not even confined to me. It affects my son, my brother, my new stepfather, Denny, and everyone in my inner circle of friends and just grows. My dirty little secret is like an infestation of bugs that refuse to die. Every life that is negatively impacted by my abuse is like the bugs recolonizing — the abuse lives on. Some days, I wonder if I'll ever win. Even though Kevin Buckhold is in jail and will likely die there, he always seems to sadistically have the last laugh. Look at tonight: from behind bars Kevin Buckhold has still managed to invade our evening.

Straightening my spine, I decide I won't give my former step-dad that luxury. I take a towel I had set aside for the therapy pool and use the corner to wipe my eyes. After I place the towel back on the counter, I deliberately walk into Jax's arms and place my arms around his chest and hug his body, placing my cheek against his warm pectoral muscles. His heart rate is beating faster than it was the last time he held me in his arms, and the sound is comforting. It's almost as if our bodies find each other's rhythms to be soothing and complementary. As soon as I settle into his arms, a sense of peace settles over me. It's as if something has clicked into place and I have found my true center.

As soon as Jaxson hears me sigh, he takes it as a sign that it's okay for him to touch me. With excruciating slowness, he raises his hands and brings them to my shoulders and carefully pulls me closer for an embrace. We stand silently for what seems like several minutes before Jaxson murmurs, "Donda, I feel like I need to say I'm sorry."

"Why? It wasn't your fault. You didn't know any better. Sometimes, I lose it. There's no rhyme or reason. It's random. I can go months, sometimes years and nothing will trigger me, and then the silliest, stupidest thing like a slip of the tongue from a total stranger, or a voice on television or a movie poster or ... who knows ... will cause me to evaporate into a pile of nothingness. All the progress I've made goes away and I'm a scared fu—freakin' eleven-year-old, stacking furniture in front of her door again."

The muscles in Jaxson's face tighten as he grimaces. "That's why I have to apologize. I have to apologize for the fact that you ever had to live like that. No one on the planet should ever do that to another person No one should ever have to live in that kind of fear. It's a good thing you told me what's already happened to your stepfather in prison, because if you hadn't, I would be tempted to do things that would put my medical license at risk. Scum like that don't deserve to breathe the same air as the rest of us, much less be part of the medical profession, I can't believe that his colleagues played any part in protecting his sickness and promoting him like that. It just blows my mind."

"I know it's hard to believe, but I saw first-hand evidence that it happened. They knew how my mom was treated, and they saw the after effects of the beatings, but they let my step-dad practice in their dental group, and they never said a word. In fact, they shamed my mama publicly and made her look like she was to blame. It was part of the reason she didn't feel like she had the power to escape. I hold them partially responsible for my abuse. As nearly as I can tell, they enabled my step-father and encouraged him; they darn near did everything except hold the camera and sign him onto the porn websites where he did his dirty work."

"Wow, did they really keep him on after he was arrested?" Jaxson asks, shock lacing his voice.

"Oh no, once Tyler had his threats caught on video in front of a law enforcement officer, they had no choice but to back off — at least publicly, but they allowed him to use company resources to hire a defense team, so they still backed him in the end."

"That's appalling."

"Appalling pretty much sums up Kevin Buckhold. That's a succinct way to categorize his whole personality and approach to life. Most of the time, I'm able to put it behind me. Meeting you and peeling back all of these layers of my life has left me vulnerable to a lot of emotions and feelings I haven't brought up to the surface for a long time. As exciting as all of this is, it's also very, very scary."

Jaxson hugs me tightly and then pulls away before he takes a few seconds to examine me carefully. I feel like an insect exhibit at the zoo by the time he's done. Finally, he starts to speak somberly, "I need to ask you something, and I don't want you to take this the wrong way."

I immediately stiffen as I warn, "Sentences that start that way never end well."

"There's a very real possibility this one might not either," he concedes. "However, I'm asking this with the very best intentions. I can't help but wonder if it might be easier and healthier for you if maybe I wasn't in the picture. I seem to bring you lots of stress and strife. Maybe I should just bow out now."

Instinctively, I want to verbally lash out at him — but to be fair, it's not a thought I haven't had myself. It would be rather unfair of me to blame him for something I've considered too. I take a deep breath and steel myself against the answer I'm afraid I might receive. "Is that what you want to do?"

Jaxson violently shakes his head. "Are you kidding me? Leaving is absolutely the last thing I want to do. But if it keeps you from feeling pain, I'll go."

"Jaxson, I think I'm going to feel pain either way, and I'd much rather feel pain with you in my life than without you."

———————◆●◆———————

After such a rocky, emotional start to our date, I was beginning to wonder if we were ever going to get on more solid footing, but once we are in the therapy pools, it evens out a little. I'm not sure Jax doesn't have almost as big a sadistic streak as my physical therapist. Unbeknownst to me, he filled one therapy tub with really hot water and one tub much cooler. He claimed that there was a valid therapeutic reason for this, but I think he just wanted to see me shriek when I innocently got into the wrong one without knowing there was a difference. After the initial shock wore off, Jaxson and I settle into a more traditional date mode. I have to laugh out loud when I see he has decorated one of those bedside tables with a little tablecloth and a candle to serve some snacks and juice. Gabriel must've told him I am a sucker for Eddie Murphy movies because he queues up *Coming to America*. Eventually, the ritual of switching tubs becomes tedious and we decide to curl up in a big fluffy towel and watch the rest of the movie.

Actually, it's more accurate to say I'm trying to watch the movie, but Jaxson is busy watching me. It's very disconcerting. I know guys find me attractive, I'm not stupid — but the heat in Jaxson's gaze is almost a palpable thing. I squirm under the intensity of it before I finally give up and ask, "What are you looking at?"

The corner of Jaxson's mouth quirks up . "I thought that was pretty obvious, I'm looking at you."

"Well, Dr. Shepherd, do I pass muster?"

The color of his eyes seems to deepen. "Make no mistake there's no doctor in this room tonight; I'm just plain old Jax, a guy who is very appreciative of your spectacular beauty. In case I didn't tell you earlier, you look stunning. I'm an incredibly lucky guy."

I blush a little as I reach up and trace his pectoral muscle with my finger and comment, "I didn't do so shabby either; you're just as pretty to look at in any light." His surprised intake of breath spurs me to go further, so I lean forward and kiss the notch on his chest below his Adam's apple. His heart is beating so fast that I can almost see his pulse race as if it's going to break right through his skin. Without much thought, I lean over him and place an open mouth kiss on the rapidly beating pulse.

His answering groan sends a thrill through my whole body. Suddenly, I feel like I've been given an infusion of high-powered energy bars.

Just as I'm about to move the target location of my kissing, I hear an odd ring tone, followed closely by a frustrated moan. "How in the world does she know I'm on a date? She lives almost one hundred miles away," he mutters as he scoots out from behind me to dig his phone out from his pocket.

Jaxson glances back at me and winks. "I'm gonna tell her what she interrupted."

With a bemused smile, he answers his phone, "Hey Ma, I'm not sure how you do it, but you somehow still manage to chaperone my dates when I'm thirty-seven years old. I swear I'm being a gentleman —"

Suddenly, his body language tenses and I hear him say, "You didn't tell me you were going to the doctor; I would've gone with you, Mom. The whole reason I went to medical school is to help people, especially people I love. Your doctor will likely order more testing. He'll need to go by more than just a suspicious mammogram."

I flinch when it seems as if Jaxson reels from a physical blow. "You already have biopsy results? When did you have a biopsy? Did you have it done at OHSU? I probably could've called around and gotten some names of Oncology technicians for you who would do you right," he offers. He listens for a bit, before he finally shakes his head. "Mom, how many times do I have to tell you that you're not a bother? You're my mom. It's as simple as that. I'm pretty much booked straight through until next weekend, but I'll be up Saturday. Don't make me anything fancy. You promise? A pot roast is fine. Just throw it all in the crock pot. I don't care. I'd offer to bring food, but I know that you would never go for that. I love you too."

When Jaxson hangs up the phone and turns around slowly, the naked fear on his face takes me instantly back to that awful family dinner not so long ago where my own mother announced her lung cancer and I recall vividly my instant fear that it was a death sentence. Without saying a word, I get off of the couch and walk over to him and pull him into a tight hug as I whisper, "Please try not to worry; we'll tackle this together — one day at a time."

Chapter Twelve

Jaxson

The role reversal is sudden, shocking, eye-opening and comforting, all at once. As a born caretaker and nurturer, I never expected to be in the role of needing one. In a sense, this news should not have come as a shock to me. For God's sake, I'm a doctor. I'm familiar with breast cancer on the cellular level. It may not be my current specialty, but it doesn't mean I didn't learn about cancer in medical school. My rotation on the oncology floor was one of my favorite rotations. The doctor who was in charge during my rotation was so passionate about his work, I considered specializing in oncology, but ultimately, my fascination with the mechanics of motion kept me in the field of orthopedics. It was a very close call for me, so it stings a little my mom didn't even feel comfortable enough with my medical expertise to tell me she was sick.

Before I could work myself up over it too much, Donda spent time sharing with me about how her mother handled her diagnosis of lung cancer. Apparently, when her mother Gwendolyn was first diagnosed with lung cancer, she tried to push everyone away, even her friends and family. Donda and her brother were among the last people to know about Gwendolyn's diagnosis. Gwendolyn's comments to them were much like what my mom told me over the phone. My mom and I have talked a bit more over the telephone in recent days, and it turns out Donda is spot on and my mom didn't exclude me because of her lack of faith in my medical skills but rather because she didn't want to worry me as her child. I don't understand my mom's logic, but apparently it's a common thing between mothers and sons because Donda admitted that she would probably be reluctant to include Gabriel in such a conversation as well.

It seems I made a bit of a tactical error when I brought up Donda's name in conversation. My mom put two and two together and now she wants to make amends for interrupting our date. Donda has been a remarkably good sport about it though, even though she's nervous, she still agreed to accompany me today.

When I told her that my mom has a collection of sunflowers in her kitchen, Donda made her a napkin holder and sugar bowl out of clay and painted it in bright bold colors for my mom to match her kitchen decor. My mom loves to collect folk art at garage sales, so the idea of having custom-made knick-knacks for her will thrill her to pieces.

"I wish Gabriel was here to break the ice, he's pretty good at this kind of stuff. He can just talk about his comic books or his video games or the basketball team and everything is fine. He doesn't have issues in his past that he has to avoid talking about. I just never know how to respond to small talk because there are places it leads to where I'd rather not go, so I never know what to talk about. I do okay, but I'm not great. My mom taught me to cook some things, but with my food issues, I wasn't into learning about that stuff. I was just really weird about food. I'm better now, I can cook some, but it's not something I love to do. Now that my little brother married Kiera — who is like Betty Crocker reincarnated, I don't even have to worry about it anymore. Shoot, between Kiera and Heather, basically all the cooking in the house is completely done. My mother is in total homemaker heaven when the three of them get together and have little mini challenges like they have on the Food Network or at least that's what it seems like to me —"

I reach across the car to grasp Donda's hand. "Donda, that's the absolute last thing you need to worry about. My mom is the easiest person on the planet to hold a conversation with. She will talk your ear off. I doubt you will even have a chance to get a word in edgewise. This is not the inquisition, I promise you. My mom will be pleased as punch she has a brand-new set of ears that have never heard her stories before."

"Are you sure? Compared to you or your sister, I'm not really all that impressive.

"Ms. Bold, you are plenty impressive to me and I have every reason to believe that my mom will read you exactly the same way I do. You are fun, courageous, smart and witty. If all else fails, you can show her that video that you took of Gabriel and me playing basketball in the driveway and her heart will be melted in one big puddle. You got this covered."

"Don't forget, my mom made her a chess pie. I wanted to make sure I made a good impression."

"In that case, she may want to keep you and send me home." I squeeze her hand for reassurance.

Although it's tempting to hide behind all the lighthearted banter, it's still going to be a tough visit. I don't know how I'll handle the line between medical professional and concerned son. Even though I'm here to be supportive of my mom, I can't forget all the medical knowledge that's been crammed into my brain for all these years. I know that once she tells me what's really going on, I will want to look at her medical records and figure out how severe things are, so it's an awkward tight rope. I also don't want to crowd my mom and make her feel like I'm taking over her medical care because she's fully competent to make her own decisions, but I know I'll feel compelled to give my opinion probably more strongly than I should. I'm not sure I'll be able to separate my professional instincts from my family duties as her son.

Donda seems to notice my sudden tension as she runs her hand lightly up my arm. "Are you okay?"

"No, not really. I'm trying to prepare myself for how difficult this conversation is going to be … along with the many more we will have over the next few months."

"Jax, you do it one day at a time, there is no other way." Donda replies. "I can't tell you the number of times I wanted to rush in and save my mom. I wanted to argue with her, her doctors and especially Denny. I don't know if anything I would've done differently would've changed the outcome; in fact it might've even made it worse. My mom is doing well now, but watching her go through all the chemo and radiation and being so sick was gut wrenching for me. It gave me a whole new appreciation for how tough it was for her to watch me go through my struggles with anorexia and bulimia and then with the drug and alcohol addiction, I never felt so guilty — even when I was going through my active addictions. It's weird, I never saw what it was like to be on the other side until my mom had lung cancer, and after I saw what it was like to be the caretaker. I wanted to go back and take back all those years when I put my mom through hell."

"How did you deal with all that?" I am curious to know about how it affected her relationship with her mom.

"The strange thing is that the cancer may have been the best thing to ever happen to my family," Donda muses.

After seeing my confused and stunned look, she continues, "No, really it's true. I went into the whole situation not trusting men at all after what happened between me and my so-called step-dad. As it turned out, the person my mom turned to in this whole situation wasn't my brother or me, it was Denny. Denny is my sister-in-law's dad. At first, we thought Denny and my mom were just friends — and maybe they actually started out that way, but eventually they fell in love. Given my history with men, it was hard for me to trust that Denny had my mom's best interest at heart. Little by little, I realized he did. Over time, he began to build a relationship with me and treat me like a daughter — or shall I say, like a man should treat a daughter. He treated me just like he treated Kiera, with respect and dignity. Our relationship grew and I began to trust him. Soon, we began working together as a team to help my mom. Together with my brother, I was able to help him pull off a surprise wedding. It was the most amazing, romantic thing I've ever done in my life and it made Denny and I partners-in-crime. It's also the first time I've truly ever been friends with a man and I think I really like it. In a weird way, I don't think it would've ever happened if it hadn't been for the cancer."

"That's really a great outcome, but how is your relationship with your mom? Did she resent your interference?"

"No, that was the other surprise. We were able to clear the air about things that happened to me when I was a teenager and really talk about the future and how we wanted things to be going forward; it was like having a new beginning with the slate wiped clean. I can honestly say, for the first time since before my dad passed away, my mom and I are friends again."

"Wow, that's not the kind of story I usually hear when people talk about their experiences with cancer. Normally, I hear the other side of the coin. I hear stories about it tearing families apart and battle lines being drawn, I'm glad it didn't work out that way for you."

"In all honesty, I had a lot to do with the estrangement with my family. I started to believe all the things Kevin Buckhold had told me about myself — that I didn't measure up to them, that somehow I was something less than the rest of my family. I had internalized his garbage and started to believe it about myself. I think that's part of what made me a target for people like Ricky and his friends. I was stupid enough to believe anything they told me. I became so unsure of myself that I isolated myself from everyone including my family. It took a scare as big as cancer to show me that it wasn't really all about me and my problems."

"I think you're being a little hard on yourself, you were fighting some serious battles. It's not as if you were complaining about a hangnail or something," I argue.

"Yeah, but being unable to control my eating or addictions is not exactly the same as being a paraplegic or an amputee like some other members of my family," she replies with an exaggerated eye roll.

"That's where I am going to disagree with you. There is ample evidence to say addictions are in large part genetically based and the same is true of eating disorders. Would you blame someone for having diabetes or cystic fibrosis?"

"No, of course not. That's stupid. There's no willpower involved in diabetes or cystic fibrosis — but there is with drug and alcohol abuse."

"Donda, addiction is a really complicated thing, there are a lot of factors involved; you can't just chalk it up to willpower. You can't dismiss bulimia and anorexia so easily either," I insist firmly. "I know that it's your natural tendency to want to shoulder the blame for everything, but this isn't all on you. You've done an incredible job of handling your addictions, but they are not your fault."

"You know, that's the other thing I learned with my mom's cancer. A lot of things don't make sense, but that doesn't make them my fault. I want you to remember that when you talk to your mom. Just because it sucks doesn't mean that it's your responsibility."

<hr>

As Donda and I walk up to my mom's driveway, I turn her words over in my head, '*Just because it sucks doesn't mean that it's your responsibility.*' I can't tell you how many classes and workshops I've had in medical school on avoiding burnout, keeping proper mental balance and maintaining proper doctor/patient distance. None of the professionals have ever boiled the dilemma down to such a perfect, succinct statement before. It's a struggle I've faced my whole life being the son of a single mom trying to decide what's my role as a son versus the "man of the house". I repeat those words in my head like a mantra so I can keep the right amount of distance and perspective and actually help the situation. *Just because it sucks doesn't mean that it's your responsibility. Just because it sucks doesn't mean that it's your responsibility. Just because it sucks doesn't mean that it's your responsibility.*

Donda sees me moving my lips and asks, "What in the world are you doing?"

"Putting your excellent advice to work so I don't overwhelm my mom with my good intentions," I answer.

"I think you are stressing yourself out before you need to. She might actually ask for your advice. She probably didn't want to do it over the phone. Try not to get ahead of what's going on here. I know it's hard not to, but let your mom explain before you jump to conclusions."

I brace myself for what I might see when I open the door because it's been several months since I've been able to go home and I don't know how long my mom's been sick without telling me.

I breathe a sigh of relief when she opens the door wearing her characteristically loud yoga pants and an oversized sweater. She is wearing a ridiculous amount of color for one relatively small human being, but that never seems to stop her. I can't stop myself from doing a quick visual assessment. Her color seems good and her eyes are clear and she's moving around well. I'm so caught up in my exam I don't notice that Donda is tapping me on the shoulder.

"We forgot to get the cooler out of the backseat. Can I have the keys?"

A little dazed, I turn to her and reply absently, "I'll get it. I think everything will be fine here."

Chapter Thirteen

Donda

MRS. SHEPHERD LOOKS AT me intently. "Remind me to ask you some day how you tamed the lion. I expected Jaxson to be fussin' at me something awful, but you seemed to have calmed him down. You must be something really special."

I look behind me to see if she's talking to someone else. With me, Jax has been the definition of cool, calm and collected, I can't imagine that he would ever be considered a lion of any sort. "I don't know if I've been all that special, I crashed my car in front of your son and then almost fell off a ladder. Oh, don't forget the time I yelled at my son in front of him and accused Jax of being a jerk. I don't think I'm so special, Mrs. Shepherd."

"Child, if you're not making a fool out of yourself sending him booby pictures on your phone while you're making crazy duck lip faces, you're a far cut above the women who've been throwing themselves at him recently." She shudders.

Although her words make me laugh, I also cringe at

the thought of sending anyone those kinds of pictures. "No thank you, Ma'am. My teenager has taught me all about Internet safety. I wouldn't dream of sending those kind of pictures, he's told me about the websites those pictures can end up on. I had nightmares for weeks."

"Oh, so your son does that for you too? I'll never forget the first time Jaxson showed me how to use a cellphone, I thought the thing would bite me. Now, you can barely pry it from my hands. Those things are so handy when you go shopping; you can look up coupons on the fly. You don't even have to clip them anymore — it's the darnedest thing. My girlfriends who don't know how to use smart phones are always jealous when I can save money when we go out to lunch. Now my Jaxson told me about your son but I don't remember how old he is? Oh, look at my manners. Come on in the house —"

I stand for a moment in her doorway uncertain what to do next because some people are picky about shoes in their house, but I don't see any shoe holder at the front door. As I looked down at Mrs. Shepherd's feet, I see they are bare and I am paralyzed with indecision for a moment.

Normally, I would wear a different type of shoe, but the knee injury has messed with my serious love affair with high heels. Briefly, I chew on my bottom lip and Mrs. Shepherd finally notices I'm not following her. She sees my tennis shoes and says, "If you feel comfortable, kick your shoes off, we don't stand on ceremony around here."

As I'm looking for a place to sit down, Jaxson comes in the front door and sees my dilemma. He sets the pie down. "Allow me." He kneels in front of me and takes off my tennis shoes and sets them inside the coat closet.

I look up at Mrs. Shepherd. "I have to compliment you on the fine job you did raising such a phenomenal son. He is a perfect gentleman."

"Jaxson, where did you find this extraordinary young woman? Can you make sure you keep her?" Mrs. Shepherd responds with a wink.

For the first time in about four hours, I actually take a full breath and let it out. I was so nervous about this meeting, I could barely eat all week. It seems to be going pretty well.

Mrs. Shepherd notices the cooler sitting on the table and exclaims excitedly, "Ooh, did you bring me goodies?"

"Don't look at me," Jaxson instructs, as he points toward me. "This one was all Donda's doing."

I blush as I respond, "Actually, I don't even get most of the credit for this one; my mom does. I have this bossy friend who likes to sometimes act like my personal doctor and he keeps telling me that if I don't stay off my knee, it will never get any better. Since I don't want to stress him out any more than he already is, I'm inclined to listen to what he has to say. This time I didn't make it, but my mom says if you ever need anything to call her. She recently went through a similar struggle and she says to tell you that she's got 'wide shoulders, big ears, and a quiet mouth'."

Mrs. Shepherd shoots Jax a dirty look as she accuses, "Well … I might want to take your mom up on that since some people can't keep our family business private."

I start to unload the cooler. "He didn't tell me much of anything on purpose, I happened to be there the night he got the news. He wasn't being a gossip. It was just a matter of timing."

"Seeing how lovely you are, I can understand why my son was so upset when I interrupted his date. I suppose I'm not really all that upset you know what's going on because Jax needs someone to talk to about this. You seem like you might be the perfect person for him to have around if you have been through this with your own mother."

"It's not an easy place for anyone to be in. If I can help in any way, I'd be glad to." I take the pie out of the cooler and show it to her.

When she sees what I brought her, she turns to Jaxson and says, "You must like this one, you don't talk about your southern roots to just everyone."

Jaxson puts his arms around both of our shoulders, as he admits, "I do. I like her a lot."

Mrs. Shepherd looks at me with tears in her eyes as she pleads, "I know there aren't any guarantees in life, but Jaxson is my baby and I'm sure you understand as a mom. Please try your best not to break his heart. He's been through more than you can imagine."

I can't help but tear up either. It's such a precarious time. So much could go so wrong or so right. It's like making all the cuts before I make an intricate stained glass piece. Everything can look like it's coming together just fine, but if one piece doesn't fit correctly, it can throw everything off. When you're working with glass, if you're having a really good day, and everything's working fine, everything seems to flow well. Yet, if you're having a bad day and things start to break, it all seems to cascade like a bad dream. As well as things are going right now, I can't help but wonder how long we can hold it together without it shattering into a million pieces. I don't want to share that with Mrs. Shepherd so I simply respond, "Your son means the world to me and my son. I will treat him the best I know how."

<hr>

As the lively lunch wraps up, I can't help but draw parallels to the very strange family dinner we had a couple years ago involving my family. That same weird tension is present: the feeling that something big is going to happen, but not knowing what it is. The difference is this time, I know something is coming. The last time, I was completely blindsided by the announcement. I was more distracted by the surroundings of the restaurant because it held bad memories from my mom. I totally was not expecting a completely unrelated announcement about cancer. This time, it's different because the news isn't coming as a complete surprise to anyone. The only thing we're waiting for is a discussion about the seriousness of Yvette's cancer — after I gave her the napkin holders and sugar bowl, I was upgraded to first name status.

I'm still getting used to people being happy to see my arts and crafts projects. When I first started doing this stuff, it was just a way to fill my time and give me something constructive to do with my hands. I found it relaxing. It was a way to get my mind off of less productive thoughts. I started off with stained glass and intricate beading projects and then I discovered painting. At first, I started with tiny canvases, but as my confidence grew, so did the size of my work. On a whim, when I worked at a toy store, I asked the manager if I could redecorate because the inside of the store was in such bad shape. Much to my surprise, he gave me free-rein to do whatever I wanted to do. I took full advantage of the offer and painted full murals of traditional toys on the walls. A local restaurant owner saw my work there and asked me to paint a vineyard scene on his Italian restaurant, so I did that. From that, someone asked me to paint their coffee shop and suddenly I had more than just a hobby; but it still surprises me that people will pay me to do what I do for fun.

Glancing around the table, I suddenly realize people are staring at me. I blush as I sit up a little straighter and pay attention to the conversation around me.

"I asked you how your studies are going?" Yvette prompts.

"Sorry," I mumble. "I was just thinking about how life has changed for me recently. School is okay, I guess. I am so not like my little brother. I may never make it out of school because I can't decide what I want to do. I started out as a criminal justice major, but it wasn't really what I wanted to do, then I went into healthcare but I'm not sure it really suits me either. I've changed course again and I wonder if maybe I should get my degree in something design related. I feel like maybe I might just be throwing it all away one more time."

"Honey, the world is all about change. Nothing stays

the same. I don't know why we teach our children they have to choose a single path and stay on it. Even Mother Nature doesn't do that. Rivers change, the beaches change, the weather changes. Everything grows and changes — why not us? It would be a sad world if we all stayed the same people we started out to be at eighteen. Now, I don't know how it's all going to work out with your college situation, but these things have a way of unknotting themselves and smoothing out. You just need to be patient and ask for some good advice. I know I get in a world of hurt when I try to figure problems like that out in my head."

I can't contain a giggle as it erupts from me, "I'm not sure how you pegged me, but you've got me nailed. I've got expert skills at thinking myself into a real tizzy-fit. Asking other people for help is not big on my to-do list."

Yvette laughs out loud at my confession and reaches across the table to give me a fist bump. "Well, it takes one to know one. I didn't say all of my 'so-called wisdom' came the easy way."

Jaxson has been watching our interaction with blatant amusement, but he suddenly gets serious. "Mom, speaking of seeking outside help, I think it's time for us to talk about what's going on with you."

Yvette takes a drink of her coffee before getting up from the table and grabbing a three ring binder.

The cheerful Art Deco design of the three ring binder is a little disconcerting. My mom used to have one of those binders for all of her medical information too. Just because you can dress up the outside, doesn't make what's on the inside any less devastating.

I peer over the edge of my large glass of soda at Jaxson and I realize that the tips of his fingers are white against his ceramic coffee mug. I reach across the table to grasp his hand as I mouth the word, "Breathe."

Jaxson nods tightly as he visibly tries to relax. He turns to Yvette and asks, "What do you have here, Mom?"

"You know my Zumba class? There's this nice woman there and she's a nurse. When I told her that my mammogram didn't look so great, she told me to start this notebook. She said I might not need it, but if I did, it would be helpful. Turns out she was right. I've got all my medical stuff in here. I kept it all and asked for extra copies of my records in case you might want to look at them."

"Mom, why did you go through all that stuff by yourself instead of asking me for help?" Jaxson asks as he scrubs a hand down his face in frustration.

"Jaxson, I didn't know if it would be all that serious. If it was, I didn't want to get you in trouble. You know I watch *20/20* and that *Dateline* show and doctors get in trouble all the time for getting their relatives special treatment. I figured if I need something extra like experimental treatments or special drugs or something really expensive or if I want something fancier than my insurance company wants to provide me, and I put your name down as my son, they might think you are giving me special treatment. I didn't let anybody know that you are my son because I don't want to get you in trouble before you even get your first real job. That's why I haven't said anything to anybody," Yvette explains.

"Mom, I'm still your son, whether I'm a doctor or not. I know the rules. I won't put my whole medical career in jeopardy to help you. However, I do know what's out there and I can tell you about things — without breaking any rules."

"Well, I didn't know where those lines were and you are so busy with your job as a resident, I didn't want to get you in trouble with your new bosses. Besides, you can't really do anything until we know what's wrong with me. The doctor I first saw said it could be cysts. I read on the Internet that it was better for me to drink decaffeinated coffee if I wanted to get rid of any cysts. I tried that, but when I went back for the biopsy, they decided it probably isn't cysts. A week from Thursday, I need to have a lumpectomy."

"Mom, have you gotten a second opinion to decide whether a lumpectomy is better than a full mastectomy?"

"Jaxson, I have lived with these breasts for many decades, I just want to see how severe the cancer is before I go choppin' them off. Now, I know there hasn't been a man in the picture for quite some time, but that doesn't necessarily mean I don't ever want one. My bosom was one of my best features — if the doctor says I can keep it, I'd just as soon do so — thank you very much."

I can see the features of Jaxson's face tighten as he struggles for balance. "Mom, did somebody explain to you the risks inherent in that approach?"

"Good heavens, yes! I've done so much research, I could probably write a book. I might not have a fancy college degree like yours, but you forget that I helped keep your grandfather's eye clinic afloat since I was old enough to handle a typewriter and a calculator. I went to nearly all of his medical conventions with him. He was always going to more of those than he ever needed just to sell glasses. I know my way around medical speak, that's for sure. Whatever I don't know, I figure out on the computer."

"Mom, I'm not trying to suggest that you're stupid or anything, I want to make sure that the doctors went over the options with you and didn't cut any corners. I want to make sure you're getting the best care possible. Did you tell Jordan about this? How is she handling it all?"

"No, I haven't told Jordan yet. She has a big show this weekend. I figured I would tell her on Monday after all the hullabaloo has worn off. She deserves a chance to celebrate all of her hard work before I tell her about all of this. She's been working on that campaign of hers for eight months now. Did she tell you it's going to be featured in Vogue?"

"I'm thrilled for Jordan, but you know she'll be really ticked off when she finds out you've known about this for a few weeks and didn't bother to tell her. If you think I'm a control freak, Jordan runs circles around me."

Yvette just shakes her head. "Son, tell me something I don't know. That girl has been trying to keep up with you from the moment she was born. I believe 'focused' should be her middle name. I'm surprised she's not actually in medical school with you."

"If dead things didn't completely creep her out, she probably would be, but she couldn't ever get over dissecting things."

"I expect she'll probably be on the first plane out as

soon as I tell her anyway, I don't think a couple days will make much of a difference for her. If she operates the way she usually does, she'll take a couple of weeks' downtime after a big show anyway. I'll call her tomorrow evening and let her know. It's not like she has a life outside of her job anyway, I worry so much about her. As far as I know, she isn't dating anybody seriously. She was dating a model named Jordan for a while. Everybody thought it was cute: Jordan and Jordan. I knew it wasn't serious — she treated him like a dress-up doll, not like somebody she was truly interested in. I don't want her to think I'm interfering or anything, but she's getting up there and she might not be able to have kids."

"Mom —" Jaxson starts in a warning tone.

Yvette looks over at him and glances apologetically at me, "I know, I know. I shouldn't interfere. It's not really my business, but I was really hoping for more grandchildren one day. Jasmine was gone in just a blink." She gasps suddenly as she turns to Jaxson. "Oh, maybe I shouldn't have said anything. Does Donda know about Jasmine?"

The pained expression that streaks across Jaxson's face is enough to prompt me to answer for him, "Yes, he told me all about that time in his life. It was one of the first things he shared with me. I'm so sorry for your loss."

Jaxson finally finds his voice. "Ma, I think we have bigger things to worry about than Jordan's dating status right now. Starting with planning for Thursday. Who are you planning to have with you for your surgery?"

"If you or Jordan can't do it, I was going to have Rosemarie from church take me. You know, she used to be a CNA. I figured if I got sick after surgery, she wouldn't mind cleaning up after me."

I can tell that Jaxson is getting upset as he has to blow out a breath before he states wearily, "Mom, how many times do I have to tell you that you're not a bother. Just call me when you have a final surgery time and I will be there to pick you up and take you."

"Can Donda come too? They're going to do all sorts of private, female stuff. I know you're a doctor but I'm your mom and I don't want you to watch them draw on me like I'm a giant chalkboard. It's just too — I don't know, it's just too something," Yvette explains as she throws up her hands dramatically.

I just met Yvette today and it seems like a bit of a personal request, but I don't want to argue with her. I do CNA work too, so I guess I'll have one more client for a while. I look at Jaxson and shrug. "I'd be happy too."

CHAPTER FOURTEEN

JAXSON

I DIDN'T HAVE ANY idea how much one family dinner would change things between us, but even without spoken words and formal definitions, Donda and I seem to have moved to official couple status. Many other couples talk about this step for weeks, if not months before taking it, but we simply migrated into it. It's not without its technical challenges though. It's not as if I live right next door. We have to juggle my job, her part-time job, her new business along with Gabriel's school and sports. I finally had to add a new calendar app to my phone to keep track of it all.

Tonight, Donda has a meeting with a prospective client for Claim Your Space in Wilsonville, so she is staying over at my place. Tomorrow, we will be picking Jordan up from the airport and the next day is my mom's surgery. My mom's illness is bringing a whole new dimension to my work. I can't count the number of surgery consults I've sat in on where the physician has simply blown through patients' questions as if they're nothing, but now that I've sat in the other chair, I find myself pausing longer at the doorway to make sure there are no last-minute questions before I leave the room.

As I put the finishing touches on the salmon before I put it on the grill, I hear Donda pull into my carport. Before I can even get out there to help her, she's headed up my stairs to the kitchen, balancing a couple of packages in her arms. I rushed to take them from her. "I hope you don't mind, I brought some dessert. I had to go check out some tapestries at this little boutique and there was a cute bakery right next door. I feel disloyal not going to Joy and Tiers, but this place looked sensational. I couldn't decide on just one flavor, so I got a bunch. I hope you're hungry."

"You could always claim you're doing product research for Heather. It's always important to take one for the team, I suppose. In my book, there's never any such thing as too much cheesecake."

"She was so impressed you could pick out the lemongrass in her tart the other day. You have earned a lifelong fan. She can spot a dyed-in-the-wool foodie from a mile away, I thought you said you didn't like fancy food," she comments with a raised eyebrow.

"Oh, I like it just fine. I like other stuff better though. My roommate in med school thought he was going to be the next big Food Network mega-star, so he was always throwing stuff together and making us guess what was in it. If we couldn't guess what was in it, he'd make us do the dishes. I became a quick study in herbs and spices. Even though gourmet food is not my highest priority, avoiding doing dishes is always preferable when you have loads of homework."

Donda laughs out loud. "Smart and handsome, I knew there was a reason I keep you around."

After I put the cheesecakes on the counter, she laces her arms around my neck and gives me a long, deep kiss. Had the timer on the fish not gone off at that very minute, I would've been tempted to throw in the towel on dinner completely. This woman has some serious kissing skills. I could stand here in my kitchen and make out for hours. I'm in no real hurry to change my itinerary but Donda pokes me in the side and says, "Don't you think you should take care of that? We don't want to set the kitchen on fire."

I pull away with a large grin on my face. "I'm sorry, I thought that's what we were doing already."

"Oh, you are such a funny guy, but salmon going to waste is a big deal. We can light fires later on. I'm starving."

"All right, if you insist," I relent as I pull the fish off the grill and slide it onto the plate with the salad. "Would you like to eat at the table or in the hammock?"

"How do we eat in your hammock?" she asks dubiously.

I point toward the corner of my living room where I have created a library of sorts, complete with a huge indoor hammock. "Very, very carefully — it takes practice. I got good at it when I was in school because I spent so much time reading in it, I got used to having all my snacks there too."

"That's impressive, but I think I'll stick to the table

for now. I have a gift for making a mess out of myself. Seriously, I am intrigued by your version of a man-cave. I guess I made some assumptions about you based on your car. I expected you would have the latest and greatest technologies and a TV the size of a small planet."

I move my medical journals and mail to one side and set our plates down onto the table and pull out Donda's chair before I answer her, "It would be nice to have a ginormous TV, but I have other priorities. The only reason I drive a nice car is because I inherited the car from my grandparents. I'm driving a hand-me-down, and as nice as it is, I would much rather have my grandparents here."

"I'm so sorry, Jaxson, I had no idea. I saw this luxury car I'd never be able to afford in a million years and thought you bought it. I should know better than to make assumptions."

"You had no way of knowing about the history behind my car," I try to reassure her.

Donda starts to eat before she continues the conversation, "I guess it's pretty lucky that I have the type of kid who is likely to be more impressed by your version of nirvana than most."

"I think it's safe to say. I came in the other morning from an overnight shift at the hospital, and he was completely sacked out in the hammock with a huge stack of books around him as if they were teddy bears," I recall.

"He does seem comfortable around here and around you. I'm so glad you have such a great relationship. I've never seen him take to someone like this. He's always been reserved, even around his teachers and coaches, but he doesn't seem to be that way with you. It's unnerving. The only other person I've seen him open up to like this is my brother, Jeff. I understand Gabriel took you to a pickup basketball game with Mindy and Jeff, how did it go?"

The corner of my mouth lifts in a smile as I remember the unexpected afternoon. "Your niece is a riot. She had some interesting nuggets of relationship advice for me but beyond that, she is a phenomenally good basketball player and her relationship with your brother is remarkable. If it weren't so readily apparent by their appearance, you would never guess she's adopted. Those two are as alike as two peas in a pod. I know you told me your brother is a serious sort of guy, but those two together are like a comedy team."

Donda grins affectionately. "It's true, Mindy Mouse brings out the happy in my brother like no one I have ever seen except, maybe Kiera. She was the first one to ever truly understand all of what makes my brother tick and Mindy and Becca are as important to my brother as oxygen. Just out of curiosity, what relationship advice did Mindy have for you?"

"Oh, I don't know, it was kinda weird — I figured maybe she got it off of one of those Internet horoscope sites or something — but she told me not to let my past haunt my future and to trust what I want to believe, not what others tell me. I just thought it was funny since it was the first time she ever met me and she sounded like a fortuneteller. What could she possibly know about my life? She said vague stuff like honoring my past family and treasuring my new one — it was like the usual schtick you see on all those television shows with TV psychics. I was a good sport and played along. It was strange though because Gabriel seemed all sorts of freaked out about it."

Donda looks pensive for a few moments. "There is no logical, empirical — to use your term — way to prove to you what we've all come to understand about things Mindy and Tara say. It has become a well-established fact that if one of them says something about your life, you best sit up and take notice. They rarely make commentary about your life which doesn't turn out to be true. I don't have any solid facts or data to back me up, but the two of them are spooky. I don't know how they know what they know. I don't know if it's a gift from God … or a curse from beyond. I don't know if it's witchy-voodoo, an inherited talent, or a sixth sense — I don't know. Whatever it is, the two of them share a bond, a gift, or curse — something sets them apart from the rest of us and it's spooky, weird, wonderful and amazing."

"You know, there have been some powerful new treatments for mental health conditions including mass hysteria and delusions?" I offer, with more than just a little tongue in my cheek.

"Go ahead, joke. I was a skeptic at first too, but it didn't take too many instances for me to become a true believer. Those two are amazing. If I were you, I'd think back over all the things she told you and write them down. At some point, you'll need to know the information she gave you in some form or another. I know it seems silly, but her predictions have never been known to be wrong."

"I'll keep that in mind. Would you like to retire to the

hammock for dessert?" I ask as I push back from the table.

"That sounds wonderful, although I can't guarantee I won't fall asleep; today has been a really long day."

"How did your meeting go?" I inquire.

"I don't know if I'll be able to be competitive for the job. I think it's a little bigger than my business can handle. It's even bigger than the Pennington job and that job has about stretched Claim Your Space beyond all of my capacity. I think I need to get more money in the bank and expand my business a bit before I can take on bigger jobs. I need more space and more people."

"That makes perfect sense. Not every job will be a perfect match for your company. It's okay to say no if something doesn't feel okay. You don't have to take every client who walks through the front door."

"I guess in my head, I know that, but my heart is afraid to start turning away people because I'm afraid they might stop coming to my front door if I turn people down."

"Turn you down? I don't think so. I've seen your stuff, it's totally gorgeous just like you are," I comment as I lift her into the hammock and crawl in after her. I forgot what it's like to have two people in a hammock. Immediately, we sink together into the middle.

Donda shrieks as she's startled by the unexpected movement. She chuckles in a low husky laugh as she comments, "This is unexpectedly cozy. I am beginning to understand the appeal of the hammock." She looks at my jeans and sweatshirt with speculation. "It seems to me that you are over dressed for this occasion."

I struggle to sit up without disturbing the hammock. "I guess you have a point. Is there anything in particular you'd like me to remove?"

Donda looks startled by my unorthodox question. She seems to think about it for a moment before answering, "As tempting as it is to be greedy, I think I'll stick to the basics and ask you to remove your shirt so I can revel in the awesomeness of your chest."

I'm not quite sure how to respond to the compliment, so I shrug. "I can handle that."

I gingerly sit up and drag my shirt over my head. Donda pensively watches me while she chews on her bottom lip. Abruptly, she sits up and whips off her blouse leaving only a lacy tank top behind.

My surprise must've been evident on my face because she laughs softly as she comments, "It wouldn't have been fair if I expected you to get naked without following suit."

"Naked, huh? Is that where we're headed?" I ask.

"I hope so. We've been flirting around the idea of this for months. I don't think there's much about each other that we don't already know by now. I've decided I've been a pretty good girl this year and I deserve to put my past behind me and move on. I'm going to give myself the gift of happiness and this year I'm going to specifically define happiness as you. In a weird way, I'm giving myself you for Christmas." Donda reaches down and hooks her thumbs under the hem of her tank top and peels it over her head. She throws her knee over my body and leans over me as she slowly kisses me.

"Merry Christmas to both of us," I whisper softly

after she leans back to unbuckle my pants.

"Happy Holidays, Jax," she replies with a sexy grin.

I groan as a thought occurs to me. "Donda, please don't kill me — but, I talk a bigger game than I play. I haven't thought about protection in years. I haven't been in a relationship for a while. I don't have anything available," I admit with a sheepish grin.

"That's all right, I've got you covered. I am protected and I'm compulsive about testing. On some level, I'm still paranoid something will pop up from the Jerk-Wad. Don't worry, everything's fine — it's just my own excessive compulsion because he made me dirty," she explains with an exasperated sigh.

"We don't have to do this. If it's too soon, I understand," I reply, while rubbing her back in small circles.

She sits up against my thighs,. "No, I won't let him have that piece of me anymore. I belong to me and only me. If I want to share myself with someone else, because I really like you and want to feel close to you, it's my business and only mine. I refuse to feel guilty or ashamed for wanting to love you."

In that instant, I can see the look of raw desire and fear of rejection spelled out in her wide-eyed gaze as she grimly watches for my reaction, clearly expecting the worst.

Choosing my words with great care, I pull her body over mine and whisper against her temple, "You never had one reason to be ashamed. All the shame was on him. You are beautiful inside and out. Donda Kristen Whitaker, I've never looked forward to loving someone as much as I look forward to loving you."

I wake up to sounds of violent cursing coming from the kitchen, I can't believe we fell asleep in the hammock; I haven't done that since my days of pulling all-nighters in medical school. I guess in a sense that's what we did last night in the most pleasurable of ways.

"Why can't you have a normal coffeemaker like everyone else's? Do you realize your coffeemaker is more complicated than the one Heather has at the bakery?"

"Maybe it would be easier to operate if you waited until daylight hours to try. It's our vacation, remember?"

"We have to go get your sister at the airport, *remember?*" Donda counters.

I scramble around to find my watch or cellphone on the little side table beside the hammock and when I do, I about have a heart attack on the spot. "Oh great! Donda, we should've been out of the parking lot ten minutes ago! Jordan is a stickler for punctuality. We better hope her plane was held up by weather."

"Why do you think I was trying to make you coffee, Einstein? So much for my romantic morning after —" she trails off.

"I promise to make it up to you at some point. Let me get this started and I'll hop in the shower. Since you're already dressed, will you go start the car and turn on the seat warmers?"

Donda snorts at me. "Do I look like I'm the type of person who has a car with seat warmers?"

I lean over and kiss her before I get a couple of travel mugs down from the highest shelf in my kitchen. "You're absolutely brilliant, I'm sure you'll figure it out. I've got to get in the shower before I get into any more hot water with my little sister. She'll be stressed out enough about Mom, as it is."

———— • ————

"You losing your sense of direction in your old age?" my sister greets me with a look of impatience marring her expression.

"No, just chronically lacking sleep. I forgot to set my alarm."

Jordan sticks her tongue out at me. "Fine, I see where I rank on your priority list. Right behind a good old-fashioned nap — even though you haven't seen me in forever."

"Sorry, Sis, a man's gotta do what a man's gotta do," I quip.

Jordan's head swivels around as she notices Donda. She immediately gives her a clinical assessment — like she does every model she ever sees. "Pretty bone structure, but a little less refined than you usually go for," Jordan judges tactlessly.

Donda laughs out loud. "If you meant that as a compliment, you missed the mark, because it sucks. If you meant it as an insult, it also sucks, because it's true. I don't think I have a refined bone in my whole body. However, I will give you points for humor, because it was kind of funny."

Jordan draws in a surprised breath at being

confronted so directly.

Donda sticks out her hand. "Hi, I'm Donda Whitaker."

I rush to intercede. It is important to me that this meeting go well. I want the last two of the three most important women in my life to get along as well as possible. It'll be a delicate balancing act. Every woman in my life is opinionated, passionate and strong. I slide my arm around Donda's waist protectively. "Donda, this is my beautiful and smart little sister, Jordan. To be honest, she could give Gabriel a run for his money. Unlike me, she was an All-Star point guard instead of just a benchwarmer."

Jordan looks confused and I realize my mom hasn't told her anything about Gabriel. Belatedly, I realize that it's probably a tactical error to tell her about Gabriel in the middle of the crowded Portland international Airport. Unfortunately, I can't take back the words, so they're just hanging there in the air. Finally, Jordan turns to Donda and asks, "So, is Gabriel your son or are you trying to pull some sort of scam on my brother?"

Donda narrows her eyes as she looks at my sister and replies, "Of course Gabriel is my son. Would you like to see pictures? Don't worry, I'm not trying to trap your brother in a baby smack down, I didn't even know him until he rescued me from a hit and run."

"Jordan, before you make any snap judgments about Donda, please get to know her. You guys have a lot in common. She's a phenomenal artist like you. If you want to know the truth of it, Donda didn't pursue me at all — in fact she tried to ignore me. It was me who went after her."

"Jaxson, I find that really hard to believe, she's so far away from your usual type," remarks Jordan as she studies Donda.

Donda draws herself up to her full height as she stares back at Jordan and responds, "I know you'll never believe this, but your brother is so far from my ideal type — if it weren't for my son pleading his case, I would've never spoken to him again."

Chapter Fifteen

Donda

As I'm waiting for Jaxson to come back from dropping Jordan off at her hotel, I want to kick myself for my inability to keep my sarcastic mouth shut. I don't know why I can't seem to learn my lesson about that kind of stuff. It's not like Jaxson doesn't have enough stress in his life.

Things are so tense between all of us, Jordan doesn't even want to ride to the hospital with us. She decided to rent a car and pick up Yvette and take her to the hospital herself. Jaxson is trying to play it cool, but I can understand why he would be devastated. I'm sure he wanted to give his mom last-minute medical advice on how to advocate for herself with the doctors. My smart mouth got in the way. I should have known better than to get riled up by this stupid chick turf war — especially since I know she's no threat. I don't know why I let it get so personal. She was just watching out for her big brother. I'd be stepping up for Jeff too, so I'm not sure why I got all butt-hurt about it. Talk about your stupid, unnecessary drama. Just sign me up — I'll be right there with my personalized T-shirt for the occasion. Now, Jaxson and his family are paying the price for my stupid pride and need to be right all the time.

On the way to the hospital, I try to apologize to Jaxson again for my over-the-top behavior. He brushes it off saying Jordan did her best to provoke me. He explains that in Jordan's industry, she is often called upon to make snap judgments and she often carries them over to her personal life. He seems to think things will be better this morning, but I'm not so sure. I'm trying to keep my focus on supporting Jaxson because I can tell he is having a difficult time being on this end of things.

In a weird way, Jax reminds me a lot of my brother. As a lifeguard and an attorney, Jeff is fine with things when he is in control, but as soon as he has to step back and allow other people to take charge, Jeff's fears multiply. I think that's where Jaxson is this morning. As we wait for the parking ticket at the gate to the parking garage, he is about to drum a hole in his steering wheel with his fingertips.

"Jax, isn't one of your former mentors going to scrub in?" I ask.

Jaxson nods. "Dr. Nishimoto actually cut his vacation short so he could do this for me. I was honored."

"See, you have eyes and ears in there even though you can't be in there yourself. The best thing you can do for your mom is to try to breathe and relax and not let your nerves add to hers."

"You know, as a doctor, I have counseled my

patients about the positive, expectation-free, let-God-and-the-doctors-take-care-of-it-all approach for as long as I can remember. It is so hard to put that advice to work when you're the one sitting in these seats."

"I've been on both ends of the spectrum. My mom was a very reluctant patient. She didn't want any of us to take care of her because she didn't want to be a burden. I have a feeling your mom will be much the same way because she reminds me a lot of my mom. They seem to be cut from the same kind of cloth. Strong and quietly feisty."

Jaxson gives me a double take as he slides his arm around my waist and we walk side-by-side into the hospital. "Clearly, you haven't spent enough time around my mom if you think she *quietly* does anything."

"A poor choice of wording. I just meant your mom and mine both have this inner core of strength they don't always show to other people — but it's there, nonetheless."

"That's very true of my mom. People tend to underestimate her because they think she's all bluster and noise. Most people don't realize she is a very strong woman underneath all the window-dressing."

"What I needed to hear as a patient was everything was going to be okay, regardless of how scared I was. I never let anyone know I was completely freaked out because I didn't want to stress out my family anymore than they already were. If someone gave me permission to be scared and said they'd be there anyway, it made me feel so much better about the situation," I admit.

Jaxson backs me up against the wall in the little

alcove in the hallway. "In case I don't get to tell you this later, thank you so much for keeping me grounded through this. Your advice means the world to me."

I shrug as I respond, "You're welcome, I'm not sure I'm saying anything profound, I'm just trying to help. I know this is really hard. I'm here for you — whatever you need."

"That counts for everything, trust me," he responds with the first genuine smile I've seen from him all day.

Jaxson grabs my hand and walks me into the hospital room. I don't know if I would have willingly gone if he wasn't holding my hand. I didn't say anything to him about how difficult it was for me to actually go inside because he has enough on his mind, but it's taking all of my focus and concentration not to end up on the floor. I don't have a single good memory in my life related to hospitals or treatment centers. They are the stuff of my nightmares.

Fortunately, or unfortunately I don't have much of a chance to stew in my own nerves because as soon as Jordan sees me, she lashes out at Jaxson, "Really, did you have to push her in my face today, of all days?"

Yvette reels around in surprise on her daughter as she chastises her, "Jordan Cassandrea Shepherd! Where in the world are your manners? For the record, I personally invited Donda to come here today."

"Sorry, Mama," apologizes Jordan. "It seems awfully convenient that she's inserted herself in our lives right when our family is the most vulnerable. That's all I'm saying."

I silently take a deep breath as anger flares deep in

my gut. I have been called many things in my life, but I am deeply ethical. I take responsibility for what I am, but I won't take responsibility for things I'm not — and I am not running a con on anyone.

I am still trying to decide what I should say when Jaxson steps in front of me and holds up his hand to Jordan as he declares, "That's enough. You don't understand what's happened in the last few weeks. In fact, you don't know much of anything about Donda at all. Therefore, you should have no legitimate comment about my relationship with her or when we fell in love."

Jordan rolls her eyes at Jaxson. "Oh, great! You love her now. I don't even know how you can begin to believe in happily-ever-after after what happened with your first wife."

Jaxson's expression grows hard as he addresses Jordan, "I don't remember that topic being up for discussion. My relationship with Donda is separate from my former wife and not up for debate. Just like you haven't asked me for permission to date the 1,486 guys you've dated over the past few years, I don't have to give you a complete accounting for my choices. It's simply not your business."

I'm watching the drama unfold in front of me and I feel like a fly stuck on flypaper. I'm not sure what to do. Yvette asked me to be here but I feel like my presence is disruptive. Jaxson needs me here as well. I glance up at Yvette to see how this is affecting her and the expression on her face compels me to take action.

"Okay, the two of you need to go out for coffee, yoga, sumo wrestling, or some crap like that — but the bottom line is you don't need to be here. Until you can work out whatever is going on between you, you're upsetting your mom. So, go. I've got to do some girly stuff with your mom anyway," I declare as I pull some nail polish remover out of my backpack.

"I'm fully capable of doing 'girly stuff' with my mom," Jordan insists.

"I'm sure you are," Yvette concedes, "but right now, Donda isn't trying to pick a fight with anybody. Go work it out with your brother, I've got bigger stuff to deal with right now."

Jordan lets out a huge dramatic sigh as she complains, "Why doesn't anyone understand Jaxson is the one who started this by bringing a stranger in here?"

"Jordan Shepherd, have you lost your marbles?" Yvette challenges. "First, I already told you I invited Donda to be here today. Secondly, even if I hadn't, she'd have every right to be here because she's your brother's girlfriend."

Finally, the tension gets to be too much for me and I look to Jaxson. "Jax, I know you want me to be here, but would it be healthier for your family if I wasn't? I know better than anybody how uncomfortable it can be when someone comes in from the outside who seemingly doesn't belong. I don't want to be your version of Denny."

Yvette pipes up in my defense, "I don't know exactly who Denny is, but I want you to stay."

At the same time, Jaxson answers, "I *do* know who Denny is, and he's exactly the kind of reason you need to stay. At first, things were not okay between you and didn't seem to click, but eventually you guys worked things out. I think it's just a rough spot between you and Jordan and you guys can come to a truce. I don't know what's gotten into my sister, but she's not usually this way."

I roll my neck and pick at the paint under my nails. "Look, I don't know. I do know your mom and I feel stuck in the middle between whatever's going on between the two of you. If you guys can go work it out sooner rather than later, that would be great."

The room is tensely silent for a few moments before Jordan speaks up with an amused smirk, "I don't know if you noticed, but I think we just got sent to our rooms by your girlfriend."

After the door closes behind them with a quiet whoosh, Yvette sinks back against the pillows and closes her eyes as she dryly comments, "Well, that was hardly the warm fuzzy family moment I had envisioned this morning."

"Don't worry about it. It's pretty much how it used to be between my brother and me. It's just been recently, since my mom had cancer, that we've been able to have a civil conversation," I disclose. "Sometimes, I wonder if that's just the way it is between siblings."

Yvette wipes her palms across her eyes as she asks in a quiet voice, "Don't they understand I love them both?"

"I think they do. Fear and anxiety make us do weird things," I answer carefully as I take her hand and examine her nails. "Do you mind if I take your polish off? The anesthesiologist is going to want it off anyway."

She gasps in dismay as she exclaims, "Oh no, I

didn't think about that. Sylvia did such a beautiful job on my nails this week too."

I pat her on the shoulder. "I'll fix you right up after surgery. I got pretty good during all those years I practiced being a nail technician on my little brother."

I figure things probably will be okay with Yvette when she winks at me. "Perhaps that might explain why the two of you don't get along so well."

———◆———

Whatever Jaxson and Jordan did during the coffee break seemed to work wonders; I no longer have to pull daggers out of my back as we wait for Yvette to come out of surgery. That doesn't mean I'm not completely going out of my mind with nerves and anxiety. It's exhausting to try to pretend to have it all together when inside I'm a complete mess.

Jaxson is busy reading some medical journals and Jordan is on the phone so I decide to try to focus on something besides Yvette and the abhorrent hospital background. I pull up my email accounts for Claim Your Space and start checking them. Gabriel has set up my smart phone so I can basically run my whole office from it. It's strange for me to think that anyone can reach me any time of day or night. I miss the days when you could clock into your work and clock back out when your day was done. It seems like these days, no one's day is ever finished. I receive an email from my friend at the television station and an odd file I don't recognize. She warns me not to open the video unless I have Wi-Fi access.

"Oh great! I have no idea how to set up any kind of access. I can't even function without my resident computer nerd," I mutter to myself.

Jordan peers over my shoulder. "Problem?"

I'm too exasperated to be startled, so I'm uncharacteristically unguarded . "It's nothing, I need to open this file for work and I don't know how to set up access to do it. My teenager usually does all that stuff for me. I don't even know how to turn on Wi-Fi when I'm not at home."

Jordan takes a quick look at the model of my phone and says, "I can set it up for you really quick. I'll just set up a hotspot on my phone for you. I've got tons of data; my company pays for it and they don't care how we use it."

"Are you sure? I don't want to be a problem," I hesitate.

"Yeah, I'm sure. I need to think about something, *anything* other than Mom right now. The alternative is watching reruns of Barney I think I remember watching when I was a kid and that's pretty scary."

"I hear you. I was here with my mom a couple years ago. I wish I could tell you there is an easy way to get through this process, but there's just not. It's something you get through the best way you can. I appreciate the offer of help though. This email seems important, so I should probably check it as soon as I can."

Jordan puts her hand out and raises an eyebrow at me as she waits for me to hand her my phone. "Do you mind?"

As I hand her my cellphone in the well-lit atrium style waiting room, I realize some of her makeup has come off.

Jordan notices my increased scrutiny and declares with a sigh, "Look, I'm not contagious okay, I'm too tired to explain it all right now."

A startled laugh escapes me. "Why would I think vitiligo would be contagious? That's just stupid."

"You wouldn't believe the number of stupid people on the planet. I'm glad you're not one of them."

After fiddling with a few more buttons on my phone, she hands it back. "That should work now."

I open the email and wait impatiently as the file takes forever to load. Jordan comes over to stand beside me so she can see what I'm watching.

Much to my shock, it is a video of the outside of the Pennington mansion, complete with theme music and a video montage of me painting my latest mural on the wall of the third guest room in the back. At the end, the jaunty letters across the screen read, "You can Claim Your Space! Sunday morning 10 a.m. Pacific time. Join us for this exciting new home improvement show."

The video fades to black and I stand there in stunned silence.

I feel Jordan's cool hand on my upper bicep as she escorts me to a seat and sits down with me. She squats down by my knee. "Donda, I know this is a lot, but this is a good thing, right? You got your first show! Your work is beautiful, by the way. My brother wasn't kidding when he said you're talented."

"What am I doing with a show?" I fret with panic in my voice. "I'm just starting to get my business off the ground. I've got no business hosting a show. What was I thinking?"

"You might just be getting this reincarnation of yourself underway, but you've been an artist for a long time, correct?" Jordan confirms.

"I guess in one form or another. Mostly I think I'm scattered — especially when you compare me to my former premed, current lifesaving-lawyer brother."

"I know all about overachieving brothers, remember?" Jordan commiserates. "Still, today is about you and what you accomplished. Getting your own show is huge. You should be proud of yourself."

"I guess so. Right now, I guess I'm in shock. It started out as helping a friend with his film school project. He used to film me for fun and I knew he interned at the TV station, but I never thought anything about it. After I did the one project for the reporter, she was thrilled and said I should have a show, but people say those kinds of things to be nice all the time. I never thought anything would come out of it," I ramble.

"It's all right to be rattled. I feel that way every time we book a big show, I always want to pinch myself and wonder if it's my life I'm really leading. I'm just a little girl from the suburbs in Oregon, what am I doing booking huge shows with major fashion magazines in New York?" Jordan looks around before commenting, "Why isn't my big brother in on this momentous news?"

I scan the waiting room. "I'm not sure. The last I checked, he was reading up on some medical stuff for some surgeries he's going to assist with soon."

I can tell when Jordan finds Jaxson standing over by the bank of vending machines. He is talking on his cellphone and gesturing wildly with his hands. Suddenly, Jordan sways on her heels and lets out a pained gasp. Her mind apparently went where mine did: *Maybe it's the worst possible news and they're breaking it to him privately, doctor-to-doctor first.* Jordan buries her face in her hands and pleads, "Oh please, don't let it be Mom.

CHAPTER SIXTEEN

JAXSON

MY FAVORITE BOOKS AND movies are the ones where they mess with the concept of time. I really wish I could do that today. Just a few hours ago, my life felt perfect. My mom was feeling optimistic about the outcome of her surgery today, my Chief Resident was happy with my performance and Donda was wrapped around my body like the lovely, exotic creature she is. Now, my feeling of contentment has been blown to smithereens and I'm not exactly sure when it happened. One moment, everything seemed fine, and then it wasn't.

I'm totally bowled over by the fact that Jordan doesn't like Donda. I figured they might have a lot of things in common since they both work in creative fields. I know since Marquette pulled her crap with Jasmine and then got away with it, Jordan's been crazy protective of me, but let's face it: it's been almost fifteen years since Jasmine died. What happened between Marquette and me has nothing to do with Donda. My sister needs to learn to leave the past in the past. I can't make it better, I can't bring Jasmine back and Marquette has paid the only price she'll ever pay for what she did. There's no point in rehashing everything and embarrassing Donda. It would just upset Mom. It all seems to be working out better now. Jordan seems to be talking to Donda and there doesn't seem to be any hostility between the two of them. They must be watching YouTube videos or something on Donda's phone.

I wish I was over there with them, but I can't be because I'm stuck on the phone with the hospital. A patient they operated on the other day has developed an unusual infection in his bone, so they are going over the procedure with a fine-toothed comb. The attorneys for the hospital want to interview me to see if I broke protocol, but I didn't even touch the patient. It was standing room only in there. Specialists were called in because of the severity of the fracture. Some more senior physicians were attending and other residents wanted to step up so I took a backseat and watched. I'm confident about my role in the surgery so I text him and remind him about the video of the procedure. Of course, because it's text, my suggestion gets interpreted as attitude when I was only trying to be helpful. I seriously don't have time for this today.

I'm getting worried about the amount of time it's taking them to do Mom's procedure. A lumpectomy should be standard and short. However, she's been back there a while. The nurses should be coming forward and notifying us soon that she's doing fine and is in step down. Weirdly, it's not what's happening so I'm becoming increasingly stressed out over my mom's situation, not to mention what's going on with my sister and work and the distressed expression on Donda's face. I can't tell what's going on, but she looks like she's been hit by a truck. Mercifully, the bureaucrat on the other end of the phone finally decides to let me go.

As I walk up behind Donda, I hear Jordan tell her, "After this whole deal is done, I'm going to get so drunk, I won't remember anything until next Thursday. We might as well turn it into a celebration of your news. You want to join me?"

I can feel Donda instinctively stiffen in reaction to those words. I place my hands on her shoulders. "Good news? What did I miss? Was it something about Mom?"

Donda shakes her head no. "No, it was a work thing. They picked up the series about Claim Your Space. We thought maybe you had heard something about your mom because we saw you on the phone."

"No, I haven't. That was my work. Sadly, I don't have such great news. Unfortunately, I can't talk about it — let's put it this way: it's not happy news — nothing worth celebrating. However, we should totally celebrate your news. I knew it would happen for you. Your work is phenomenal. I can't believe you haven't been 'discovered' long before now."

"Thank you, but I think as my boyfriend, you are supposed to be a big fan," she answers with a grin. Turning to Jordan she says, "I don't really do the drinking thing anymore, but if my overprotective personal doctor here says I'm clear to dance, he owes me a night out on the town. That might be fun."

I watch anger settle over my sister like fog on a fall morning. Jordan shoots me an angry glare and compresses her lips into a thin line. She turns her back on me and responds to Donda, "I don't know if I'll be able to fit it into my schedule. It depends on how it works out with my mom."

———•———

My mom was slow to come out of anesthesia, but otherwise everything seemed to go okay with the lumpectomy. Right now, all she wants to do is get all the wires and needles out of her and go home. I don't blame her. It's been a long day. I'm not sure what's going on between everyone. I'm stressed and at a loss to explain the dynamics. One moment, everything seemed okay, and the next moment, it all seemed to blow up in my face again like it did this morning and I'm not quite sure what happened.

Abruptly, Jordan announces, "Donda, would you mind driving Jaxson's car back to Mom's house? I need him to drive the rental car back to the house with us. I'm getting a bad migraine. After we drop Mom off at the house, I need to go to the pharmacy to get a prescription filled."

Donda appears surprised, but replies, "Not a problem. I was a valet during one of my many offbeat jobs in my lifetime. I can drive pretty much anything even with a stick."

"You sure have led an interesting life," my sister comments almost dismissively.

"That's putting it mildly," responds Donda with a tight grin.

Mom was dizzy and tired on the way home, but the transition went well. Donda stayed behind to take care of her while I take Jordan on her errands around town. The tension in the car is thick. I'm so tired. I don't even know what day of the week it is, let alone what everyone is fighting about. I finally pull the rental car into an obscure spot in the corner of the parking lot.

I shut it off, turn to Jordan and bluntly ask, "I'm too tired to guess. What has crawled up your butt?"

I am shocked at the amount of rage in my sister's eyes. "I don't know. Maybe I should ask you. What, or maybe I should say who, is crawling up yours? I thought maybe you learned your lesson with Marquette, but maybe not. This Donda — she's pretty, I'll give you that. She appears to be talented enough. For Pete's sake, Jaxson! This girl has 'messed up' tattooed on her forehead. Do you advertise for women like this in your life?"

I feel like one of those cartoon characters I grew up watching. I can feel rage roll up from my toes to the top of my head. If it were physically possible for steam to be rolling out of my ears, it probably would be. I have to grit my teeth and take a few moments to take several deep breaths before I speak. If I don't, I know I will say something to my sister I cannot take back. Our mother is facing a potentially terminal illness. This is not the time to blow up our family. I need to remember that during every second of this conversation. This is bigger than me and my ego.

When I can speak reasonably, I turn to look at

Jordan and say, "You really have no idea what you're talking about? The only similarity between Donda and Marquette is that they were both impossibly young when they became mothers and life had a way of screwing them both over before they were big enough to have a voice to fight back. That's it."

"Why her!" Jordan argues. "You're a doctor; you're so successful, you could have anyone you want. You could have a business executive or you could have a traditional housewife to stay home and do nothing but whatever you want her to do. You could have a socialite out of Martha's Vineyard ... you could choose your wish list — why would you want a junkie?"

I level an even stare at her as I try to keep my voice even as I explain, "Let's get this straight. Donda is *not* a junkie. She has more than a decade of sobriety behind her. A history of substance abuse does not make you a bad person. Let me see if I can make this clear enough for you. Donda *is* my wish list. She's bright, witty, funny, creative, compassionate and stubborn as heck. She's an amazing mother and is beautiful to our mother, in case you haven't noticed. I can't ask for anything more."

"That's the other thing: don't you think it's convenient she comes pre-packaged with a perfect little family? Do you really want to be raising another man's mess? You have no idea about all the crazy stuff I saw when I was a nanny. Blended families are a recipe for disaster. Women like Donda would go out seeking men like you. When I used to take the kids to the park, I would hear these women strategizing about how to catch a good guy with their kids; it was sickening."

"I agree, kids should not be used as shiny trophy pieces. But it's not happening here. I was the one who chased Donda. She's been putting up all sorts of caution flags. She's been burned as many times as I've been, if not more. She watches out for Gabriel's well-being like a fierce lioness. There is no way she's putting him out there as bait for a handsome guy who happens to want to be a dad. Don't get me wrong, Gabriel is hands-down the coolest kid I've ever met. If I can step in and give him any guidance or mentoring along the way, I'd be more than happy to, but he doesn't need any help from me. He's remarkable all on his own. Donda has done a phenomenal job with him."

"Isn't it weird playing daddy for a kid who's not yours, knowing Jasmine would've been about the same age?" probes Jordan.

"Some days, it brings me to my knees. I don't expect it to get any easier as he gets older either; he'll have the prom and graduation and his marriage to get through. All those milestones will be like reliving Jasmine's death all over again. Yet, I can't separate the two, Gabriel comes with Donda. They're a package deal, if I love one of them, I love them both. I don't get to pick and choose because one hurts my heart more than the other. I have to suck it up and deal."

"That's not fair of her to ask! That's super selfish of her," Jordan insists, indignant on my behalf.

"Jordan, are you even listening to me?" I ask, frustration seeping from every pore. "Donda hasn't asked for one thing from me. Not. One. Thing. I have a hard time getting her to take grocery money from me when I stay at her place and eat her out of house and home. She doesn't cling to me and ask me to make never-ending promises, she never asked me an ironclad commitment for forever, and she certainly never made me promise to fall in love with her. I did anyway. It wasn't something I planned to do, and it complicates things in my personal and professional life — but there you have it. I'm a resident, my mom has cancer, I'm in love with a single mom of a teenager who lives in a different city than I do."

"Jax, are you sure? You thought you were in love before and look what happened —"

"You are my sister and I love you, but you need to get a grip. I am not the same person I was at eighteen, and neither are you. Things change. I'm looking for completely different things now than I was back then. I was young and dumb and not careful. Life has taught me a lot of hard lessons, but you make it sound as if I don't ever deserve to move on. That's just not fair. Are you saying because things didn't work out the first time, I don't ever get to fall in love again?"

"You know me … I'm not even sure I believe in love and family at all. I think the whole thing is a crock-o-poop but that's just me. Personally, I think you could do a lot better than her. I suspect she's a mess you don't need in your life." Jordan sighs as she studies me closely. She finally shrugs. "I suppose if your heart has spoken, there's not a lot you can do. I want to go on record as saying I don't trust her and all she's about. I've seen too many manipulative women use their kids to try to get into a man's life. Look at you: you're handsome, you're successful, by all appearances, you have bucket loads of money. Why wouldn't she go after you? You've got everything she needs and more."

"Geez, thanks a lot. Maybe she just likes me for me. Did you ever think about that? Maybe I'm just a nice guy who is smart and funny and pushes her buttons. Maybe I provide something she needs besides a wallet, a status symbol, nice abs and a night in the sack," I retort.

"Oh, gross! Like I needed to envision my brother making love to anybody. Thanks a lot for the visual," declares my sister as she sticks her tongue out at me.

"*You* brought it up by suggesting that maybe I was some kind of cardboard cutout of a boyfriend worth nothing more than my value on a spreadsheet. I just wanted to make sure you have the whole picture. I didn't want you to shortchange me."

Jordan rolls her eyes at me. "There you go being like every other guy I know: vastly overestimating your skills in the sack. It happens every time. You all think we don't care about anything other than that. It's so laughable. If you knew how little we all think about it, you'd be embarrassed and disappointed."

"I am so not getting into this discussion with you. You are my little sister. Don't you have girlfriends to talk to about this kind of thing with?" I tease.

Much to my surprise, my usually confident sister slouches in her seat. "No, not really. All of my friends are either married with families or getting married and they don't understand why I'm not. They've all decided I'm some sort of weird man-hater. They don't understand why I don't have a compelling need to settle down, get married and have kids. I've never been one to go along with the crowd, but it makes me stand out among all my friends. They just think I'm hating on their lifestyles, I'm not really. I just don't want it for me. They don't seem to understand the difference. I don't have a whole lot of people who want to hang with me anymore. Even if I did, these days, I'm not sure if they want to be around me because of who I am as a person or who I know in my job. It's bizarre."

"Jordan, I hate to say this, because it'll sound all preachy as your big brother … but, sometimes you get back the energy you put out there. You're quick to place judgment on everyone else's choices and lifestyles, maybe you're just getting back some of the negative energy you're pumping into everyone else's face."

"Are you calling me a witch?" she asks incredulously. "So much for family loyalty."

"Just giving you something to think about, Sis. If the shoe fits wear it well, Cinderella." I cuff her cheek like I used to do when we were kids.

"Just remember, I gave you some stuff to think about too," Jordan retorts defensively.

"Trust me, I'm not likely to forget this conversation anytime soon. Now, let's go get your stuff so we can go home and check on Mom." I take the keys out of the ignition and put them in my pocket.

I feel like a character from a television sitcom as Donda and I are back in my childhood bedroom getting ready for bed. Originally, I figured Donda would go back to my place tonight and I would stay with Mom. Unfortunately, an unexpected bout of post-anesthesia nausea modified those plans. For some reason, my mom has decided Donda is the only person who can truly understand her puking woes. Perhaps it's because Donda is trying to keep her spirits up by telling her all sorts of amusing, awkward stories about when she was battling morning sickness with Gabriel or helping her mom with the side effects of chemotherapy, but my mom has decided it's Donda's job to help her cope with everything which might embarrass her. Fortunately, I was able to persuade Jordan to go back to her hotel room and deal with her migraine, so I don't have to handle the additional complication of that relationship as well.

Speaking of headaches, I am precariously close to breaking out with my own stress headache myself. I massage my neck and temple in an effort to delay the onset.

Donda comes in from the bathroom drying her hands on a paper towel. "Poor baby," she murmurs as she walks up behind me and rubs my neck. "I think you need to take your own advice and go get some physical therapy on this. Your back doesn't seem a whole lot better. Were you able to convince your sister I'm not the personification of evil?"

I'm startled by the random nature of her question, but as usual she got to the heart of my conversation with Jordan. "I'm not sure it was quite that bad, she was just being sisterly."

"Come on, I can pretty much guess what she thinks about me, Jaxson. I'm guessing not a lot of it's good — in fact, I would bet you dimes to dollars she told you to dump my butt as quickly as you could."

I grimace slightly. "The conversation did have those overtones, yes. How did you guess?"

"If my brother was an up-and-coming hot-shot orthopedic doctor, and someone like me came hanging around, I'd have a few concerns as well too."

"Does it make you mad that people are judging you about your past?" I ask, confused by her acceptance of Jordan's discrimination.

"Heck *yes,* it makes me mad! It's like I can never grow up from the confused kid I once was, but they were my mistakes and I need to own them. That's not to say I don't wish almost daily I could wake up with a clean slate and have no one understand what I did in the past. Some days, I wish the collective memory of the whole world would blink and the past would not matter. It wouldn't matter to us and it wouldn't matter to anyone else. Wouldn't that be a cool world? We can both benefit from learning from our mistakes but have the true forgiveness of everyone around us. Imagine how amazing it would be to be able to just move forward without being weighed down by what happened to you in the past. Sometimes, I like to imagine I'm operating in that kind of world. That's how I get into the headspace to paint some days. I create a magical place on those walls where people can pretend the present doesn't exist — a parallel universe where everything is perfect, happy and ideal."

I rest my forehead against hers. "Is it all right if I come to inhabit the parallel universe with you? After a day like today, I've decided I don't like it much in this world."

CHAPTER SEVENTEEN

DONDA

"MADISON, I DON'T KNOW why I'm even doing this. I'm telling you, she doesn't like me. I don't see how this little get-together will change anything. It'll be awkward as heck. We're all going to be there pretending to have a good time like we've been lifelong friends or something and I can tell that she'd rather grind me into the ground under those impossibly high stilettos of hers."

Madison fluffs her hair and blots her lipstick on a piece of toilet paper before she winks at me. "Did you forget I'm from Boston? I miss good old-fashioned chick fights. Things are way too laid-back on this coast. No, seriously — will you relax, please? We've all been working far too hard. When was the last time we all got to go out together? Even Aidan and Tara are here and when was the last time we were all in the same place? Although, I can't believe they're trying to go to a regular club, but Aidan says his security has checked out the place and we should be able to go without being mobbed by fans."

Kiera wheels over to me and she is wearing a little

green cocktail dress which flares out at her waist. "Yeah, this is the first time I've been out since I weaned Charlie. I'm feeling footloose and fancy free for a change. I wonder if Jeff even remembers what it's like to go on a date?"

Heather fans herself a little. "I don't know, Kiera — Tyler and Jeff have had their heads together like two kids plotting revenge at recess. It's hard to say what the two of them have cooked up for tonight." Heather looks up at me and asks, "You and Jaxson haven't been discussing marriage plans have you? Our gang is a little too fond of surprise weddings for my comfort. I'm too tired to pull one off at this point. Did I tell you the last big cake order I had, the bride wanted a nine tier wedding cake?"

My jaw goes slack. "Nine tiers? Was this one of your Hollywood weddings?"

"No, that was the kicker. This was just a bride who wanted to one-up her friends from high school. She was having the wedding at a small church and then the reception at a local golf club. I've done smaller weddings at this golf club before. It's nice, but it's not nine-tiers-of-wedding-cake-nice. I felt bad for her mama and daddy because they wanted to give their daughter everything she wanted. However, that cake was just too over the top."

"What did they do?" I ask resisting the urge to nervously chew on my eyeliner pencil. "When I was thinking about marrying Gabriel's dad, I couldn't even afford grocery store wedding cake let alone a nine tier cake from a private bakery — I'm sorry, Heather, I don't mean any disrespect, but your stuff is ex-pen-sive."

Heather laughs at me. "Donda, trust me, I know. If

I didn't make my own wedding cake, I'm not even sure I could afford my own work. I tried to talk the bride into a smaller cake, but she just wouldn't be budged, so the parents ended up taking out a second mortgage on their home. I thought it was too much — but who am I to say anything? I'm only the cake decorator. I know my forearms may never be the same. At this moment, I have a hate/hate relationship with my piping bag. I am so ready to go dancing, you have no idea. Even though Tyler and I live in the same house right now, I've been working so hard he might as well be deployed. I can't wait to spend some quality time wrapped up in my soldier tonight."

"Fine. I get the hint — everybody wants a nice date night. I promise to be on my best behavior. I can't make any promises about what will happen. My very presence seems to make Jaxson's sister angry."

Tara gives me one of her spine-chilling, spooky looks as she instructs, "No, you can't control Jordan, but you can control yourself. You need to do what you do best. Get lost in the music. Let it wash over you and fill every pore. Forget all of your pain and hurt and feel the joy of the music as you dance. Don't forget this has been a really tough time for Jaxson too and he really enjoys dancing. Although he might not be as skilled at dancing as you are, it's as good for his hurting soul as it is for yours," Tara stops speaking for a moment. I thought she was done but then almost as if it's an afterthought she adds, "Donda, I once lost my ability to hear the music because I let my past rule my future, don't make my mistake."

I take a deep breath and let it out as I try to absorb Tara's words. I learned a long time ago you have to let

Tara's advice soak in a while. You have to let it wash over you and sink in where it can. She never tells you directly what to do, she just speaks in riddles and rhymes. You have to pick out what applies to you the best way you can.

I lean down to adjust the buckle on my shoe and then stand straight up. I let out a quick whistle as I direct the Girlfriend Posse, "Let's go 'wow' ourselves some men and influence some people."

———◆———

I don't videotape much of my life. Honestly, I just don't think about it. I know I've got a camera on my phone, but I always forget it's there. In this case, it would have been helpful to have remembered it. Well, maybe not so much helpful as fun and ego building. Jaxson's reaction to the dressed up version of me was worthy of having its own script in a romance movie.

Jaxson's reaction is extreme. It makes me wonder how bad I look on a daily basis. He assures me the two are not related. He loves my dressed down look fine; but he can appreciate having a fine treat every once in a while. Jaxson's admiration of my dress made it worth the time Heather, Tara and I spent picking it out. There isn't very much dress here actually, there are wide cut outs at the waist and the back is pretty much non-existent. I had to trust Tara's fashion advice on this one because Heather's advice tends to be a little over-the-top for my taste, but Tara says I look respectably sexy. I'll have to take her word for now.

As we sit down at the table, Jordan studies my dress carefully. "Wow, I saw that design a couple weeks ago at a show, I didn't realize Ka'lka was planning to bring them to market so quickly."

Aidan speaks up on my behalf, "That's probably because she didn't. Ka'lka gave it to Donda. We're working with Ka'lka on outfits for the Grammys and as soon as she saw how tall Donda is, she insisted she find a place to wear that dress often."

I look down at the knit, body-conscious dress with the clean lines and simple embellishment at the waist. "I like your friend, Aidan. She designs great dresses. Unlike most dresses, this one is comfortable to wear. If I don't get a chance to tell her thank you, will you let her know I really love it?"

Jordan's jaw goes slack. "You're telling me Ka'lka gave you a fifteen thousand dollar dress? For no other reason, than just because? You don't have to do any endorsements, show up at any celebrity parties or anything?"

I start to choke on my drink as I instinctively gasp. I turn to Aidan and Tara. "You guys never told me this was valuable. I thought it was a leftover dress that didn't fit one of the people from your show! There's no way I would wear a dress this expensive. I wouldn't even put it on my body! I sweat when I dance; I'm going to ruin this thing. I don't have that kind of money."

Tara narrows her gaze at Jordan as she responds to me, "First of all, Ka'lka gave you the dress because she wanted you to have it. It would be rude of you to give it back, regardless of how much it's worth. Designing dresses is how she expresses her creativity just like I dance and you paint walls. It's how it's done. It's just because someone has decided her art is worth a lot more right now. Secondly, every dancer worth their stuff knows how to get sweat out of a costume. It's a skill you pick up. It's no big deal. So dance away."

Kiera nods. "What Tara doesn't know how to get out of your dress I can probably figure out. You wouldn't believe all the nasty stuff I get on my clothes, being in a wheelchair. Go and have a good time and don't worry about your dress, we've got you covered. After all, we are the Girlfriend Posse."

"Girlfriend Posse?" Jordan inquires with a puzzled expression.

Tara examines Jordan carefully before disclosing, "Girlfriend Posse is the term we came up with for the group of us who are very close friends. We always have each other's backs at all times under any circumstances without any questions asked. Over the years, our group has gotten much larger as our family has grown through marriage and relationships. If you want to open your mind and your heart to the friendships we offer, you are welcome to join our group. However, among the things we don't tolerate in our group are prejudice, prejudgment and meanness for sport."

"Wow, already making snap judgments about me without even knowing me, huh?" Jordan replies with a sour expression. "I suppose Donda has told you all sorts of terrible things about me."

"No, actually the only thing she really told me about you was your name. The rest of my impression of you came from you. The good news is you have the rest of the evening to change that," Tara responds.

Jaxson is laughing as he comes back to the table. "You should've warned me not to play video games against these two," he declares pointing at Tyler and Trevor.

I raise an eyebrow at Tyler,. "Isn't it a little unfair and dishonest of you not to disclose you've been playing Pac-Man in Aidan's man cave for close to five years now?"

Tyler looks a little chagrined. "Okay, so maybe we shouldn't have wagered against him. That may have been a little unfair, but in our defense, we didn't know what advantage his surgeon's hands might give him."

I throw a cocktail napkin at him as I respond, "Yeah, yeah, tell it to the judge, Officer Colton. Sometimes I have a hard time believing people think you're a good influence on my son. I think it's the other way around; I think Gabriel keeps you on the straight and narrow."

I pivot to Jaxson. "Dare I ask what they won from you?"

"I'm not sure exactly, because it's crazy loud in here. As far as I can tell, I'm supposed to be helping out with something involving the Oregon Supreme Court, a lake somewhere, some driftwood and a damsel in distress. I think I'm either drunk or very confused," Jaxson replies with a shrug.

I look over at my brother who has pulled Kiera up onto his lap. "I better not hear you're involved in this," I threaten.

Jeff looks up from his conversation with Kiera with a blank look on his face, "Involved in what?"

"Whatever scheme these two bozos have come up with to try to con my boyfriend into helping them with the gargantuan project they're working on with William to redo his pile of sticks he affectionately calls a boat —
"

Jeff shakes his head and chuckles. "Nope, not me; I try to stay as far away from that thing as I can. It's like EPA waste. You think you know what you're looking at, but the next time you look at it it's even bigger than before."

"What is this thing?" Jaxson asks.

"Trust me, you're better off not knowing. William is a very nice man, and I'm sure he was a great Supreme Court justice in his day and he probably served Oregon well, but boating is not his thing."

"This is a relative of yours?" Jaxson attempts to clarify.

The table erupts into a cacophony of "Yes, no, and sort ofs."

Jordan looks around the table in complete astonishment as she comments, "One would think that would be a yes or no question, right? You don't get to pick your relatives."

Heather pipes up, "Honey, it's not so simple in this group. You sort of can pick your family in this group or you can wait long enough and family members might marry each other," she finishes with a laugh. When she sees Jordan's frustration at her response, she continues her explanation. "It started out pretty simply. Denny is Kiera's daddy. Kiera lost her mama early on. William — the former Oregon Supreme Court Justice, and avid fisherman, has been Denny's friend since childhood. Denny made William and his wife, Isobel, Kiera's godparents. When Kiera was little, she came to Boston to have surgery; I was also at the hospital and became her best friend. When Kiera grew up, she went to college and met Tara and also became her best friend. When Kiera got married, Tara and I were her bridesmaids. A dashing young musician, Aidan, played the piano and was smitten by the beautiful Tara. Jeff and Kiera were not done with their matchmaking quite yet. Jeff had this annoyingly handsome, yet bothersome giant of a cowboy friend he had known since high school who seems to find me quite fetching. I couldn't resist Tyler Colton and I fell in love."

"Well, someone should contact the Hallmark Movie Channel," Jordan snaps sarcastically.

Madison just peers at Jordan over the top of her martini as Trevor kisses the back of her neck. "Just wait, you haven't heard all of it yet."

Jordan rolls her eyes and says, "You mean there's more? You all have to be making this up."

Tyler straightens to his full height and responds in a deep voice, "No ma'am, she's not kidding. We'd be happy to show you marriage licenses if you'd like."

"Geez, I was just kidding, get over yourself. Go on with your story, I'm sure it's romantic like everyone else's story."

"Actually, it is. The next love story took us by surprise. My sister, Madison, was on the run from a stalker, but the rest of us didn't know that. Trevor was one of Tyler's Army buddies who came to stay with us while Tyler was deployed to help me run the farm. He came to Madison's rescue and helped catch the stalker. In the meantime, they fell in love."

"Hey, I saw your story on the news, your stalker turned out to be your ex-wife or something, right?" Jordan asks Trevor.

"Yes, it was one of those, 'you can't make this stuff up because it's stranger than fiction' things," Trevor confirms. "In a weird way it was all worth it because I have an amazing wife and daughter I would've never had if I hadn't lost my leg and ended up at the lieutenant's house with my crazy ex-wife chasing Maddie."

"Maybe I should take back my remark. Maybe you really should contact the Hallmark Channel. You guys have some pretty remarkable stories," Jordan concedes.

"Wait, you haven't heard the granddaddy of all romantic tales just yet," I remark.

Jordan's eyes widen in surprise. "You mean, there is even more? What do you guys put in the water out here?"

Madison snorts with laughter. "I've often thought that myself. You know, it's too bad Denny is not here to tell the story because he is a phenomenal storyteller. The rest of us are left to piece the story together from the outside so we don't know exactly when the love story came together between the two of them."

"The two of who?"

"I'm sorry, I forget that not everybody knows everybody in our little group," Kiera answers, taking a sip of her iced tea. "Gwendolyn is Jeff and Donda's mother. Their father was in a boating accident when they were kids. My dad is Denny. My mom died from a brain tumor when I was a toddler. After Jeff and I got married, my dad and Gwendolyn started spending a lot of time together. No one thought too much of it because our families spend a lot of time together and we had just adopted the girls so it was natural to socialize with each other and our parents were both active. They liked to get out and do things together. Somewhere along the way, their friendship changed into love. Our parents married each other in a beautiful ceremony. It was an amazing tribute to our families and to love, to the past, to the present and the future. It was a rough couple of years and it was great to see such hope come out of it."

A dark expression comes across Jordan's face as she addresses Kiera, "That's great. I'm glad the family thing has worked out for all of you. I think statistically it's not realistic to expect it will work out for everyone — but, I wish you the best." She slams her drink down on the counter and heads off toward the women's restroom.

I look up at Jaxson with concern. He brushes his fingers across my brow. "Don't worry about it, she'll calm down in a few moments. I think she's got something going on back at home which doesn't have anything to do with us. I don't know what it is. Maybe she's got man problems or something. Come on, I promised you a few turns on the dance floor, don't let her spoil our fun."

⸻ • ⸻

The dance floor is dark and seductive as Jaxson pulls me into his arms. It's a silly, almost girly thing but Jaxson is the perfect size for me. As a tall woman, I often feel like I tower over the world around me. It's hard to feel dainty and feminine when you often have to stare down at men in your life. I know I'm strong and capable, but sometimes it feels good to be cocooned in someone's arms.

I haven't been dancing in a while and when I do go dancing, I usually try to stick to the light, flirty songs because I *really* like to dance. It's like something comes over me and I forget I'm in a public place. I tend to interpret the lyrics through my body movements, so I have to be careful what I dance to. My kind of dancing is okay if I'm jammin' in Tara's dance studio with the Girlfriend Posse, but it can get me in a little trouble if I'm dancing in a club full of strangers. Back in the days when I was chronically not sober, I never noticed how much danger I put myself in. Now that I know the risks, I'm horrified at what I must've been like when I was under the influence. Let's be honest, I'm lucky I wasn't a bigger mess. I must have angels living on my shoulders — come to think of it, they probably have condominiums there.

Jaxson swings me around in an elaborate dance move and then collects me back into his chest and kisses me thoroughly, reminding me he isn't some random dance partner at the club. The stakes are high and oh so deliciously personal.

I pull him closer to deepen the kiss as the song ends. My fingers curl around his strong biceps so I don't fall down. My knees are trembling and it has nothing to do with my injury from the accident. The desire coursing through my body is easily short-circuiting my brain. I can feel the heat of Jaxson's hands at my waist.

A sound starts to break into my consciousness as I break away from the kiss and notice the cocktail waitress who served us our drinks is discreetly clearing her throat beside us. I quickly stand upright and wipe my lips with the back of my hand. I feel like I've just been busted at the prom making out with my boyfriend under the bleachers.

"I'm sorry to disturb you, but are you Donda?" she asks, hesitantly.

I nod my head to confirm. "Yes, I'm Donda."

"Your friend needs you in the restroom," the waitress informs me.

I grab my cellphone and throw my purse at Jaxson as I sprint toward the bathroom. "I'll be right back, Kiera probably needs help to get into her chair."

I quickly open the bathroom door, half expecting to see Kira sprawled on the floor, instead I find Jordan sitting on the bathroom vanity. "It's nice to see you surgically remove yourself from my brother's lips long enough to see if anybody actually needs help. You know, I see family is actually pretty important to you. That's cool. But this whole thing you've got going with my brother — it won't work, you know that, right?"

"What thing?"

"This whole bogus family thing," Jordan responds with venom.

"Don't pretend you haven't dangled in front of him what he's always wanted but couldn't have because of what Marquette snatched away from him. Don't worry, Jaxson knows who his real family is — your family is not his real family."

"Jordan, I'm not trying to substitute my family for

yours. I like your mom," I insist.

"You have a mom, why don't you stick with your own?"

"Jordan, I don't understand, I'm not trying to take your mom either. I've got my own mom," I answer defensively.

"Exactly!" exclaims Jordan triumphantly. "You've got your own brother, and your own mother in your own life, why are you bothering my family?"

I'm completely perplexed and befuddled by her question. I take a few moments to try to wrap my brain around it, but no matter how I take it apart and put it back together, it doesn't make any sense.

I open my mouth to speak but she interrupts me.

"I'll make him choose, you know. This vision of a perfect family your friends and family present, it's not real. I just want you to know. It's all an illusion that goes away. You blink and it's gone. Don't go thinking you got it all just because you've got family and the perfect postcard life."

Her words absolutely horrify me. If she were to present a choice like that to Jaxson, it would completely crush him. I can't imagine a crueler thing to do. As I take a moment to study her in the mirror, I have no doubt she would do it in a heartbeat.

I know to help the person I love, I'll have to do something which hurts him deeply — that's the worst.

<hr>

Heather and Kiera might have understood my

decision last night when they escorted my sobbing body home and fed me warm tea and Oreo cookies until I could breathe without choking on my own snot, but it appears my son isn't quite as supportive of my decision. I cringe as I unfold the scrawled note he left attached to my purse.

WTF Mom! I thought you were going to give Jaxson a chance.

CHAPTER EIGHTEEN

JAXSON

AS A DOCTOR, I'M getting used to my life changing in the blink of an eye, but I'm getting sick of it happening in my personal life too. Every time Donda and I get on some sort of even ground, something blows up in my face. I thought we were having a great time with her family and friends when we went out dancing. Sure, my sister was being a little petulant, but I didn't think it'd be enough to derail the whole evening. Jordan can revert to her teenage self quickly when she has alcohol on board. Honestly, I was just prepared to let her sit and sulk for a while because she always comes around. I was stunned when my girlfriend ditched me at the party — so much for celebrating Donda's good news — I don't know what happened. One moment we were practically making love on the dance floor and the next moment I'm pathetically waiting for her to come out of the bathroom.

Donda must've turned off her cellphone because phone calls are going directly to voicemail and my text messages are being completely ignored. There's not any indication she's reading them. I hope there isn't something more serious going on. Marquette used to cut everyone out of her life too when she was going on a drug binge. I hate that my mind goes there, but I don't know what else to think. Everything seemed normal when she went into the bathroom at the bar and then it wasn't. I've seen that pattern too many times with my ex-wife.

Right now, I don't even have the luxury of thinking about it much — three days of black ice has taken care of that. There have been multiple MVAs in the last few days, not to mention orthopedic injuries from slips and falls. Between elderly people falling on stairs and kids having sledding accidents, it's pretty much been a free-for-all in the surgery suites.

As I scrub into surgery on a teenager who rolled over an SUV that had four-wheel-drive, I'm relieved that Gabriel wasn't able to get his car quite yet. I give myself an inner eye roll at the direction of my thoughts. They haven't even been gone a whole month yet I think about them all the time.

Fixing the compound fracture didn't take quite as long as I had expected, I guess I'm getting more proficient with time. As I change back into my street clothes and collect my cell phone from my pocket, I notice there's a text message from Gabriel.

Need your help ASAP — G

The message was sent about thirty minutes ago. I look at my watch and realize he might be at lunch so I return the message, *Just got out of surgery, what do you need?*

Can you meet me at the school?

In an instant, my plan to go home and crash evaporates. If Gabriel is reaching out to me, perhaps he knows something about Donda. I haven't heard anything from her in weeks. I'm starting to get really worried. I can't let this opportunity go by without touching base with Gabriel.

I suppose so. Don't you have class? I respond.

I'll explain when you get here.

Maybe he's only being cryptic because he's on the phone, but it's not like Gabriel to be cryptic. In fact, since we became friends, the teen is pretty much like a never-ending fountain of words. I'm honored he brought me into his circle of friends and since he discovered that my mom is a crossword puzzle aficionado, he and my mom have been having little competitions online. Still, something about the way that he's communicating with me now, makes the hair on the back of my neck stand up on end. It seems more than usual teenage angst.

After I show my ID at the front desk in the school office, I asked where I should wait to meet Gabriel and I'm puzzled when the receptionist informs me he is waiting for me in the vice principal's office.

Wordlessly, I allow her to escort me to the principal's office. Weirdly enough, it doesn't feel any different now than when I was a kid. You would think now that I am a doctor, I would somehow feel more in charge of the meeting. I don't. I guess old feelings die hard. I swallow hard before going inside the office and taking a seat beside Gabriel.

I'm surprised when the Vice Principal reaches out his hand to shake mine and remarks, "It's always nice to meet the fathers in these situations, I'm Vice Principal French. I'm new to the district, I don't think we've had a chance to meet yet."

I open my mouth to speak, but then think better of it and observe the situation for a bit longer before I comment.

"Where's Mom today?" the Vice Principal asks as if he's suddenly Gabriel's new best friend.

I can feel Gabriel stiffen beside me. "She is working. She had an important meeting in Eugene and she won't be back until later this afternoon."

"Gabriel, why am I meeting you here instead of having lunch?" I ask as I rub my throbbing temple.

"Some things can be said and I just let them fly, you know what I mean? Other things have no business being said," Gabriel responds, frustration clipping his words.

"What happened?" I ask, relatively sure I don't really want to know.

"For the record, it's not my fault I'm a better fighter than Brady is. If the jerk is going to call somebody's mom a crack whore, he should really have some skills behind his words."

"Hold on, I think maybe you should tell me the story from the beginning," I reply.

"Okay, I've got nothing to hide," Gabriel straightens in his seat and leans forward. "You would've done the same thing as me. I was just minding my own business. I got out of my fourth-period class early because we had state testing and I was finished. I went to the library to work on some of my drawings for my comic book. Brady came up and started talking smack. He said his dad was on the task force that put my dad in jail. That's no big flippin' news story, everybody knows my dad died in jail. Then he started in saying my mom is a dirty crack whore and the only reason she stayed outta jail was that she flipped on my dad."

I have to bite back curse words.

"When I told him he had no idea what he was talking about, he called me a 'lying piece of sh —'" Gabriel's speech breaks off as he scrubs a hand down his face. "Brady claims that he knows she's been going to NA and AA meetings because his dad has an inside source and she better watch her back. He plays football, so he's wider than me even though he's not taller than me. He tried to intimidate me by grabbing my sweatshirt and pulling it tight against my neck. I've known how to get out of a hold forever because Aunt Tara teaches self-defense classes. I jumped up out of my chair and spun out of the hold and just stood up. He was so surprised that I was able to get away from him, he went and told the librarian I was the one who was picking on him and that I had threatened to start a race war. So, for whatever reason, Brady is sitting in his class and I am sitting in here."

I turn to the Vice Principal. "Is that true? There were two kids in the fight; did you release the other student before an investigation was done?"

"Well … umm," the Vice Principal stammers, "Brady O'Toole is one of our star athletes and he's never been a disciplinary problem before."

"Sir, with all due respect, I think you should check

Gabriel Whitaker's academic record as well," I suggest.

As a rosy hue takes over his body, the Vice Principal turns back to his computer and types in Gabriel's name. He softly whistles through his teeth as he exclaims, "I see Brady is not the only All-Star athlete. It seems you are an academic All-Star as well."

"I guess his question remains unanswered, if Brady was the first aggressor, why is Gabriel the one sitting here in your office?"

"He should've contacted a school official to intervene," the Vice Principal blusters.

"Had he done so, would the response have been any more even-handed?" I ask pointedly.

"It's hard to tell without having been there to witness the incident. Without both parties here to interview, I can't determine what happened, but I find that Gabriel's account is credible and since he doesn't have a disciplinary history either, I'm going to give him the benefit of the doubt. State testing is done for the day and to avoid any further conflicts today I will excuse him from the rest of his classes today," the Vice Principal instructs staring at me. I have mixed emotions about this solution since the other kid involved gets to stay in class, but as I glance over at Gabriel, he looks exhausted.

I look over at Gabriel and ask, "You have anything else you need to finish up here today?"

Gabriel shakes his head. "I guess not."

"Sorry for the inconvenience, Mr. Whitaker, I'll sign you out." the administrator states as he shakes my hand.

As we're walking to the car, Gabriel comments,

"That was beyond weird."

"Not real familiar with the inside of the principal's office?" I guess.

"Not so much. They call me the Archangel around here because I get good grades. It's a little annoying being known as the goody-two-shoes."

"You could be known for far worse things, trust me."

Gabriel opens my car and throws his backpack in the backseat and then slouches down in the passenger's seat before continuing to explain, "Yeah, I know. People always assume that I'll be nothing but a thug just because of where I came from. My dad was on trial for dealing drugs when I was in preschool. Some people still remember that. They assume I'm going to grow up to be the same way. It's weird, they never assume that I'm going to grow up to be like my uncle Jeff who is an attorney or my great grandpa who was a war hero. They think I'm going to be a junkie like my dad. I barely knew him."

"I know what that's like. My dad disappeared when I was just a baby. I did my best to be mediocre. I just wanted to fit in with my friends and make it okay for my mom and sister. I didn't really get serious about life until I got my girl pregnant. Instead of trying out for hoops to make it as a walk on in college, I was bagging groceries and worrying about how I would keep the heat on so my kid didn't freeze to death."

"Your girlfriend didn't help with the bills?" Gabriel asks.

"Well, by that time Marquette was my wife. Her parents were pretty traditional, and they were having a hard time with the fact that she got pregnant so young and getting married before the baby arrived just seemed like the right thing to do. Jasmine was so little when she was born, she wasn't even quite six pounds but, I swear all six pounds of her were in her lungs. Man, that little doll could cry so loud, I think the neighbors of the neighbors could hear. I know now that Jasmine probably had something called GERD, but all I knew then was she was the fussiest baby I ever saw. She cried all the time. It seemed like we could never do anything to make her happy. Marquette couldn't deal with it all. She wanted to go back to the life she had before she was a mom. She started to hang out with friends she had made in our new apartment complex. You can imagine that on my meager salary and the bit my mom was able to help out with, we didn't live in a very nice place. I was so busy trying to keep a roof over our heads, I didn't realize I was losing Marquette in the process. In the end, I lost everything that mattered to me."

I glance over and see Gabriel's face cloud with emotion before he turns away. It's quiet for a bit before he blurts, "If you've lost everything once before, why did you throw it all away with my mom? I thought what you had with her was good. I thought you liked us. I thought you liked *me*. I thought we were like a real family for a change. I thought we were different." Gabriel stops as his voice starts to break and he uses his sweatshirt to wipe tears from his eyes.

"Gabriel, I do like you. I do consider you like my family. I changed nothing. I didn't call it quits. Your mom quit on me. I don't know what happened. Your mom won't talk to me, she won't return my calls, when I stop by the house, she won't answer the door. I don't have a way to reach her. I have no idea why were not together anymore."

"Seriously, that's it? You're gonna let my mom quit that easy? Dude! You're a doctor! You gotta have more in you than that! If she was dying, would you give her thirty seconds of CPR? No! You'd give it everything you had. You would work on her until your arms could give no more. That's what you have to do with my mom. My mom is scared to death — she's worried that she's not worth it. She doesn't want you to sacrifice your relationship with your sister and your mom for her. She doesn't believe she is worth your love —"

"Crap! You mean all this is because of the stuff Jordan was saying? She believed the garbage coming out of my sister's mouth? You've got to be kidding me! First of all, my sister doesn't know anything about my relationship with your mom. She thinks she knows what went on with my relationship with Marquette, but she doesn't know about that either. My sister's in a bad place and she seemed to be lashing out at everybody and trying to inflict the most pain possible."

"Congratulations, she succeeded. I haven't seen my mom in this shape since right after she got clean. I hope your sister is proud of herself," Gabriel remarks bitterly.

"I triggered a relapse?" I exclaim, scrubbing my hand down my face in horror.

"No, my mom is still clean. She's tougher than that, but you're not doing a lot to restore her faith in men, I can tell you that much. What she wants more than anything else is someone that's going to be there, come hell or high water. Unfortunately, you weren't. You called it quits at the first sign of trouble. I gotta say Doc, I thought you had more guts."

My first instinct is to argue with Gabriel to give him a list of excuses as to why I couldn't have done more. As I try to organize a coherent rebuttal, I realize the kid is spot on. Regardless of my commitments at the hospital or the weather emergency, I shouldn't have let Donda close me out of her life, she's too important to me to allow her to simply close herself off and to disappear from my life.

I pull the car over into a parking lot with a roadside coffee stand and shut the car off, and turn my full attention to Gabriel. "There isn't one thing you haven't said to me that isn't absolutely true. Though, I'm not sure I would characterize what I have going on with your mom as a game. It's very serious. I love your mom; I don't see that changing anytime soon. In case you're wondering, I love you too. When I lost Jasmine, I never thought I would be part of another child's life. It's cool you let me be part of yours. I don't know what will happen between your mother and me, but I'm grateful for our friendship."

"What are you going to do to fix it, Doc? My mom can't deal with much more sadness. She deserves better," he challenges.

"Honestly, I don't know. You'll probably be the first to know when I've got a plan. There's nothing I want more than to make your mom happy."

———— • ————

As we pull up to the Pennington property, I notice that

there aren't any of the rigs from the filming crew around. The only vehicle I see there is Donda's. The two college kids she's been working with don't even seem to be around.

Donda obviously wasn't expecting any company, and she's not thrilled to see my vehicle. Her displeasure is clear from her posture. She looks ready to throw me off of the property with just the power of disappointment coming from her gaze. Her displeasure grows exponentially when she sees Gabriel in the front seat of the car.

Gabriel tries to defuse her anger with the polite approach first. "Mom, I thought you were going to be down in Eugene at a meeting with the expert in historical architecture?"

"I was; unfortunately she missed her connecting flight in Denver and we had to reschedule for another day. That doesn't explain why your butt is not sitting in chemistry class right now."

"We had state testing. I finished early so Vice Principal French told me I could go home early," Gabriel hedges.

I grab my lunch cooler from the backseat of the car and hand Gabriel his backpack as I remark pointedly, "After we go in the house and get comfortable, he can tell you the rest of the story."

"Geez! I'm sure I don't even want to hear this!" Donda throws up her hands. "I've got to go take care of my brushes before they dry out. I'll see you inside."

"I guess what happens in Jax's car doesn't stay there," Gabriel mutters under his breath.

"Some things, sure. Almost getting suspended from school? I can't keep that hidden from your mom. You know that."

Gabriel drops his head in acknowledgment. He looks back up at me and takes a deep breath. "Jaxson, this isn't going to be good. She's really, really mad."

I put my hand on his shoulder as we walk up the porch steps and tease, "Well, like you once told me, since she's already mad, you don't have far to fall."

"Somehow, that's not reassuring," Gabriel swallows hard. "My mom has a very long memory."

———◆———

Even after Gabriel and I spend several minutes explaining the events of the day in a light most favorable to him, the atmosphere around Donda is thick with tension. It's so frosty in the room, I half expect to see icicles sprout from the elaborate chandeliers. I'm not sure if Donda is more furious at Gabriel or at me. She just keeps looking at him with tears welling in the corner of her eyes. "Why, Gabriel, why? Of all the people on the planet, why him?"

"Mom, I thought you were in a meeting and I didn't want to bother you. Grandma is getting ready for a big wedding this weekend and she was getting a big flower shipment today. You might not trust Jaxson right now, but I do. He's my friend."

"Gabriel Enrique Whitaker, I am your parent, Jaxson is not."

"And whose fault is that, Mom?" Gabriel responds, his words dripping with sarcasm.

I flinch at his bitter tone. Still, I feel the need to address   Gabriel. "That's not an appropriate way to talk to anyone — especially your mom. It's not my place to get between the two of you. That's the last thing I want to do. If you can't be respectful to your mom and let us work out our differences, I can't be your friend."

"Mom, that's not fair. Why can't you just talk to him? What's the big deal? It seemed like you guys were going to make it. I don't understand! I'm going upstairs to work on some homework. Can't you guys at least try to work it out? I know you guys probably don't see it, but you're tight. Try not to screw it up by being stupid." Gabriel pitches his backpack over his shoulder and stomps up the stairs.

For a few moments, Donda and I sit in stunned silence as we listen to Gabriel slam a door in the distance. In general, Gabriel's a low-key kid. He can say a lot with a few well-chosen words, so for him to have an outburst at all is pretty unusual.

"It would seem he has an opinion about our relationship," Donda observes dryly.

I wince as I hear music filtering through the ceiling. That can't be good for his ears, but I remember doing the same thing when I was a teenager.

"So it would seem." I could've left it at that, but I elect not to play it safe. This may be my only opening to say what I really want to. I decide to lay all my cards on the table. It can't be much worse than it's been the last few weeks. I move to an ottoman sitting in front of the couch where Donda is seated. I sit squarely in front of her so I'm looking at her face-to-face. "Donda, he is not the only one that has an opinion about our relationship. I'm still not sure exactly what happened, but I gather it has something to do with my sister. I want you to know that her opinion of us has nothing to do with how I feel about you. If I haven't made it clear enough, I love you. I also love your son. If my sister continues to be the Queen of the Prigs over this, she can just go back to New York. I don't need that kind of crap. She just needs to grow up and realize my past is not my future."

Turning her face away to hide her tears, Donda replies. "I've learned the hard way that I can love someone and still tear apart a family, I'm not sure I'm ready to do that to you. Yvette needs you and your sister right now more than anything in the world. The two of you need to pull together. You don't need me in the middle of you. Maybe it's too late for the two of us — there might just be too much pain in our past to overcome."

I lean forward and rest my forehead against hers. "What about you and Gabriel, don't you deserve to be happy?"

"Gabriel deserves all the happiness in the world. Me? Not so much. I think I've screwed enough people over in my life that I might not have any good karma left."

"We'll have to agree to disagree. Many of the things that happened to you were never your fault. The ones which were your fault were a reaction to the crap you'd already gone through. I don't know if you use up any of your karma points that way. As far as I can tell, once you got a handle on what was eating away at your soul, you did a remarkable job of turning your life around by being an amazing mother and role model to your son. He thinks you invented sunshine, sugar, and all things good."

Donda's whole face lights up. "I'm such a lucky mom, even when he makes me so angry that I could spit nails further than my pneumatic nail gun, I know I am so blessed that he's mine. He has made it so easy to be a good mom."

"What are we going to do about us? I miss you so much it's difficult to concentrate on my job or anything else," I press as I run my fingers through her hair and along the delicate shell of her ear.

"Jaxson, I can't give you an answer right now. There are too many things up in the air in both of our lives. You have to sort out what's going on with your sister first. I can't be the cause of another family breakup. I almost caused mine to disintegrate. I won't do that to yours, especially not while Yvette is so sick."

I expected a lot of things to happen when I professed my undying love for Donda and Gabriel, but this was not one of them. I try desperately to hide how much her words have gutted me as I pull her to her feet and give her a tight hug and whisper in her ear, "If you decide we're worth fighting for, let me know. I can't do this halfway in/halfway out dance anymore. You know where to reach me if you ever make up your mind."

As I walk out to my car, I send Gabriel a text message. I*'m sorry, I gave it my best. I think your mom just needs time and space.*

CHAPTER NINETEEN

DONDA

IF YOU LOOK UP sadness in the dictionary and it has a picture, it would have the expression on Jaxson's face as he pulled away and kissed me on the forehead and quietly left the house without a word. If you would've asked me if I was capable of shattering such a strong man into a million pieces, I would've told you it was impossible. Yet, I watched it happen in front of my face. I want, with every fiber of my being, to call him back and say I've changed my mind, I've made a mistake, it should've never happened this way, I don't know what I was thinking, I must be insane. I wish I was under the influence of some mind-altering substance — but I'm not.

I walk over to the front door and look out of the stained glass. I don't even know what I'm looking for. Maybe I was hoping he would refuse to leave. How ludicrous is that? I practically ordered him out of the house. Why would I hope that he would stay?

Abruptly, I catch a glimpse of myself in a mirrored wall hanging. Strangely, I'm shocked to see the same devastated, shell-shocked expression on my face. I don't know why this surprises me because I feel hollow inside. Anger starts to overtake my numbness as I think about the circumstances as a whole. Why am I letting someone else control my destiny again? Haven't I figured it out by now? Why can't I just allow myself to be happy? I know Jordan is his sister, but — come on — doesn't she have some responsibility to respect what makes Jaxson happy? If we're good, who is she to say I'm not enough for him?

I've never been good at being able to self-talk my way out of an emotional down spiral like this one. Although I can give stellar advice to other people, I seem to miss all the very obvious red flags in my own life. As much as I want to talk my way out of this mess by myself, I know it's time to call in some semi-professional outside help — or at least as close as I feel comfortable consulting right now. Digging my phone out of my purse, I dial Tara's number and breathe a big sigh of relief when she picks up.

The first thing I notice when Tara greets me is that she sounds really tired. Tara is never the loudest voice in the Girlfriend Posse, but this is quiet even for her, prompting me to ask, "Are you okay?"

Tara can't cover the hitch in her voice. "I will be. It's been a rough day. We just got back from the fertility specialist. Apparently, I have an awkwardly tilted uterus and hostile cervical mucus. I didn't realize that stuff could have an attitude, but apparently it does. It makes it more difficult for me to get pregnant. We thought that maybe it was just the issue with my ovaries, but it's a bunch of things. You know, it's funny; when Aidan and I first got together, I was really worried I might get pregnant. I was afraid I wouldn't be a good mom because of my past. Aidan helped me work through all those fears and I started to believe I could do the whole mom thing right. Now that I'm mentally prepared to be a mom, it's like my body is betraying me."

I feel a wave of guilt as I remember how easily I got pregnant with Gabriel when I wasn't even trying. In fact, I was attempting to prevent it, but he arrived whether I was ready or not. "I'm so sorry Tara, I'll just call back another day," I offer apologetically.

"No, don't do that. I just need some time to work through this. I'll be fine. It's not like we didn't know it was coming. We knew something was wrong, we just weren't sure what," Tara insists. "Tell me, what has you reduced to tears, and why is Gabriel about to punch a hole in the nearest wall?"

"He better not be punching any holes in the walls… we're at the Pennington place right now. I can't say I blame him. I feel like punching a few myself."

"Why are you doing this to yourself, Donda? I thought Jaxson makes you really happy."

"I wish I knew. It seems like there's a part of me that has to sabotage every bit of good in my life — like I can only be so happy without destroying myself. I don't know why. It's almost as if I believe all that stuff Kevin Buckhold spoon-fed me about myself. I know I'm not really worthless garbage, but for some reason, I always end up treating myself that way."

"Donda, have you ever gotten proper treatment and counseling for your sexual abuse? You were systematically abused in horrific ways for years. The incest was probably the triggering event for both your eating disorder and substance abuse issues — not to mention the stress of knowing Gwendolyn was being abused and the added responsibility of trying to keep your little brother safe. That's a lot of mental torture."

Even though she can't see me through the phone, I shrug helplessly. "No, I didn't really get treatment for the incest. I'd already done so much stuff around my eating disorders and the drug and alcohol abuse that I felt like the sexual assault was just one more layer of stuff. I felt like everyone had been poking around in my head and body forever. I couldn't deal with any more intrusiveness. What more could they possibly learn about me? I had already bared my soul to half the world. I didn't want to share any more of my secrets. What would it help? It couldn't take away what the Jerk-Wad had done to me. It couldn't give me back my childhood. My first sexual experience will always be forever synonymous with the worst horror movie I've ever seen. I will never forget the smell of his cologne mixed with his sweat and adrenaline, the feel of his hand against my mouth as he tried to silence my screams of pain and the feel of his forearm against my midsection as he held me still in a vice grip so tight I could not get away. The smell of his sour breath as he tried to first sweet-talk and then threaten me into silence haunts me to this day. I can't leave a room without breath mints within arms' reach. The sick part is that it worked — for years it worked."

"That's why it's important to talk it out with professionals and other survivors. Because when you do, you'll realize that you are not the only person who feels like they could have handled it differently. If I'd had the courage to come forward and accuse my rapist earlier through the right channels, it's possible other women might not have been victimized. Can you imagine the guilt I feel about that? I beat myself up about that for so many years. I finally had to gather the courage to let that burden go so I could love myself and love Aidan. If I didn't do that, my rapist would win all over again. I simply couldn't allow him to have that much power over my life."

"You really think it would be helpful to dig all that stuff up again? It happened so long ago. Why should I unbury it all? It's not like I don't have enough stuff going on in my life right now. Why should I give that creep one more second of my time?"

"I wish you didn't have to. Unfortunately, it sounds like your former step-dad is still the loudest voice in your head. Until you can sort that out, you might not be giving yourself a fair shot at happiness. It would be a real shame if you let your future walk right out of your life because voices from your past are overwhelming you."

I can't hold back my sobs any longer. After I collect myself, I ask in a broken whisper, "I don't even know where to start."

I can almost see the gentle smile on Tara's face. "Lucky for you, I keep my sexual assault survivors group in my favorites. We have a meeting tomorrow night, would you like to go with me?"

I wipe the tears from my eyes with the back of my hand as I make my decision. "I guess I don't have anything to lose. Right now where I'm at pretty much sucks moose balls — to borrow a phrase from my sister-in-law."

My hands are shaking so hard that I can barely bring the cup of hot coffee to my lips without spilling it all over myself. Tara and I are meeting in the back of a very nondescript truck stop in the middle of nowhere. I know that no one is paying us any attention in the bustling shop. Even as late as it is, the turnover is high and the waitresses are hustling. The motherly looking waitress takes one look at me as she delivers my chocolate cream pie and asks sympathetically, "You all right, Sweetie? Can I get anything for you?"

I dab my eyes with a napkin. "I'm fine, thank you. It's been a hard day."

"Carol's chocolate pie will cure just about anything that ails you. I hope things look up soon. I've been there, I'll tell you what, pie and coffee is on me."

"Oh, you don't have to do that!" I protest.

"Consider it my random act of kindness from one sister who's been hurt to another. Just pay it forward someday."

"Thank you so much. That's really nice," I remark through a teary smile.

After the waitress leaves the table, Tara turns to me and says, "Don't worry, I was so shaken up after my first meeting that I almost couldn't make it home. It's pretty common to feel this way."

"I didn't know my story was so similar to everyone else's. I thought my story would be weird because I was just a little girl. I thought most people who'd been through this would have been victims like you see on TV, assaulted by some strange person in an alley or on a college campus. I know people like Madison who were taken advantage of in bars or on dates like you were. I didn't realize that there were so many people like me who were hurt by family members or other people that were supposed to love them. It was like listening to variations of the same play read by different actresses putting their own spin on the lines. It was so surreal. To hear it from so many generations was weird too. That one woman was almost eighty years old, right? The woman that brought her daughter, the daughter was only thirteen — even though their stories span generations, they were almost identical. That alone makes me want to curl up and cry for days."

"I know. It's profoundly sad. On the other hand, we've made progress because now we have a safe place to talk about it. It's no longer a secret no one can acknowledge. We can all support each other and collectively use our strength to fight back."

I set my coffee cup down on the table and look at Tara intently. "I know I keep asking this, but, I really need to know. How do you fight back? I'm almost forty years old and I still have nightmares. When Jaxson touches me a certain way or says a certain word or slips and calls me baby or honey, I'm right back to that scared eleven-year-old. Does that ever stop? Sometimes I look at Jaxson and realize what he's been through and I think to myself, he's already had enough trauma in his life, he doesn't deserve to have a basket case like me in his nice ordered world."

"Donda, I could've written those same lines. I had the same arguments with myself when I first got together with Aidan. The truth is, love makes very little sense. I believe we fall in love with the person who is strong where we are weak. If you think about it, it's the perfect plan. In our case, before Aidan, I was completely ignoring the creative, artistic side of me. I pretended it didn't even exist. By doing that, I was killing the part of myself that made me happy. Aidan recognized in order to be balanced, I needed to have the discipline of martial arts but I craved the creativity of dance and painting. He created an environment where I could thrive. He didn't try to change or diminish my skills, he helped me grow them. I think that's how you know you can believe and trust in someone. If they take you as you are and allow you to grow and change without being threatened by your success, to me that is the definition of true love."

"He's talking about making us a family, you know — the forever kind of deal. The other day, he mentioned adopting Gabriel. He's that serious about us. What if I can't rise to the standard of being a doctor's wife? I remember what it was like for my mom trying to fit in with the wives of the dental practice, it was a disaster. They hated her from the very beginning. What if it's like that with me? It's not like I'm exactly country club material. I'm more like a chicken-wings-at-your-local-bar kind of chick. I don't exactly fit into the upper echelon of society. What if they find out about my past? I know that sometimes people even hassle Gabriel about it at school. I'd hate for my ex-fiancé and my poor decisions to reflect badly on Jaxson's career."

"From everything I have seen, Jaxson adores you. He's nothing like Kevin Buckhold. He won't undermine and sabotage you. He's not an emotional or physical abuser like that Jerk-Wad. Your step-dad set out to destroy Gwendolyn. He did nothing to support her with his peers. Jaxson simply would not allow anyone to treat you that way. We live in a whole new world of social media now. Everyone has a past. There isn't anyone who doesn't have to deal with some aspect of their personal history. He chose you knowing your past. I'm sure that Jaxson is prepared for any fallout. From what you've told me, he has his own complicated past he's had to explain to people. This is nothing new to him."

"I think you're probably spot on. Gabriel tried to mouth off to me yesterday because he was angry about what was going on and Jaxson wanted nothing to do with that. He shut him right down. Jax told him in no uncertain terms he was not to speak to me that way. Gabriel seems to really respect his opinion too — even though I could tell that he was furious with us both. Jaxson also made it clear that he doesn't really care what his sister or mom thinks of the situation; he has chosen Gabriel and me. I don't know what to think about that. His mom is sick right now. She needs both of her kids. I don't know if I could forgive myself if I caused another family riff like I did with my family. We're just now coming together – mostly because my mom got cancer. I don't want to screw up anyone else's family."

"You know, I think I have to side with Jaxson on this, I don't think it's you who's screwing everything up. I think it's Jordan who has issues. Maybe Jaxson needs you fighting on his side and maybe he's just too afraid to ask you to stand up for him? After all, the woman he loved before let him down in a huge way and it's probably really difficult for him to trust that you're actually going to come through for him when it counts."

Tara's words hit me like a slap in the face. I take a few bites of my chocolate cream pie as I process her words. Even though just a few moments ago, the pie had tasted heavenly, now it sits in my mouth like dry sawdust. My stomach clenches as I stop to think about how many clues I've missed. How long has Jaxson been asking me to stand by his side? I cringe as I think back a couple months ago to that first morning when we went to go get Jordan at the airport and the dread on his face as he realized we were running late. As I think back on the interactions he's had with his sister, they are nearly all combative and uncomfortable. I take a long sip of my coffee before I let out a deep breath and confirm the stark truth, "I don't know why I didn't see it before, but you're right. I missed it all. I was too busy playing the victim to realize I need to be helping Jaxson fight the battle. It's a wonder the man doesn't hate me by now. No wonder Gabriel is so mad. He's always really good at seeing all the pieces of the puzzle and understanding how they fit together."

"What do you plan to do?" Tara asks.

I squirm in the booth as my stomach flips over again. "Well, I guess I'm going to avoid having strong coffee together with pie and emotional topics. It's totally not settling well." I have to abruptly stand up and run toward the bathroom. I practically ran over the waitress on my way. "Sorry, it's been a really bad day," I mumble as I rush past her to empty the contents of my stomach into the toilet in the ladies room. A feeling of dread washes over me. Since I have battled back against my bulimia, I've done everything in my power not to throw up. It would be so easy for me to fall back into the old patterns, especially when things are up in the air and chaotic in my life. It would be so tempting to have one thing in my life that I completely control. Still, I know even though I start out in control of what goes into my mouth, it would quickly spiral out of control and turn around and rule my life. I can't let it progress to that point.

Although I'm juggling a million balls in the air right now, I need to take a little mental health break so I can marshal my strength to focus on what's really important in my life right now. I'm sure this is all just accumulated stress. Between Yvette's cancer, my mom's follow-up appointments, the garbage with Jaxson's sister, and the trauma of rehashing my past so I can explain it to Jaxson, I've just taken on too much. All that doesn't even account the stress of starting a brand-new business on television.

What if I totally screw it all up this time and tackled more than I can really handle? I'm so exhausted. Perhaps I need to step away for a bit. I should take Gabriel over to the coast for spring break. He likes to go over there and visit the aquarium. He likes to take his sketchbook and get inspiration for his Comic book series. It would be good for us to get a chance to talk and reconnect and figure out how to communicate about what's going on in our lives. We've drifted apart since I started Claim Your Space and began dating Jaxson. I want to let Gabriel know nobody could ever replace him in my life. It doesn't matter if I've fallen deeply, madly in love with Jaxson; Gabriel is still my number one guy and always will be.

Finally, I feel steady enough to get up from the crouching position in front of the toilet bowl. It's disgusting in the bathroom; I can't believe I voluntarily put myself in this position for many years. Unfortunately, there is no way of escaping my twisted, sad past. I can't explain or justify my weird decisions I made. I suppose in a way it was trading one form of pain for another. I had more than one therapist explain that I was trying to make myself less and less attractive to the Jerk-Wad. I rinse my mouth out with some water and stick a TicTac in my mouth.

When I return to the table, Tara's eyes are filled with concern. "Is everything okay?"

"Wouldn't you, of all people, know that?" I tease.

"Usually, I would, but I am not really getting a clear picture of what's going on here," Tara admits, looking puzzled.

"I'm sure it's just all the anxiety from the last few days just catching up with me. I've been running on adrenaline, Red Bull and coffee. Filming has been running a little behind on the project, so now we're in a big time crunch to finish. Mrs. Pennington has guests coming soon."

"Donda, I'm serious. What are you going to do about your personal life? I think you need to get that straight pretty soon," Tara cautions.

"I'll just add it to my pile of things to sort out. They are all knotted together; I don't even know where to start. It's like giving me a scrap ball of yarn. Every place I start to fish out an end of the string to start with, another one pops free. I don't even know where to start with the mess that is my life I've got so many loose ends and none of it makes sense."

"You look so exhausted. You seem like you're going

to fall asleep mid-sentence. I'm going to take you home. We can talk more later in the week after you've had a chance to sleep on it."

I wish I could say that sleeping on it gave me a whole new fresh perspective, and I suddenly figured out what to do with my life. Unfortunately, that's not at all what happened. When I woke up the next morning, I found an email from my station manager informing me that they had entered my television show into a design contest. Apparently, this contest is between all networks and cable outlets and it will increase visibility and ratings — not to mention it has a substantial cash prize for the winner. The only downside is that instead of having two months to finish my project, I now have only three more weeks until the final reveal must be completed. After calling in my staff of art intern students, we decide that we are in a position to complete the project on time with the new deadline, so *You Can Claim Your Space* becomes my first and only priority for the next three weeks.

Although Gabriel is not thrilled with my decision, he has had to make similar decisions for his comic book and website, so he understands sometimes your art has to come first. I hope that if and when I ever get a chance to explain it all to Jaxson, he will understand.

Just as I'm about to prime the wall with gesso for a large mural in the breakfast nook in the dining area of the newly refurbished bed-and-breakfast, a car pulls up the long drive. I'm confused about why anyone would be here because I sent the interns home hours ago.

When I answer the door, I'm surprised to see that it's Yvette. She takes one look at the shocked expression on my face and hastens to explain, "Gabriel came over and did some yard work for me. He was telling me about the long hours you've been working, so I brought you some dinner in case you didn't have any."

"You came all this way to bring me dinner?" I try to make sense of her comments. She lives a long way away. If Gabriel went up to her house to do yard work, he is so grounded. He needs to talk to me before going that far away.

"Oh, I'm sorry I should've explained. I am putting new floors in my place and the finish they put on the hardwood floors makes me cough like crazy. Jaxson thought it would be better if I stayed with him until my place airs out. I got bored because he's been working crazy hours recently, so I decided to organize his pantry. He had tons of this seven bean mix for soup. I decided to make some and ... well you know how that goes, when you make a little soup, it turns into a lot of soup. Gabriel says you like this kind of stuff. He worries about the way you eat."

I roll my eyes. "Yvette, there isn't anything my child doesn't worry about when it comes to me. All in all, I'm pretty healthy. I do have a rather unhealthy addiction to caffeine, but I don't think it's going to kill me. However, I do appreciate the soup. I haven't had a chance to run out and get anything for dinner."

"Well, that's just a blessing. You and I will sit down and have some dinner. I brought soup and French bread. I even brought some of that dark roast coffee you like."

"If I wasn't covered in paint, sawdust and other junk I'd rather not identify, I would give you the biggest bear hug right now. My stomach has been growling for longer than I can remember today, but I've been too busy to eat. Every time I think about getting out of here and getting a bite, something else pops up and distracts me. It's been completely crazy."

Yvette clicks her tongue at me as she chastises me, "You need to take better care of yourself. You have a growing boy who depends on you."

I walk over to the kitchen sink, wash my hands and wet a paper towel to wash my face with, before I sit down at the makeshift table we made from two sawhorses and a piece of plywood. I roll my head around in a slow circle trying to relieve the tension in my neck. Finally, I look at Yvette and concede, "You're right. Some days, it just seems too much to handle by myself. I don't know how you did it with two kids, Yvette; my hat is off to you. Most days, it's all I can do not to feel like I'm drowning."

The expression on Yvette's face is pensive and tight for a few moments before she finally breaks her silence and declares, "I know I'm probably speaking out of school, but I just have to ask, what happened between you and Jaxson? The two of you had more heat between you than a welder's torch. You seemed to complement each other beautifully. I haven't seen my baby's eyes light up like that for years. He was so happy and now he's not. Can you tell me what happened? Nobody can explain it to me."

"Honestly, I don't know if I can explain it either. My best explanation is that I got scared and stupid. I don't have the best history of family relationships. My brother and I don't always see eye to eye and as I've told you, I had a strained relationship with my mom in the past. When Jordan clearly didn't get along with me and she fought with Jaxson, I thought the best thing to do would be to back off and let Jaxson and Jordan have time with you while you were recovering from your surgery and deciding on treatment options. I didn't want to disrupt your cancer treatment by causing additional drama between your kids." My justification sounds lame to my ear, even as the words flow from my mouth in my disjointed explanation.

Yvette just throws her head back and laughs. "Child, if you could get those two to get along for more than a half an hour, you could claim an accomplishment I haven't been able to do in a lifetime. Those two have been like oil and water since the day Jordan arrived on this planet. Jaxson was so disappointed too. He wanted to be the doting big brother, but Jordan wanted nothing to do with that business."

My eyes widen as I process her words.

"I love my daughter, but that girl has been competing against the whole world since she was old enough to string two words together. It didn't help any that things seem to come easily to Jaxson. He was always so bright that he didn't have to put much effort into his schooling. It just kinda happened for him. He's a naturally gifted child, even when he didn't want to admit it. He went through a stage where he just wanted to be a regular kid who could fly under the radar and do what all the other kids were doing."

"Jax? Fly under the radar? Fat chance of that!"

Yvette nods. "Right? He didn't want to be known as a smart kid or even a talented athlete, he wanted to be average, but since you know my boy so well, you know there isn't anything average about him. His dedication to other people is extraordinary, and he's so smart I don't even know if I understand the full extent of it all. He does a good job of hiding behind his 'I'm just an average guy from the neighborhood persona' that sometimes he fools even me."

"Was his relationship with Jordan always this bad?" I ask. "I can't help but wonder if my presence here is making things even worse."

"Well, I think seeing Jaxson with a new woman in his life is difficult for Jordan because she didn't really approve of Marquette. She tried to talk Jaxson out of dating her even before she got pregnant with Jasmine, but Jaxson didn't really listen to his sister because she was still in junior high when all this happened. He figured she didn't really have any basis for understanding what he was going through. Guys always underestimate female intuition, I think.

I smile at her assertion.

"When Marquette went off the deep end and got involved in drugs, which basically led her to forget about Jasmine in the car, Jordan placed a lot of the blame squarely on Jaxson. She feels like if he would've listened to her advice to start with, he would've never found himself in that position and beautiful little Jasmine would've never passed away. In some ways, I don't know if she's ever fully forgiven him for his choice to continue to date Marquette in spite of her objections."

I grimace as I observe, "So, basically what you're telling me is that if Jaxson and I follow our hearts and continue to date, Jordan will basically never get over it and always be waiting for something to go wrong in our relationship like it did with Marquette and Jasmine?"

Yvette nods sadly. "I won't lie to you and tell you it's not the most likely possibility. Jordan has a big old chip on her shoulder that she's not willing to put down. If you don't mind, I'd like to tell you something else too. I don't tell very many people this story but I think it's important for me to tell you."

I tear apart a few pieces of French bread and dunk it in my soup. The pained look on Yvette's face makes me more than a little hesitant to hear what's coming. As far as I know, things are progressing pretty well with her cancer treatments. She did not have to do anything other than a modified lumpectomy and some follow-up radiation treatments. Then again, I've been blindsided by cancer news before, so I'm practically holding my breath as she speaks, "Up to this point I've kept this a secret from Jaxson, so if you feel the need to share this with him, he might find it painful. Use your discretion please. I don't want to hurt him."

My stomach drops to my toes as I listen to the pain in her voice. Up until this point, Yvette has been charming, funny and upbeat. Her shattered demeanor is more than a little disconcerting. She looks out the kitchen window as if she is watching a movie from years ago, I doubt she even remembers I'm still in the room as she starts to narrate a story only she can see, "I can't even begin to tell you how much I loved Roger Smithstone. I met him at church camp and I thought my parents would love him, but they didn't. One of my aunts knew his mama was half white and that was just not acceptable for my parents. We had family pride to think of, or so I was told. It was long ago drilled into my head that if white folks could have family lineages to be proud of, so could we. My parents forbade any contact between the two of us; we couldn't even write letters. Of course, we were devastated and tried every way we could to circumvent the rules. It worked for a while until my mother found a stash of letters from him. Then I was grounded from my girlfriend's house who was acting as a go-between for us. My parents were so upset at his family they threatened to get his father in trouble at his job. I stepped away from Roger, thinking it was the best thing to do given the circumstances."

I nod sympathetically and hand Yvette a clean paper towel to wipe the tears collecting in the corner of her eyes. She gives a tight nod of acknowledgment as she continues her story, "Not too long after that, I met Jaxson's father. I know now that he was probably just a rebound relationship — but back then we didn't use those kinds of terms. I was just looking for someone who would treat me right and fill the void left by Roger. I was too young to understand I was there for all the wrong reasons. I don't think he was a terrible man, I just think we were the wrong people for each other at the wrong time. He wasn't ready for the responsibility of a wife and son. We tried hard, he even tried to straighten himself out in the military and give the marriage a second shot, which is how Jaxson got a little sister. The second go around didn't last much longer than a week and I doubt Jaxson even remembers him being around. I tried to keep him away from Jaxson so he wouldn't break his heart if he didn't stick around."

"You and I have more in common than I ever would've imagined. I tried to protect Gabriel whenever Ricky came around too. Somehow I think I instinctively knew he wouldn't have the staying power he needed to be a real dad. I'm sorry you had to go through the same garbage I did."

"I didn't tell you the story to make you feel sorry for me, I told you my story because I don't want you to make the same mistake I did. Even though I got two great kids from taking the path I took, I can't help but believe that I missed out on marrying the love of my life because I let other peoples' opinion about my life overrule what I knew to be true in my heart. I don't want you to make the same mistake with Jaxson. I don't want you to disregard how you feel about him — just to make other people happy. Lord knows that the two of you have been through enough in your lives to be able to make intelligent decisions about what makes sense for your family. It's not like you're impulsive teenagers or anything. If my daughter isn't happy with Jaxson's decision, that's just too bad. She has her own life to live. I can't make your decision for you, I can only help remove obstacles, and I hope sharing my story with you today has helped bring some perspective. All I want from the two of you is for you both to be happy. When my son is with you, he's the happiest I've seen him since before Jasmine died. I hope the two of you can work it out. I'd like to see the sunshine return to my son's expression."

As I stand to give Yvette a hug, I whisper in her ear, "There isn't anything I'd like better than to make everyone happy again. It's the worst feeling on the planet to know I have two very unhappy guys in my life. I just want to make sure I am making the decisions for all the right reasons this time."

"I understand. Anything that makes those two so happy can't be wrong, can it?" Yvette replies as she hugs me tightly, pats me on my shoulder. "I'll leave you and Gabriel a place at dinner this weekend."

CHAPTER TWENTY

JAXSON

WHEN I DECIDED I was going into orthopedic medicine, I envisioned a more sedate practice where I would be helping people overcome congenital disabilities or perhaps cope with the challenges of growing older. I hadn't anticipated spending quite so much time in overnight shifts at the ER. This is starting to be a really bad habit. I stand in the bathroom of the locker room and splash ice cold water on my face as I try to energize myself after a hellacious shift.

It was insane! Four different complete compound fractures from the same MVA. The road conditions tonight didn't even warrant such a severe crash. This one was purely due to street racing. It was completely preventable. Now, these teenagers will be facing months and months of painful rehab because they had to show off for each other. It makes me wonder if there's any point in doing the same song and dance every freaking weekend. I swear it's like Groundhog's Day. I did almost the exact same surgery last weekend. The only difference is instead of lower extremity fractures, most of the ones in last week's accident had upper extremity fractures. It's such a waste.

Just as I'm about to collect my belongings from my locker and go home, I hear my name being paged over the overhead system. My first inclination is to pretend I didn't hear it. Yet, I know how the paging system works and ignoring it won't help, so I head to the information desk to see what's going on. Much to my surprise, my little sister is standing there. She greets me with a perky grin as she hands me a cup of coffee, "I figured you might need this. Are you free for breakfast?"

Jordan practically recoils at the searing look of fatigue I send her way as I respond, "Sorry Sis, not today. I'm totally beat. I couldn't even stay awake long enough to get the food. As soon as I can get home, I'm going to hit the sack and sleep for about three weeks."

"Does that mean you won't be at Mom's this weekend?" she asks.

"I'd love to be, but I don't know if I have it in me. I've been working so many back-to-back shifts I don't even know what time of day or exactly which day it is."

"Well, I guess it's a good thing you're not wasting your time on that Donda lady, she was bad news — to shamelessly use her kid to get attention — that's all kinds of wrong. You're better off without her."

I scrub my hand on my face as I tamp down my temper enough to formulate a response, "Jordan, this will have to be one of those times where we reach a truce and decide we will never resolve this. I'm not better off without Donda. In fact, I'm worse."

"If she's so into you, then where has she been?" challenges Jordan.

"I wish I knew," I concede. "It's like she's dropped off the face of the earth. She's back to not answering her phone or anything else. Knowing me, I probably did something to tick her off again."

"You won't listen to me, just like you didn't listen the last time, the woman is bad news," Jordan asserts.

I give my sister a quick hug as I take my scrub hat off, "Jordan, look, it's been a long few days. I'm tired and I just want to go to sleep. I'll sort this out another time. I appreciate the offer of breakfast, but being social is not what I need right now. Thanks for the coffee, I'll talk to you later."

⬛◆⬛

As I stand under my shower and wait for my head to clear, I begin to think about what Jordan said. Unfortunately, she makes a compelling case. Where has Donda been? It's not like I didn't lay out my whole heart for her to see. I made my intentions pretty clear. What could she possibly be waiting for? Am I not good enough for her? Is it because I don't have any money? Is she waiting for a sugar daddy like Jordan said? I don't really know. I thought what we had was good, but maybe I've misread the situation. What if she's using my mom's health as an excuse not to commit? Perhaps she didn't like me much to begin with.

I hate being played. Actually, I don't think anybody really loves it, but I seem to have a special gift for falling for women who specialize in playing nice guys like fine instruments in a well-tuned orchestra. The more I think about it, the more it becomes apparent she's up to something. Otherwise, why string me along like she did, making me think things are going along smoothly and then all of a sudden drop me like I'm the proverbial hot potato. Granted, she had a litany of excuses: Her business was just taking off, she didn't want to upset Gabriel's school schedule since he was a new starter on the basketball team, she didn't want to interfere with my success as a doctor, she didn't want to step in between my sister and me or influence my mom's medical treatment. It was always something. What if it wasn't about the small things, but about us as a couple? Why couldn't she be honest with me? She's had weeks to contact me after our little heart-to-heart conversation where I told her how I feel, and there's been nothing but radio silence. I don't even know what it means. Did she reject my declaration of love, or is she's thinking about it? Is she deliberating different options? Is she waiting for the relationship to die a slow painful death without having to end it? I don't know and it's driving me crazy. I don't want Jordan to be right. It makes me angry, but it's becoming increasingly clear she might be.

I close my eyes as I wash the shaving cream off my face. It must've been a few moments too long because I sway in the shower as I nearly fall asleep standing up. Lethargically, I turn the water off and throw some shorts on and collapse into bed.

It seems like just minutes later that my doorbell starts ringing like crazy. When I pull my cell phone off my nightstand to check the time, I am startled to discover I've been sleeping for nearly nine hours. I snag a T-shirt out of a basket of clean laundry that's sitting on my couch on the way to the front door. I don't know who I was expecting to find, but it definitely wasn't Gabriel and my mom together. Apparently this is the day to bring me food. Both Gabriel and my mom have their arms full of food for me. I raise my eyebrows in question at Gabriel and he shrugs. "I learned a long time ago from my Aunt Heather, if I want to eat well, I help her in the kitchen. Your mom's recipes are the bomb."

"I agree. My mom is a phenomenal cook, but that doesn't explain why you're cooking with my mom or even *where* you were cooking with my mom. Last I checked, my mom is staying with me. I know I haven't been getting much sleep recently, but I'm way too tired to figure this out without an explanation," I declare as I try to stretch my back out.

Gabriel grins at me. "Hey Doc, don't you think you should see a doctor about your back?"

I shake my head at him in bemusement. "Yeah, yeah, whenever I have some free time. So, what's the story about the breakfast buffet, which smells amazing, by the way?"

My mom picks up the tale, "Gabriel is quite an accomplished cook; he helped me feed the entire crew this morning. Let me tell you, it's grown to an impressive size these days, but with all the extra help, I think she'll meet the deadline with a little room to spare. She is so talented. I am so impressed with her skill. She puts Martha Stewart to shame."

As I start to put all the puzzle pieces together, my agitation grows. "Mom! Are you telling me you've been hanging out with Donda all day? Why does she have time to spend with you all day, but she can't even bother to return a phone call?"

"*Dude!* Get a grip. My mom isn't exactly hanging out with anybody right now. She barely has time to take a pee, let alone socialize with anybody. Didn't you hear? They knocked like six weeks off of her schedule for the Pennington job so she could meet the time constraints of some contest they entered her in. Some executive somewhere decided to enter her into this thing because it would be good for ratings, but they didn't bother to check with my mom to see if it might absolutely kill her first. I think they forgot she's recovering from a car accident. She's been working nearly round-the-clock trying to get this thing done. I'm sorry if she hasn't taken the time to update her Facebook status for you. Oh wait . . . under her contract, she's not even allowed to do that because all of this is under wraps and top-secret. Maybe if you tried to talk to her you would know."

"I did try to talk to her. I told her where I stand, I was waiting for her decide if we are worth it," I respond defensively.

"I don't even think my mom has time to have coherent thoughts about anything other than meeting her deadline. This time, I don't think it's all about you."

My mom chimes in, "I have talked to Donda and I know she's been doing a lot of thinking about the two of you. She just hasn't had a whole lotta time to do anything about your relationship."

"I'm glad I rank right up there with her top priorities," I remark sarcastically.

"Jaxson Shepherd, you can just check your attitude at the door. If you think your job is somehow more important than Donda's, you've got another thing coming. She's been a single mom for more years than she'd probably like to count and she's trying to start a business with the whole world watching. I don't see you over at her house helping. I see you moping in the corner like a little boy who wasn't chosen to play tag. I promised myself I wasn't gonna try to get involved with the two of you — but son, you need to get over yourself. Gabriel's mama is one of the nicest, kindest woman I've ever met. That actually might be part of the problem. She is trying to put everyone else's needs before her own — including yours. Think about that when you accuse her of being selfish and having other priorities. The reason she's taking it slow and careful is because she's trying to watch out for what's best for you. You might disagree with her methods and motives, but she's doing it because she loves you."

Gabriel nods. "Your mom's right, you know. My mom knows she's made a lot of mistakes in her past. I think she blames herself for things which aren't even her fault too — but whatever. She is so afraid she'll screw up again, she feels like she has to plan and plot everything so she doesn't backslide and cause anyone else any more pain. I'm asking you not to give up on her before she finds her way back to you. She just needs to give herself permission to claim the love you've given her. It'll take her a while to trust that it's real, I think."

Gabriel's deceptively simple request hits me deep. It's a reminder that I'm not the only person in this relationship who has a river of emotional history. It wasn't fair of me to lay it all out and expect her to make a unilateral decision about our relationship. Who am I to be issuing ultimatums?

My mom interrupts my inner train of thought as she starts digging through my cupboards. "Do you want me to make you some coffee? Do you want it black or do you want your fancy stuff? Your machine is fancier than the one at my local coffee shop, do you know that?"

Gabriel laughs out loud at my mom's offhanded comment. "You sound just like my mom. She hates Doc's coffee machine. Every time we stay here, she threatens to go garage sale shopping and get him an old-fashioned Mr. Coffee machine. Don't be surprised if that's what you get for Christmas. I'm warning you, you can kiss your fancy lattes goodbye. You'll be drinking camp stove coffee for the rest of your life. My mom likes her coffee as black as road tar. She tells my Uncle Jeff that if it's not strong enough to dissolve a spoon, it's not worth drinking."

I chuckle when I hear his warning. "What your mom doesn't understand about my fancy frou-frou coffee is that I routinely put several shots of espresso in it so it's just as strong as her truckers' coffee. It just *looks* like it's made for lightweights." I turn to my mom. "I'm so tired today, I don't really care what form my caffeine comes in. If you want to throw whole coffee beans in my mouth, I'd probably just swallow them whole."

Gabriel waves his finger in front of my nose as he teases, "Don't they teach you all that stuff is bad for your health?"

I shrug nonchalantly. "They sure do. They also teach you that medical professionals make the *worst* patients on the whole planet." I swing my body around and sit in a kitchen chair next to my mom as I help myself to one of the delicious looking cheddar muffins. "On that note, I think I'll have a half a dozen of these and maybe a few of those brownies I smell. When I'm done stuffing my face, you and I need to talk about ways I can step up my doting boyfriend routine with Donda without stepping on her toes. You're right, Mom, I totally dropped the ball with Donda. I could've done things a dozen different ways and made it easier for both of us."

CHAPTER TWENTY-ONE

DONDA

JUST. SHOOT. ME. NOW! I know it's going to be a totally crappy day when that's my first thought when I wake up in the morning. Seriously, I thought I knew pain when I was playing basketball at an elite level in high school, but that pain was nothing compared to what I'm feeling this morning. I don't know whose bright idea it was for me to remodel a whole bed-and-breakfast myself while filming it. I want to flog myself when I realize I don't have anyone to blame but me. It was me who thought it'd be a wonderfully creative idea to market myself while I do my first huge remodel. This is so much different from doing a few little rooms in the homes of my friends at a nice leisurely pace. I feel like I haven't slept in months. When I look at my murals to paint them, I see lines where there are none; the lines which *are* there are sometimes so blurry I can't even follow them.

I seriously need to take a break. Fortunately for me, most of my interns are unavailable today because of dead week. Many of them are required to be on campus for the next two weeks for college finals. Although it'll put a damper on my timeline for my project, it might be the break my sanity needs — not to mention my body. I can't remember the last time I was this exhausted. Of course, the fact that I'm running on paint fumes and caffeine probably has something to do with it. Gabriel has begun to bring food to me as if I'm some wild animal in an exotic animal exhibit. He cautiously sets it down next to wherever I'm working and quietly backs away as if he's afraid I'm going to have a feral reaction. Sadly, I'm so stressed out and anxious about this project, his fears are not entirely unfounded. I haven't been much fun to live with recently.

I reach up and touch my cheekbone. It's tender. Oh joy, I think to myself as I squint against the sunlight coming through my shades. It feels like I might be getting a sinus infection. Just what I need and just in time for me to go back in and do all the voiceover narration explaining the more complicated techniques I used throughout the show. That's going to make all of my lines of dialogue in the show sound really crisp and professional — not! I'll sound like Daffy Duck talking through a metal pail. My field producer will be absolutely delighted.

When I told my friend that he could film me painting my murals, I had no idea what it would take to produce a television series. I didn't know I was gonna have to do all this piddly technical stuff at the end. I figured I'd go in and paint my murals as usual and they would do their magic TV stuff and it would be a television show. I didn't realize I personally would be involved in all the magic that is required to make a coherent television production. It's a lot of extra work. If I weren't on such a huge time crunch, I would probably enjoy the process. But, right now all I want to do is sleep.

Finally, I give in to my body's needs and curl up into a little ball as I go to sleep. I guess I shouldn't be all that surprised when I wake up to my phone alarm going off. Thank God I had the foresight to set it before I crashed. Otherwise, I probably would not have resurfaced until Gabriel came back home from school.

I slowly take inventory of my day and gingerly stretch. It's immediately clear I shouldn't have pushed my body so hard over the last weeks. I feel like I'm a hundred and three years old. As I'm stretching, a burst of purple catches my eye. Sitting on top of my old roll top desk from my grandparents is a gorgeous bouquet of succulents with beautiful purple tulips accenting the arrangement. My mom, who is an extraordinarily talented florist, always thinks it's funny that of all the beautifully colored flowers I could choose, I am drawn to the ordered, structural form of succulents. I think they look magical. I can imagine some enchanted place where tiny beings frolic among the world of succulents and wildflowers. It's weird; I didn't even hear my mom come into the house to deliver the bouquet, yet it's her logo on the little gift card.

I slowly get out of bed to examine the bouquet. I am surprised when I see Jaxson's bold handwriting on the note. This is not something my mom wrote at her shop. This is something Jax wrote personally. Intrigued, I open the card only to find a small piece of paper folded inside. His note reads,

I wish I could be there to help fix it all but since I can't, your appointment is at 11:00 today.

Jax

I guess there must be other clues in the note written on parchment paper. My eyes grow wide as I open it up and notice that it's a gift certificate for a massage from a rather high-end spa in town. Personally, I have never gone, but one of the administrators at the nursing home where I work as a CNA, frequently goes there and raves about how good the service is. I have a moment of panic as I consider my options. I'm not sure I have time today for a massage, but as I lean down to put socks on, my shoulders scream in protest. Then again, I'm not sure I can afford *not* to get a massage. Clearly, I need to do something or I won't be able to function today. I guess since most of my students are off the job site today, if I'm going to take a few hours off, today is probably the best day to do it.

***

After I found out the whole story behind the small spa visit, I felt much better about it. The beautiful aesthetician who gave me my facial and tames my unruly eyebrows into beautiful arches accidentally lets it slip that Yvette used to sing with her in the church choir and is one of her favorite people. If it weren't for Yvette's advice and encouragement, she would've never gathered the courage to move to a new city and open her own day spa, so she was grateful for the opportunity to pay her back for her mentorship. When I first got the gift certificate, I felt really guilty because I know Jaxson's finances are in rough shape right now. I'd hate to think that he was choosing to spend his money on something as extravagant as this even though it's been the single nicest lunch break I've ever been on in my life. Even though it seemed like a foolish waste of time in my insanely busy week, I am really glad I took the time to pamper myself. I feel like a whole new woman. If I'm ever lucky enough to get rich and famous, I want to make a habit of coming here.

As I try to pull out my credit card to pay a tip, Sophia pushes my hand away and says, "As Mrs. Shepherd's friend, your money is no good here. I have something here for you. I'm supposed to tell you that your day isn't over yet." She takes one look at the panicked expression on my face and lets out a light peal of laughter as she pats me on the shoulder sympathetically, "Come now, it can't be so bad. You've had fun so far. I've met Mrs. Shepherd's son, that man gives a whole new meaning to the word hot. Girl, if you don't want to take him to lunch, I will —" she threatens.

I look at my clock on my cell phone and sigh. "It's just that I have a ton of stuff to do today. I don't really have all day to play hooky."

Sophia looks at me and winks. "Sometimes, you need to prioritize. If that man were mine, I would make him my top priority."

Closing the calendar app on my phone, I suddenly make a decision. I slip my phone in my pocket and take the card from her. "I know good advice when I hear it. Sometimes it takes me a little while to sit up and take notice, but I'm listening now. I'm going to go have lunch with my man before I screw it all up and manage to lose what I've got. Thanks for making me feel like an amazing human being again. Jaxson might actually remember why he fell in love with me, thanks to you."

As I'm driving to the restaurant, I feel better than I've felt in ages and I'm in the mood to celebrate with music. I'm trying to flip through the channels to find some good 80s music, when a local news report comes on. It must be a mistake. I couldn't have heard Kevin Buckhold's name — that slime-ball isn't due to come up for parole for ten years at least, why are they talking about it now? Dread sets in as I hear the context of the report, apparently a member of his legal team might have had a conflict of interest and now he and a bunch of former clients of his law office are trying to get new trials. *Crap!* How many chances does that jerk get? Why does he get to keep haunting my life?

It's a good thing Jaxson chose a restaurant close to the spa, because at this point I wouldn't have been able to drive much further without crashing my car again. I'm shaking so violently I can barely pull my keys out of my ignition. For a moment, I sit behind my steering wheel and simply try to catch my breath. Just when I believe I've started to bury the Jerk-Wad so deep in my past he can't escape, he always finds a way into my life to contaminate it. It pisses me off so much.

All the lovely deep tissue massage done to relax me is being wasted as my face and jaw are brick solid with tension. I consciously make an effort to relax because if I don't, I'll crack my teeth. It's as simple as that. I thought my days of letting him affect me this much were over, but obviously not. If hearing his name on the news is enough to make my blood boil, I can't imagine what it'll be like if he gets to go ahead with another trial. I'm disgusted with myself when I realize big tears are rolling down my face. I hate that he has this much control over me!

Suddenly, my car door jerks open and I let out a startled shout of alarm until I realize it's just Jaxson. "Are you trying to give me a heart attack?" I accuse as I angrily wipe the tears from my face.

"No, I was trying to see if you were okay," Jaxson explains as he starts to gently probe my extremities. "What's wrong? Are you hurt anywhere?"

I try to avoid his probing fingers because every joint in my body hurts from the intensive labor I've been doing in the last few days. "Yes, I'm hurt, but not from anything you think it is. I've been working crazy hours and I sometimes forget I'm not a teenager anymore. I just got some unhappy news over the radio about the Jerk-Wad. I don't even know what to think about it yet. I don't know what it means for me — or Gabriel for that matter. I don't want to let that sick jerk anywhere near my son. Who knows, maybe we need to move to the middle of Alaska or Antarctica. I don't freakin' know. I'm tired of letting the man ruin my life."

Jaxson does what he does so well and quietly collects me into a warm embrace and holds me there for several minutes until I can stop shaking and simply breathe. Once I've calmed down and I can take full breaths again without trembling like a leaf, Jaxson asks me, "Donda, when was the last time you fed yourself a decent meal?"

I sigh. "Honestly? It was the last time your mom came over and fed me. Can I tell you that your mom is one of the most amazing human beings in the whole wide world? I totally love her."

Jaxson grins. "The feeling is mutual. My mom thinks you are the total bomb. The first thing we're going to do is get some decent food in us. I feel like I have been running on coffee and energy drinks for days. I must've ticked off my Chief Resident, because he's been calling me in for every back-to-back shift there is available. I haven't even had time to heat up a TV dinner recently. We can sort out whatever we need to sort out after we've eaten. Sound like a game plan to you?"

The smells coming out of the little café are amazing and my stomach growls audibly. I grimace slightly. "I suppose that's my answer for you. Food apparently is my first priority."

I carefully scoop up the last bite of chocolate lava cake and savor it. I try not to moan too loudly and disrupt the whole restaurant. A girl could develop a pretty serious love affair with these desserts. I almost hate to move on to the heavy, serious stuff we need to get to today. Still, I know if we don't work through the serious parts of our relationship, there's no hope for us. We've been avoiding each other far too long. Simply staying apart and not answering telephone calls and texts hasn't solved anything for either of us. I know we'll have to hash it out one painful memory at a time.

Jaxson and I spend a few moments awkwardly looking at each other not knowing where to begin our conversation. He looks a little worse for the wear, and I suspect he probably thinks the same of me even though I spent the morning being pampered at his request. Finally, we start speaking at the same time. He motions me to go ahead as he concedes, "Ladies first."

I nod curtly. "I appreciate that. Thank you." I fiddle with the fringe on the funky shawl I'm wearing as I struggle to find the words I need to say. "I don't even know where to start — I'm a hard person to love. I get too focused on doing everything correctly and not hurting anyone's feelings and I forget to live in the moment and appreciate what I've got in front of me. I'm sorry I pushed you away."

Jaxson interrupts my apology with one of his own, "It wouldn't have been so easy for you to push me away if I wasn't being a stubborn moron. I'm sorry I put you in the position of having to choose between our relationship and balancing the rest of your life. I should've been helping you instead of spending all my time pouting by myself. Relationships are about teamwork and being there for each other, and I completely missed the bus on this one."

Even though I feel a sense of relief about being able to talk about all this stuff, I'm still frustrated and angry about the amount of time we wasted by being emotional idiots. "So, we're both sorry and new-agey aware and in touch with our feelings just like we're supposed to be, but where does that leave us?" I ask, as I take a long drink of my green tea. Gabriel swears it's good for me. Unfortunately, I still think it tastes like grass.

Jaxson reaches across the table and grabs my hands between his. "Donda, I can't pinpoint the moment I fell in love with you, but somewhere along the line I did. You bring a smile to my face and make it fun for me to get up every morning even when the rest of my day sucks. I love your offbeat sense of humor and your generous heart. Even when I tried not to think about you, I couldn't keep you out of my mind. You've become a part of my life. I don't want it any other way. I want to be your partner, your teammate and your knight in shining armor. I know you really don't believe in most of these things because you've been let down before, but I'd like to restore your faith."

I always roll my eyes at Heather, Madison and Tara when they talk poetically about how romantic and gushy their boyfriends or husbands were and how it made them feel all soft and mushy inside. I always thought love was a bunch of made up hype greeting card companies made up so they can sell greeting cards and flowers for holidays like Valentine's Day, wedding anniversaries and birthdays. Now that I'm on the receiving end of such words, I'm beginning to reevaluate my position. I'll admit I'm all gooey and melty on the inside too. I clear my throat as I struggle to collect my thoughts and respond, "Jaxson, I know I haven't acted like it much, but I am happier with you than I've ever been and even though I try to hold it all together and act really tough, I'd like to have my own personal knight in shining armor — especially if he's you. I love you, Jaxson Shepherd."

Jaxson gives me a devastatingly sexy smile as he stands up and walks over to my side of the table and pulls me to my feet. He lowers his mouth to mine and whispers before he kisses me deeply, "Happy to oblige for now and the rest of your life if you'll let me."

By the time he pulls away from the kiss, I'm weak-kneed for a whole other reason than I was before I came into the restaurant. Unfortunately, I'm unable to hide the expression which crosses my face as a random thought crosses my mind and Jaxson is quick to pick up on my emotions. "I was hoping for a better reaction than that," he remarks with concern.

I shake my head as I sit back down and hold his hands between mine as I tried to explain, "No, it's nothing you did. It's just my past resurfacing and swallowing almost every moment of happiness I ever have. I don't know why this always happens. It's so frustrating. I wish I could tell people how this effects my life, even years after it happened!" I lament as I practically vibrate with frustration. "Can you believe it? This guy might get another chance to be free because of some stupid technicality that doesn't have anything to do with what he did? Isn't it insane? Nobody cares about what actually happened to me, my mom, my brother or anyone else? Who knows who else he did this to. Nobody cares about what a monster he is! All they care about is some stupid procedure somewhere."

Jaxson squeezes my hands in support. He is silent for a few moments and I can tell he's thinking about the situation because he has the same thoughtful expression on his face Gabriel gets when he's trying to solve a complex math problem. Finally he says, "Before you say anything, please think about the whole situation first. I don't want to offend you, but I think there might be a solution in what you said. It won't be easy, but it might give you a voice and a way to fight back."

A feeling of dread fills me as I hear his words but

he strokes my cheek and says, "Remember, I'm right beside you. I will have your back throughout this. You've also got some powerful friends and allies in your fight. They won't let you down, you know that."

"So, what do you think we should do? So far, he seems to be the one holding all the cards. He's playing with me like a puppet."

"From what you've told me, people seem to feel sorry for the Jerk-Wad and buy his side of the story. Maybe that's because his side of the story is the only one being told in the media. I think you should get out there and tell your side. Tell people what it's like to live with the side effects of incest and abuse years later. Tell them what it was like to be an eleven-year-old girl shoving your dresser up against the door to keep him out of your room. Tell them you practically faint when you encounter the scent of his cologne in a crowded mall or in church or anywhere else. Or you can share with them the fact that you silently cry if I accidentally call you 'Honey' or 'Beautiful'," Jaxson suggests.

I wince. "Oh geez, I was hoping I was doing a better job of disguising how totally messed up I am."

Jaxson tilts my chin up so I'm looking at him. "Donda, any scars you have are beautiful to me. They are part of who you are. If Kevin Buckhold put scars on you, whether they are visible to most people or not, you should wear them as badges of honor because they made you an incredible human being."

Inwardly, I cringe because I hate the thought my step-dad has left an impact on me at all, but I know Jaxson is right. "What makes you think anyone will care what I think about him? I'm only one person. My credibility was shot over all the stuff with Ricky. Nobody's going to take me seriously."

"The world would be a really screwed up place if we were all judged by the things we did in our twenties. You have done a remarkable job of turning your life around. Look how far you've come. Your business is incredibly successful. Your artistry speaks for itself. Your son is phenomenal and you are healthy and strong."

"Even so, I'm still only one person. He's got lawyers and friends in high places. That's how he got away with so little jail time, remember?"

"Weren't you telling me about the powers of the Girlfriend Posse the other day? Haven't several of you been affected by sexual assault or domestic violence? So, it's not the voice of only one person —"

I sit up straighter in my chair as I lean forward and exclaim, "You're right, it's not just me. It's also my mom, Madison and Tara. Aidan is always saying he doesn't get a chance to use his celebrity status for the right reasons. Maybe he'll use his fame to help me stand up for other victims and give us a voice. I'll be able to fight back for once and shut Kevin Buckhold down for good. This time, I can outmaneuver him. Maybe all of his social contacts won't do him any good this time in the face of social media pressure."

Jaxson leans forward and kisses me gently. He squeezes my hands as he pulls back. He has a pained look on his face as he discloses, "It won't be easy. There is a real downside to putting your story out there. There are going to be people who will twist and turn your words around and make them ugly. I will never forget the people who tried to blame me for Jasmine's death or even the ones who went as far as to say I somehow was complicit in the planning of leaving Jasmine in the car. There were sickos who actually thought I wanted my child to die because I was tired of being poor or I didn't want to be a dad anymore. They accused me of thinking it would be easier to murder my child than to find a babysitter. It was ugly and dark and horrific to read."

I involuntarily recoil from his words as I imagine what it must've been like to read those things. "That must've been awful."

"Those comments from people haunted my dreams for months. They'd call my mother's house and leave messages on her answering machine or write to the newspaper and leave letters to the editor. I second-guessed myself about whether they were right. Was I too busy or too preoccupied to have a baby and didn't deserve Jasmine because in the split-second when I found out Marquette was pregnant, I wished she wasn't? So many times, I wanted to take that second back from the universe and relive it. For years after Jasmine passed away, in the back of my mind I wondered if my uncertainty about her existence was the reason my baby died."

"I'm sure it was devastating, but you didn't have anything to do with her actions. Jasmine's death was all on Marquette. Whether she was under the influence or not, she should've known not to leave a toddler locked in a hot car. It was a recipe for disaster. It had nothing to do with whether you became a teen parent. You've come to grips with that, right? Lord knows I about had a heart attack and said more than a few cuss words when I saw the line turn pink on Gabriel's test. I was probably the last person on the planet who should've been a parent back then."

"You do a great job now, I think you should cut yourself some slack." Jaxson rubs his chin as he thinks. "It took a lot of soul-searching for me to forgive both of us, but I had to in order to be able to move on. I don't think Marquette will ever be my favorite person on the planet, and I'll never love her the way I thought I did before this all happened, but I don't think she ever intended to kill Jasmine either. It was all a colossal nightmare which should've never happened."

"We are like poster children for things that should've never happened in life aren't we? It's like we were explaining to Jordan the other day, we could host our own Hallmark Channel and have a movie a week," I remark.

"I'm sure I've only heard part of it, but the parts I've heard are pretty dramatic. Your family doesn't like to do things halfway, that's for sure. What do you think? Do you think Gabriel would have a problem with you telling your story publicly?"

"No, I don't think he'd have an issue with it. He's asked before about whether he could incorporate elements of my story into his comic book series or his anime. I was very hesitant to allow him to do it because he's my child and I didn't want to share all the gory details with him. Gabriel didn't need to know everything about me. I didn't want to put him through the pain. Now that he's older, maybe he should know a little more."

"Gabriel's feelings should be part of your decision,

without a doubt. However, I suspect like with everything else going on, your son will probably have the most levelheaded reaction of all of us. He is one smart kid."

"I'm not exactly sure how he got so scary smart. I'll also talk to Tara and Madison and see how they react to this. Whether I want it to happen or not, if I go public with my story, the media will drag the members of the Girlfriend Posse into this situation. I know Tara and Aidan try hard to stay out of the limelight unless they need to be there. I don't want to do this if it's going to harm them."

"That's true, these things can spin totally out of control so quickly you don't know which end is up. I can't even imagine what it would've been like if Facebook and twitter would have been around when Jasmine died. It would have been complete and total chaos."

"I don't mean to sound like a wimp here, but I don't know if I'm brave enough to do this. It sounds like I need to be ready for an all-out battle, and some nights it's all I can do to close my eyes and go to sleep." I slump in my chair, feeling less enthusiastic about the idea by the minute.

Jaxson gently tugs me toward him using my hands, he lets go and gently sweeps the hair out of my eyes as he advises, "Maybe the point isn't to avoid the battle, but rather to learn how to fight harder and smarter."

"Jax, I'm scared. What if he wins again?" I ask, unable to keep my voice from breaking.

"Donda, he can't win this time. You've already won. You win because we've found love despite all the crap he did to you. Do you understand? Even if he gets out of jail tomorrow and gets to live in the middle of the Caribbean for the rest of his life, it doesn't matter. You still won the battle. You became a beautiful human being inside and out. You broke the cycle of abuse. Gabriel is one of the finest people I've met of any age. He'll be a rock star in any field he enters. I know you think you didn't have a lot to do with that, but I think you did. Your son is just like you. He is a survivor who cares a lot about the world around him. He sounds like the spitting image of his mom."

I can't control the tears as they slide down my face, "You make a kick-butt knight in shining armor. But with all due respect, I'd just as soon the Jerk-Wad not be able to live in the middle of the Caribbean *ever*. I'd like to do everything within our power to stop it from happening. If I had my way, he would live in some research facility that tests mutant fire ants or something," I offer.

"Well, I'm not sure I can do anything to make that happen, but I am totally on board with helping make sure your story gets told in the most authentic way possible. He's had control of the storyline for far too long,"

CHAPTER TWENTY-TWO

JAXSON

IF YOU WOULD'VE ASKED me just a few months ago if one glimpse across traffic at a stunning woman could completely change my life, I would've said you were crazy. I'm much too cautious and careful for something like that to happen. Yet here I am waiting at the same set of train tracks staring at the same beautiful woman. I still can't believe she sleeps beside me every night. Life is good. It's amazing how much has changed in a few short months. This time when I look over into the vehicle next to me, it's Gabriel cautiously driving his new find, courtesy of Denny. It's an older-than-dirt Jeep. It's unseasonably warm for the end of March, so he has the top down. I can't resist folding up a love note like a little football reminiscent of high school days and flipping it into Donda's lap. Her face lights up when she sees my silly note. As usual, Gabriel watches our antics with a healthy amount of teenage disdain. He glances over at me and shakes his head as he mouths the words, "You're so lame." Of course, he could've said, "You have no shame." I suppose either could've been applicable in this case. I chuckle at his response and give him an enthusiastic thumbs-up.

After Donda and I had a chance to really talk about all the expectations of our families and how they have shaped our lives, we've been able to put the past behind us. Donda was incredibly brave and sat down with my mom and told her the whole story including what happened to Gwendolyn before she told her story to any members of the media. I thought I was prepared to hear everything because I've heard many stories like this through my rotations in pediatrics and in the ER, but nothing, absolutely nothing could have adequately prepared me for the horrific details Donda shared with my mom. After a while, it was as if they forgot I was in the room. My mom has an incredible gift for drawing people out and encouraging them to share what's troubling them and she coaxed details out of Donda I had not heard before. It's probably a good thing for Kevin Buckhold that he is safely housed in prison because knowing what I know now, I'm tempted to do many things which violate my Hippocratic oath.

Donda wasn't kidding when she told me if I was part of her family, I would be part of her extended family. Even though she only has one brother, no one in the family acts as if that's the case. Tyler, Jeff's best friend from college is treated as if he's one of the family. The same is true for Donda's sister-in-law's best friends Heather and Tara. All the aunts and uncles are treated with the same amount of respect whether they are merely family friends or blood relatives.

I got a firsthand glimpse of this dynamic when I took Gabriel out with his collection of uncles to work on the legendary fishing boat of their family friend, William Gardner. I learned a couple of things. First, to call his fishing craft a boat is a real stretch of anyone's imagination and they don't actually fish much. I did learn the group of men is incredibly supportive of each other and they were surprisingly forthright about how difficult it was for them to be supportive of their spouses without being angry at the people who caused the harm. Aidan shared with me how difficult it was for him to sit through the hearing with Tara and not jump up and try to strangle the guy sitting on the witness stand. Trevor recounted having to testify in the trial against the guy who raped and stalked his wife Madison. In a horrifying twist of fate, Trevor's ex-wife actually helped her brother commit the crimes and cover them up. Of course, Denny is still dealing with the ongoing impact Kevin Buckhold continues to have on his wife and stepchildren. Gabriel and I came away from the fishing trip with a new sense of solidarity. Out of earshot of Gabriel, I also received a not-so-subtle warning from William that if I did something stupid to Kevin Buckhold, it would not help Donda. I guess it didn't take a genius to read the thunderous expression on my face. Seriously? Can you blame me, who wouldn't want to kill the slime-ball?

* * *

As I stir my coffee, I wonder why in the world I'm giving this another shot. The short answer is Donda and my mom want me to try to work things out with Jordan. Personally, I don't know if it's worth the effort. I've made my choice and my choice is Donda. If Jordan can't get over it, she'll be the one to go. It's really that simple.

Her email today is baffling. There's not much detail, and it came completely out of the blue. She just told me she wanted to meet me today for lunch. To be honest, I'm not in the mood for a huge showdown with her. If she's nasty, it's likely to be short, sweet and to the point. One of the things Donda and I talked about when we discussed our pasts is that she's not the only one who has a tendency to gloss over things she needs in her life in order to make other people happy. I realize I have let Jordan get away with way too much crap because I was trying to keep things peaceful and not rock the boat between us. Almost losing Donda over it made me realize I'm not willing to sacrifice the most important people in my life for the sake of polite Facebook updates and cookie-cutter Christmas letters. If I can't smooth things over with Jordan, I've decided I'm okay with that.

Jordan enters the restaurant and as usual, all eyes are on her. She's like a beautiful whirlwind. My sister is stunning in every sense of the word. Men and women both gawk at her until she sits down at our table. As she sets down her purse and tote bag, she opens the conversation with a dramatic declaration, "I wish you would've told me ―"

I shoot her a puzzled look. "You wish I would've told you what?"

She lowers her voice to a whisper. "You know, about Donda."

"What about Donda?" I ask, my voice full of trepidation.

As impossible as it seems, Jordan's voice becomes even softer. "You know… her past… it's just tragic."

I nod as I answer my sister carefully, "No question. It's downright horrific. I tried to tell you there was more to Donda than you ever knew, but you didn't seem to want to listen to me. Although, I'm curious to know how you found out about it all."

Jordan takes off her scarf. "I'm still working a little bit for the fashion house and one of my colleagues sent me a clip from a PSA Donda made with some of her friends. I'm assuming they are her friends because I met them the night when I was a complete witch to everyone. I wish I could take that night back. I don't know what came over me. It seemed like everyone was having such a great time being this great big happy family and everyone was all coupled up except me. I had no idea everyone had such serious crap going on under all their happiness. Anyway, my coworker sent me this PSA, not realizing it was anybody I knew. I was shocked to see Donda's story. Are they really going to let the creep out of jail? They can't do that, right? He can't rape an eleven-year-old and get out of jail! That's wrong. The video said he didn't just rape Donda, he beat up her mom too."

"Jordan, you have no idea. The PSA Madison, Tara and Donda filmed only scratches the surface of what really happened. They made it to try to counteract whatever legal maneuver Kevin Buckhold is trying to do to get a new hearing. Although, this particular issue is about Donda's case, they thought the celebrity factor Tara and Aidan bring to the table might help bring some media attention and cause some news stations to pick it up and carry it. Donda was afraid if she made the video by herself no one would be interested in her story."

My sister nods her head sympathetically. "I hate to

tell you this Jax, but your girlfriend has a point. After I saw the video, I got Donda's email address from Mom. Hey! Don't look at me like that! I was nice, I swear."

"Jordan, if you tried to mess things up between us —" I growl, trying to keep my temper in check.

"Relax, it's all good. We've been talking back and forth and she sent me the press release that goes with the longer version of the video and she sent me a long letter about the rest of her story. Jaxson, I have to tell you I'm impressed with your girlfriend. She was brutally honest about things she didn't have to tell me. She didn't sugarcoat a darn thing. You were right. She couldn't be more different from Marquette if she tried."

I let out the breath I've been holding as I mutter, "It seems to me I tried to tell you that. Unfortunately, you were too busy making snap judgments about her to actually figure out she is the most amazing person I've ever met."

"Wow! That's a pretty big thing for you to say. I met some of the people you went to school with. You know some impressive people. Not that I believe in this concept or anything, but are you saying she's your 'one'?"

"That's exactly what I'm saying. After I lost Jasmine, I never thought I would ever find happiness again. What I found with Donda and Gabriel is a different kind of happiness but I'm whole again. I will miss Jasmine every day of my life, but I don't think my daughter would've wanted me to live alone for the rest of my life. I'm going to try to live my life like Jasmine lived hers. Every second Jasmine was here on this planet, she lived her life with a sense of adventure and fun. She thought every new challenge was an opportunity to explore and have the most amazing exciting experience ever. That's how I want to explore life. I no longer want to waste my life playing it safe out of fear that I might get hurt. Playing it safe didn't save me from the biggest loss of all. I'm willing to put my heart on the line. Donda is that important to me."

"Jax, I'm sorry I ever questioned you. I was wrong."

"Jordan, I appreciate your apology, but have you told Donda? I'm gonna lay it all out here. Donda almost broke up with me because of whatever you told her about us. She was trying to protect the relationship between you and me because she didn't want to break up our family. That's how much she cares about me. If you owe anyone an apology, it's Donda because quite frankly, you were a full-on witch to her and she didn't deserve any of it."

Jordan lowers her eyes and looks at her coffee. "Jaxson, I know I can't justify my behavior. I already apologized to Donda, and she graciously accepted. She was far nicer than I ever deserved from her. If I can do anything to help you guys, I'd like to. What can I do to help keep your family safe?"

"I honestly don't know the whole answer. As a former journalist, Madison is informally spearheading the media outreach strategy. I know they were hoping it would hit some better-known viral sites and maybe hit the morning news shows, but so far it hasn't done that yet. There was some sort of continuance in Buckhold's case. Jeff told me it looked good for our side from the way the ruling was worded. It looked pretty straightforward to me, but I guess if you know the way the paperwork goes through the system, it was slanted a bit toward the State's side. At least, that's what he tells me. I guess the ruling buys us more time for the media campaign."

Jordan gets a wide smile on her face and it seems a tad mercenary. I'm nervous about what she'll say next. She leans closer as she confides, "I'm going to let you in on a little secret. Television reporters like to dress nice — real nice. Especially the ones who anchor the network news. They have this invisible competition behind the scenes to get the latest, greatest, most fashionable clothes. I can guarantee you they'll take my phone calls. I go to lots of parties. Most of the time I talk about stuff which doesn't matter. It drives me absolutely crazy. I hate making appearances just for the sake of being there. But … if I had to make appearances for a specific reason and people had to listen to what I had to say to get the goodies they always beg me for anyway, this could be very, very good."

Before I can stop myself, I wrinkle my nose in disgust at the idea. "Isn't that more than a little smarmy and underhanded?" I shudder.

Jordan let loose with a gust of laughter at my expression. "Oh my gosh! Nothing has changed. You always were such a goody two shoes. Welcome to my world, big brother. That's the way things operate in my circle. It's all about who you know and what you can provide for somebody. Look, once we can get Donda's campaign in front of people, they won't care how it got there. They'll remember her story and hopefully they'll run with it in more depth than the PSA's. Maybe she'll get some serious journalistic coverage. Perhaps a show like *48 Hours* or *Dateline* could do some investigating and figure out if this slime-ball has done anything else like this in his life. If he did it to Donda and her family, how many other families did he have beforehand? Did I tell you I've actually met John Walsh? Maybe I could call him up and ask him to profile the slimy pervert?" Jordan seems to disappear in thought for a few moments. "You know, that might not be such a bad idea — but it's been several years since I met him, he probably doesn't remember me. It was part of my college internship. He's probably met thousands of college interns throughout his career."

I hold my hand in a timeout motion against Jordan's barrage of words. "Whoa, slow down. You sound just like Madison. Seriously, the two of you should team up. She would appreciate your journalistic instincts for sure."

Jordan slumps in her chair. "I wish I could, but I have to go home to New York. Mom is doing fine after her surgery and she doesn't need me any more. My leave is up and my job is expecting me to return."

I study Jordan's body language carefully and I realize even though she looks like she could walk off the pages of any fashion magazine, she doesn't look happy at all. "Jordie, what gives?" I ask reverting back to my childhood nickname for her. "I thought you'd be thrilled to go back to New York. I was under the impression you love your job."

Jordan sighs heavily and takes a bite of her chicken wrap the waitress dropped off. "Sure, I loved it when I first got out of college and it was my first real job. I don't love it so much now. This is not what I went to school for, I have a degree. Actually, I have multiple degrees. I have a degree in Fine Arts and a degree in Journalism.

When I agreed to work for Mishka Unlimited, I never dreamt I'd still be in the secretarial pool twelve years later."

"Aren't you underselling yourself a bit? It's not like you're just one of the pool secretaries. You are the Executive Assistant to the designer," I counter.

"Jax, it's just a title. It gets me into parties, I get a parking spot and fancy stationery, but I'm still a glorified member of the clerical staff. I'm not a designer, and I'm not a journalist, I'm not anything I set out to be. I don't have anyone's admiration. The designers don't respect me and the other clerical staff doesn't like me because they think I'm kissing up to the boss. It's a terrible place to be. I'm so lonely. I don't have any real friends. It's hard not to be jealous of what you have here. You just met Donda a few months ago, and you're already tight with all of her crew. I don't know how you do that. You don't know how much I wish I had a crew." Jordan grimaces.

"If you hate it so much there, why don't you come home? I know Mom would love to have you around, she misses you something terrible."

"If I give up now, it means I've thrown away everything I worked so hard for. It would be like admitting defeat. My big plan was to go to New York and become a huge star. So much for my big plans. I guess you're the only overachiever in the family."

"Jordan, if there's anything I've learned in my big convoluted life is that just because something doesn't go according to the scripts you laid out in your mind, it doesn't mean things turned out the wrong way. It just means you and God might be reading from a different script. His might be better."

Jordan sticks her tongue out at me and made a funny face. "That's easy for you to say since everything in your life is looking perfect right about now."

CHAPTER TWENTY-THREE

DONDA

I PICK UP LITTLE Charlie and try to balance him on my hip but as I do so, the button on my jeans pops off and he sways dangerously close to the ground before I catch him and re-balance him on my hip. I turn to Kiera and ask, "Good Lord, Woman, what do you feed this child?" I look down at the button on Kiera's floor which just flew off my Levi's and amend my comment, "Come to think of it, I don't have much room to talk. I can't wait until the doctor clears me to resume running at full speed. Power walking is not cutting it for me. I can't seem to control my weight very well since I hurt my knee. This is the second pair of pants this week —"

I hear a gasp from the other side of the room and look up in time to see Mindy slap her hand over her mouth. I didn't even realize she was in the room with us because she was so engrossed in her book. I hitch Charlie higher up on my hip, walk over in front of Mindy and say sternly, "I thought you and I had an agreement. You're supposed to spill any juicy secrets involving me the minute you figure them out."

Mindy looks a little confused by my challenge. "I know, Aunt Donda. I didn't know this was a secret. I figured you and the Doc would have figured it out a long time ago — you know because he's a doctor and all. I sort of thought you wouldn't need my help on this one."

I really wish I had a Tara and Mindy decoder. Both of them totally talk in riddles when they do their weird projection stuff. I wish they would just come right out and tell me whatever it is they want to say. It would be so much easier. "Mindy, I have no idea what you're talking about."

Mindy blows her bangs out of her eyes as she tries to untangle her earbuds from her mane of curly hair, "I don't know how much more I can tell you without breaking the rules. I tried to give Jaxson a heads up months ago. He thought I was being kooky, so I don't even know if he remembers what I told him. I told him not to judge the future by his past and to give your new family a shot. Hopefully, he can figure it all out from there."

Behind me I hear Kiera give an excited little squeak. I spin around and look at her with befuddlement and confusion on my face. "What do *you* know that I don't know?" I demand.

Kiera winks at Mindy. "*You* may not be able to put the dots real close together, but I can." Keira takes Charlie from me and sets him on her lap. Charlie quickly objects to her decision, climbs down, and runs off to play. Kiera wheels her wheelchair over to the couch and motions me to sit down. After I do, Kiera asks me if I want something to drink. Impatient to figure out what's going on, I decline. I can tell Kiera is slipping into her social worker voice as she asks me questions, "I'm assuming you and Jaxson have a fully romantic relationship with all that entails?" An amused grin crosses her face.

"Duh! You know I have no complaints in that department. I am one happy camper," I answer with a snort of laughter.

"Have you been using condoms?" Kiera asks.

"No, we don't need to because I have an implant," I explain.

"When was the last time you had it replaced?" Keira asks. "I've known you for several years now, I don't think you've had it replaced since I've known you. Aren't you supposed to do those every four years or something?"

Her words hit me like a ton of bricks. "Oh my Gosh! I think you're right. The last time I was supposed to get it done, I had bad strep throat. When I got well, I just didn't think about having it redone. I wasn't dating anyone at the time. I was between jobs and I didn't have any insurance. It didn't seem like it was worth the hassle. When I called the office, and they told me to think about it for a while longer before I had the old one taken out in case I changed my mind. Life got busy and I forgot. I believe the clinic forgot the lapse too because the last time I went in for my annual exam they had me as being protected."

Mindy brings me a Sprite from the refrigerator as Kiera continues, "Okay, so this is the sixty-four thousand dollar question. Have you been having your period on a regular basis?"

I nail Mindy with a laser sharp look. "Are you for real? You're trying to tell me I'm pregnant? Oh… My… Heavens! Do you realize this means I am a single, unwed mother for the second time in my life more than a decade and a half apart? That should show people I can't learn any lessons." A bubble of laughter starts to erupt from the core of my being and I can't stop laughing until tears are rolling down my face.

After I pull myself back together and try to collect my thoughts into some reasonable order, the panic starts to truly set in. "Gabriel will be so upset. He's going to feel like I'm trying to replace him with a new kid."

Mindy shakes her head. "No, I don't think so. We talked about this stuff a lot when my mom had Charlie. Gabriel was a little sad he didn't have somebody like Becca or Charlie to hang around with."

"Great, now I feel guilty I didn't have a child sooner. Why wouldn't Gabriel say something about being lonely? Usually we talk about everything. Why would he keep this a secret from me?" I ask rhetorically, but Mindy answers.

"Gabriel always wants the best for you; he wouldn't want you to settle for just anybody, just so he could have a little brother or sister. That's not the kind of guy he is. He wants you to have somebody totally special just for you."

"I think I've finally found the perfect guy, but what if he doesn't want another child? I don't want him to feel like I am replacing his memories of Jasmine. He is Jasmine's father and I don't want to change that. I also don't want him to feel like I tricked him into a relationship with me through this pregnancy. I told him I had things covered. I truly forgot I didn't. It was an honest mistake, but I don't know if he'll believe me."

"Donda, I think you're worrying about nothing. Why would he have any reason to disbelieve you? From everything I've seen, the man is head over heels in love with you. He thinks you hung the moon. Jaxson's cut out of the same cloth as your brother. He looks all tough and gruff on the outside, but he is every bit as much of a romantic as Jeff, Aidan or Tyler. Those men are all logical and hard on the outside, but on the inside they are tender and amazing. If I were to venture a guess, I would say regardless of whether this pregnancy was planned or not, Jaxson is going to be thrilled because you are this baby's mom.

"Really? I try to keep my emotions steady.

"Really," Keira responds. "One of the first things he told me about you is that he thinks you're an amazing mother and what a phenomenal job you've done with Gabriel. I don't think he'll change his mind when it comes to this little one. So, if he thinks you did such a great job with Gabriel, it would stand to reason he thinks you would be an amazing mom for his own child. I don't think you have anything to worry about."

"Speaking of amazing moms, this will be devastating for Tara. Why can't it be her instead of me? If the universe were fair, it would be. It seems like I didn't even have to try to get pregnant and I turned out to be and she deserves it probably more than anyone I know and she's the one who ends up having problems. It just doesn't seem right."

Mindy looks thoughtful for a moment, "I don't know the answer to that. I usually do, but this time I don't. I don't think Tara does either, which is weird because she usually knows everything. I was thinking about this the other day though. Originally, Mom and Dad thought they couldn't have any kids so they adopted Becca and me — but then they ended up with Charlie anyway. Sometimes you think you know what's going to happen with your life and you make plans for that and then something else happens you weren't expecting."

I knock on the door to my mom's floral shop right after it closes for the evening. I guess I shouldn't be surprised to see Denny at the door. My new stepfather spends almost as much time at The Flower Petal'r as my mom. He greets me enthusiastically but with a hint of surprise in his voice as he stammers, "Donda? Were we expecting you tonight?" A tear leaks from the corner of my eye. "No, I guess you could say I'm a bit of a last-minute add-on to your schedule. Is it a problem?"

"Why in the world would you think that?" Denny asks me as he places his arm around my shoulder and gently escorts me into the shop. "I always have time for my favorite stepdaughter."

"Denny, I hate to point out I'm your only stepdaughter," I respond with a chuckle.

Denny squeezes my shoulders. "That doesn't mean you're not my favorite. What's making you so sad, Sweetie?"

The gentle compassion in his voice is my complete

undoing. A wave of shame overtakes my body. The sense of déjà vu is overwhelming and I sway on my feet. Denny has to brace me to keep me from falling down. My mom notices the commotion and asks in an alarmed voice, "Donda? Have you eaten today?"

My sense of mortification grows. My family's fears for me never seem to go away. They just keep resurfacing. It's been many years since I've had any kind of active relapse of my eating disorder, but my mom never stops worrying about how much I eat. As I think back through my day, I realize her advice might not be so far off the mark. It has been a few hours since I've had anything to eat or drink. "I have to eat relatively soon. However, this time I don't think that's the issue."

Denny escorts me to my favorite corner of my mom's store. It's a little tropical oasis filled with water features, soothing water fountains and exotic plants. As we sit down on a comfortable garden bench, my mom brings me a warm apple cider. After taking a few fortifying sips of the fragrant, nostalgic liquid, I motion for my mom to join me on the bench. I take a deep breath and summon the courage to say the words I never thought I'd be uttering again in my lifetime, "I've worked really hard not to disappoint you, but somehow it seems to be my special talent in life. I swear I didn't mean to land myself in this position again. It's all kinds of awkward, but I can't say I'm sad about it this time. I'm just scared. I wanted you guys to be the first ones to know officially. Mom, I can't believe I'm asking you to do this with me again — especially since I'm almost forty, but will you wait with me while I take a pregnancy test?" I blurt out, finishing my words in a rush.

My mom's jaw drops open. "You and Jaxson are going to have a baby?"

I nod tearfully. "If my hunch is correct, it would seem so."

"What a beautiful thing. You guys will make a stunning baby. I can't wait. I hope it's a girl. Gabriel will be thrilled to be a big brother," my mom gushes with a huge smile on her face.

This time, it's my turn to be shocked. "That's it? No lectures about irresponsibility and bad timing? Do you realize I've basically done the same thing I did with Gabriel? I'm single and pregnant again. It's like I'm learning impaired or something," I remark with an embarrassed shrug.

Denny gathers me into a hug and kisses my forehead. "What would be the point? If you're pregnant, there is no undoing that. It is what it is. You can only go forward from here. Hey, I saw on the news that they make these pregnancy tests which email everybody and post your status on Facebook, did you get one of those?"

Denny's obsession with technology is well known, but I can't imagine posting my results directly from my pregnancy test. "Honestly, I grabbed the first test I saw on the shelf and an extra one to be safe. Who knows? I might have the newest, most technologically advanced test on the market. Lord knows, the test was expensive enough."

My mom walks over to the floor where I dropped my purse when I was feeling faint. She pulls out the sack containing the tests, walks over and takes my hand. "Come on, let's get this done and over with. You can't make any plans until you know for sure what's going on. I know it's a complicated situation, but I can't help but root for a plus sign on the little stick this time."

Chapter Twenty-Four

Jaxson

I JUMP AS ANOTHER text message notification from Donda blares over my stereo system. Something is definitely up. Donda rarely blankets my phone in texts — usually they are short and to the point or funny goofy memes to help me get through a long day, but her text messages today have a very different tone.

I'm on my way to meet her at our favorite park. It's conveniently located halfway between where we work and we often meet here when we can catch a break in our crazy schedules. It has great secluded walking trails and a beautiful little creek. This place has become our sentimental, private escape from the world.

After I pull into the parking lot of the park, I give the voice command for my phone to play her message over my speaker system and the disembodied voice reads her message out loud, "No matter what happens today, please know I love you and I didn't plan for this."

It's probably a good thing I'm no longer driving as the puzzle pieces fall into place. I have had suspicions about what might be going on for a few weeks now. I wasn't sure whether to say anything because Donda assured me she had it all covered. Still, I'm a doctor and the signs have all been there.

Donda has been so exhausted she can barely stay awake long enough to eat dinner. At first, I attributed this to her breakneck schedule to try to complete her project in time for the contest deadline. When her fatigue continued after her schedule became more manageable, I became concerned. I added more vitamin rich greens and calcium to our diet in hopes of boosting her immune system. Ironically, I noticed the most unmistakable sign so far last night as we were making love. As I was kissing Donda's abdomen, I noticed the faint beginnings of linea nigra. In the context of our activities at the moment, it didn't make any sense, and I questioned whether I actually saw what I thought I did.

Up until this point, Donda hasn't mentioned anything about it and these days pregnancy tests are so accurate that you can almost test hours after you conceive. All right, a slight exaggeration, but not out of the realm of possibility. If all the signs on Donda's body are an indication of how far along she is, she's probably months along and not just weeks. That brings up an interesting question. Why is she just now telling me?

My phone beeps again as I receive a text message from Donda, "I'm on my way. Dweeb was late for their shift. :-("

Donda has given up calling her coworkers by their real names anymore. The administration at the care facility where she's been working as a CNA is so lax about attendance policies, it's a wonder anybody bothers to show up. Donda and I have discussions about her intentions to quit about three times a week. I have a feeling those discussions might become more urgent soon. I lean my chair back and think about all the ramifications this announcement might bring.

I'm in a weird place about this all right now. Even though I've had my suspicions for a little while, I was afraid to believe it might be true. Honestly, I don't know what to think. I've been a dad before, and it didn't work out so well for me. On the other hand, of all the things I've ever done ever, being a dad is my absolute favorite. I miss tucking Jasmine into bed at night and holding her on my chest as I sang her favorite song as she fell asleep. I miss feeding her disgusting looking gray cereal that the kids can't stand but we feed it to them anyway because we think it's good for them — the silly airplane motions, train noises and funny faces to make her open her mouth. My heart aches at the bittersweet memories. I don't know if I'm ready to do this all again. I smirk at myself as I consider the fact that it doesn't really matter if I am ready or not. If what I strongly suspect is true, I'll be a father again in a matter of a few months.

Donda pulls her car next to mine in the parking lot and throws it into park. Through her tinted windows, I watch as she takes a few moments to herself. She appears to be crying. A horrific thought occurs to me. Is something wrong with the pregnancy? Is that why she hasn't told me anything?

I leap from my car, grabbing a jacket from the backseat and go around to her side of the car and open the door. *Crap!* She's not delicately shedding a few tears, she's sobbing violently. She appears to be having a hard time catching her breath. I grab her hand and help her out of the confined space of her car and hug her carefully.

At this point, several bystanders in the parking lot are gawking at us. I grab her purse and stuff it into my backpack as I walk us to a more secluded area of the park. We have a favorite park bench there, which will afford us some privacy. As we continue to walk, Donda seems to calm down some and breathes more evenly.

When we finally reach our favorite bench, I dig through my backpack and toss Donda a bottle of Vitamin Water. It's not the healthiest thing on the planet, but it will keep her hydrated. I offer her some of my energy bar, but she turns her nose up at it. "Feeling a little steadier?" I ask.

"For the moment, but it probably won't last long," she admits. "I'm afraid once I tell you what's going on, it will change everything between us. I want you to know that these last few months have been the happiest of my whole life. I didn't plan for any of this to happen — not that I'm unhappy or anything, I don't know how you'll react to any of this and I just want us to be the way we were." Donda hiccups as a tear rolls down her face.

"Donda. Stop and take a breath. Don't worry about how you're going to tell me, because I think I already know what you're going to say," I confess.

Donda becomes still as a statue. "You do? I kind of doubt it. This is pretty earth shattering news — it rocked my world."

I can't hide my grin. "You know, when I went to

medical school, they taught me about more than just knees, ankles and hips. I'm actually pretty good at this doctoring stuff."

Her eyes widen with shock. "You knew? You've known all this time and you didn't tell me? When did you figure it out?"

"I've had suspicions for a while, but I didn't definitively put all the clues together until I got your odd text messages today. I guess I could ask the same of you … why did you keep it a secret from me? You know I have issues with that kind of thing. It would've been nice to know from the very beginning."

I try to keep a straight face, but it's difficult.

"I never planned on having another pregnancy. I knew I was having some weird symptoms, but the last time I went to see my OB/GYN, she told me I was in peri-menopause and I could expect all sorts of unexpected hormonal stuff to happen. When I started feeling nauseous, tired and cranky, I thought it was just my body doing its female thing. I never in a million years thought I would be pregnant again. Can you imagine? Gabriel is about to be an adult. I don't know if I can start over again with a baby!"

"You know, the funny thing about babies is that they tend to arrive whether we are ready for them or not. We both learned that the first time, right? If we survived it when we were barely old enough to vote, I think we can do it this time," I argue philosophically.

Donda peeks up at me through her eyelashes. "Does that mean you're not angry? Do you actually want to have a baby? We never talked about this. It just seems weird because Gabriel is almost done with high school. What in the world are we doing starting over again?"

"Honestly, I don't know how I feel about this. At first, I was upset at the thought you might be keeping it from me. I had a very bad flashback to the first time I went through this with Marquette. I didn't find out about Jasmine until Marquette was about six months along. She didn't bother to go to the doctor or take care of herself at all. She never told me why she hid everything from me. Her parents always thought I helped her hide it, but I didn't even know. It was one of the reasons her parents always hated me."

Donda looks stricken as she grabs my arm. "Jaxson, I swear, that's not what happened here. I had no clue I was pregnant. I just figured I was getting fat because I wasn't working out hard enough. I thought I was exhausted because I was working too hard. It honestly never occurred to me that I might be pregnant at my age. I thought those days were so far behind me I didn't even have to think about them."

I gather her up into a hug and kiss her temple as I assure her, "I know that. I promise I do. It's just sometimes, the ghosts of my past clash with my present and I forget where I am for a minute."

"I know what you mean," Donda wipes a tear away. "I was so sure you would be furious with me, I didn't stop to think about what it might be like if we treated this like it was good news for a change. I remember how furious Ricky was with me when I told him I was pregnant. For a while, he even swore Gabriel wasn't his. He accused me of sleeping around on him. It was this huge dramatic showdown. I practically had to beg for his forgiveness for having the audacity to get pregnant — even though he didn't want to use condoms and wasn't thrilled about me using birth control either. He accused me of getting pregnant on purpose to try to trap him into being in a relationship. When I look back, I can't believe I didn't see more clues about what a complete and total loser he was. I guess I just wanted him to be my escape from the Jerk-Wad, so I built Ricky up to be this mythological guy he wasn't capable of being. The only thing good to come out of the whole situation was Gabriel."

"I didn't have my Jasmine for very long, but the few years that I was able to be a dad were the best years of my whole life. I think Jasmine would be happy if I got to be a dad again," I   suddenly feel at peace with the situation.

———━━●●━━———

Gabriel scowls at me as he tosses the basketball back in my direction with more than a little heat. "Doc, do we want to stand here and pretend to play basketball all day or do you want to talk about something? Cuz you left your game in another zip code today."

I throw up another lead balloon, which doesn't even hit the net. The kid has a point. I haven't come close to hitting my last dozen shots. My head is in another place. I'm not even sure where to start this conversation or even if I'm the person to have this with him. I'm just trying to relieve some stress on Donda. She is making herself sick trying to decide what to do. I figured I would preemptively talk to Gabriel to see where his head is about this situation. I don't want him to feel like Donda and I are going to push him out of the family, because that's not what this is about at all.

Gabriel straddles the bench on the picnic table and throws his bag down on the ground as he grouses, "If you tell me you're splitting up with my mom, I'm going to be pissed. I thought you guys had it together this time."

I guess I should have anticipated he might view our little family meeting as something potentially negative. When I was younger, I remember dreading every time my mom called a meeting between my sister and me. "No, it's actually quite the opposite. Your mom and I have some good news — at least we think so," I clarify.

Gabriel quietly turns the basketball around in his hands and spends it on his index finger before his eyes suddenly widen. "No flippin' way! You did *not* knock up my mom, did you?"

"I might put it more politely than that, but yes, your mom is pregnant," I confirm.

"Dude! I'm starting to be a little skeptical about that medical school you went to. You know what causes babies right? My mom knows what condoms are. She hides them all over the house for me," Gabriel remarks with a bemused expression on his face.

"Your mom is still getting used to the idea. We didn't plan to get pregnant, but we're not upset with the outcome."

"You planning to stick around?" he asks with a fierce expression. "I'd hate for my little brother or sister to have a deadbeat dad like mine."

"That's one of the things I want to talk to you about

—" I start to explain, but Gabriel interrupts me.

"It's okay, I get it. I'll be out of your hair soon. I'm going to go away to college and I won't even be around. I might even be able to graduate early if I double up on my classes and be able to clear out even earlier. You guys won't even have to worry about me."

I put my hand up to stop him. "Gabriel, hear me out here first, okay? You don't even know what I plan to say. You're so far off the mark it's not even funny."

"I've seen what's happened to my friends when they get new siblings. It's not pretty. My friend Andrew had to go live with his youth minister because his mom's new boyfriend didn't like him."

"I can assure you nothing like that is going to happen to you. I brought you here today to ask you for your permission to marry your mom. I'd also like your permission to formally adopt you. I know you're almost an adult, so I don't want to presume it's what you want. I'd like to officially be your dad if you're okay with that."

Gabriel looks thoughtful for a moment before he asks, "I guess my answer depends on you. Did you make this decision before or after you discovered that my mom is having your baby?"

I have to respect his question because it's a really good one. Fortunately, I have a very honest answer for him. "I started meeting with the artist who's making the ring for your mom even before we had our big blowout at the dance party. I'm making payments on the ring and I should be able to pick it up next week. I started talking to a lawyer about adopting you shortly after we had the very strange meeting with your vice principal at school."

The look of shock on Gabriel's face is priceless. "Seriously? You and my mom were fighting back then. You weren't even together."

"It's true, we weren't talking a lot then, but I never gave up on the idea we would become a family. I never stopped loving you or your mom even though we weren't exactly seeing eye-to-eye."

"Doc, I gotta tell you, that's either completely desperate or brilliant. I'm not sure which. If you love my mom so much you're willing to put that much on the line for her, I would be honored to call you my dad."

"Thank you. I'll be equally honored to call you my son. Now, I heard a rumor that your family specializes in emergency weddings. Is it true?" I ask.

Gabriel lets loose with a snort of laughter as he teases, "I think you forgot something. Don't you need to ask my mom first? You might not know this about my mom, but she looks all modern and tough on the outside — she's really not. When she works with the senior citizens, she watches all the sappy soap operas and love stories on TV. She got screwed over with my dad, so she'll want something totally epic even if she doesn't tell you it's what she wants."

"Great ... epic, romantic, fast and on a budget. No pressure there —" I mutter to myself.

"I'll text you Grandpa's number. This'll be no challenge for my family. You guys will have time to have a European honeymoon before the baby comes."

CHAPTER TWENTY-FIVE

DONDA

I DON'T UNDERSTAND WHAT Jaxson is doing. Our appointment with the sonogram technician isn't until nine thirty. Why in the world are we leaving so early? His obsession with the nostalgic connection with the train that caused us to meet is bordering on a little cuckoo, if you ask me. Yes, it was a cute meet, I get it — but right now all I want to do is have a close and personal encounter with my pillow.

I forgot what it was like to sleep when you're pregnant. Every joint in my body hurts right now — it's like someone is coming in and stretching all my ligaments at night. I don't know if they're trying to make some sort of new sacrificial macramé out of my body parts or what, but I can barely move without wanting to scream in pain. To add insult to injury, I can't even have regular coffee. I don't think Jaxson fully understands what he's asking me to give up. Don't get me wrong, I don't want to do anything to hurt the baby, but I count on coffee to help me think. I'm pretty sure the lack of caffeine is hurting the blood flow to my brain and that can't be good for the baby either. When I reach over to turn off the alarm clock, I just about fall out of bed. I can't believe I was ever an expertly coordinated athlete. Right now, it's all I can do to get in and out of the bathtub without killing myself. I swear this wasn't so hard when I was pregnant with Gabriel. I remember going out dancing when I was about seven months pregnant with him. If I tried to do that now, I'd fall flat on my butt.

Gabriel comes in with a tray of food — of course it's all completely nutritious. I'm about to bribe my son for something deliciously evil and sugary like Froot Loops or Cocoa Puffs. I know Jax is doing his best to watch out for me and the baby. He explained because of my age I'm at high risk for gestational diabetes, but these cravings are out of control. The ridiculous thing is I don't even like that kind of breakfast cereal usually. The commercials for food which is terrible for me like Pop-Tarts and Kool-Aid seem absolutely irresistible. It's crazy.

Gabriel raises his eyebrow at me when he sees me wrinkle my nose at the orange juice, "Mom, you have to drink it. It's got folic acid in it and it's good for the baby."

I shoot him my meanest scowl. "You're as bad as your cousin, Mindy. You guys are in some conspiracy to make sure I never get anything I like anymore. I thought pregnant women were supposed to get all the ice cream and pickles they want," I whine.

Gabriel rolls his eyes. "Gee, Mom, way to sound real mature there. If you pass your glucose test tomorrow, I promise you I'll take you out for ice cream. How does that sound?"

"Does Jaxson have you on speed dial or something for my appointments?" I grumble.

"You probably don't want to know the answer, Mom. The reason I know about tomorrow's appointment is because I'm taking you, remember? Jaxson has to work tomorrow. He's helping with that bone lengthening surgery. He showed me the 3-D model on the computer. It's cool what the technology can do these days."

"It sounds like Jaxson has you half convinced to go to medical school now. What happened to your plans to go to art school?"

"I'm learning there's a lot more overlap between computer technology and medicine than I thought there was. This may be a good way for me to interlace my love of math and science together with art and computers."

"Well, I guess it's a good thing you've got some more time to decide. Maybe you can talk to your school counselor about it."

"Mom, you know they gave up on me a long time ago. They don't know what to do with a student like me. I'll have to figure it out by myself. Jaxson said I should talk to some college programs I'm interested in to see what they have to offer me," Gabriel comments with a casual shrug. "By the way, Doc says he's on a phone call with the anesthesiologist for his surgery tomorrow but he'll be up when he's done to take you to your appointment. He says to drink the juice because the sugar in it will help make the baby active for the ultrasound."

⸺•⸺

The whole time I've been with Jaxson, I don't think I've

ever seen him be so nervous. Even when his mom was going through cancer treatments, he wasn't this twitchy. It's starting to freak me out. Maybe he expects bad news from the ultrasound technician and he doesn't want to tell me. It's really strange though, because he seems to be okay with Gabriel; they're telling bad jokes with a math theme in common. Who knew there were so many jokes which have math as a punchline? I'm too keyed up to figure out whether they're funny. The boys seem to be having a good time at least.

Just as I predicted, we're held up by the train as usual. Jaxson turns and asks, "Aren't you going to turn the radio on?" I sigh heavily as I lean forward to tune his radio to my favorite 80s station. Seriously, his dedication to our traditions is starting to border on Obsessive-Compulsive Disorder. Perhaps he should talk to some of his friends at the hospital. Maybe he's been working too hard and it's starting to catch up with him. Much to my frustration, as I mess with the buttons on his radio, nothing is happening. I glance over at him and ask, "Did you know this was busted?"

Jaxson shrugs. "It's been touchy, I meant to get that fixed."

From the back seat, Gabriel offers, "Don't worry about it, Mom, I'll pop something up on my playlist."

I wink at Jaxson. "You might want to cover your ears; my kid has some interesting taste in music. It could be really good or it could be awful."

"Hey! You always tell me music is an acquired taste and I should give every musician a chance," Gabriel argues.

"Yeah, but I meant you should only give the *good* musicians a chance."

"Like this one?" Gabriel asks as he plays *Always and Forever* by Luther Vandross.

Just as I start to tear up over the emotional song, I notice my name spelled out in a huge banner on the train in front of me. I gasp in surprise as I read the banners on the next two train cars. I am totally speechless. I'm having one of those movie moments. Oh. My. Gosh. There it is! Bigger than life! Jaxson just asked me to marry him on the side of the train. *Our* train. After I catch my breath, I look around the car to make sure I'm not dreaming or hallucinating and that's when I notice Jaxson is holding a ring out to me. It's the perfect ring — not a cookie-cutter ring, but a ring that has me written all over it. It's rough and battered but artistically formed and in the center instead of a diamond there is a beautiful opal stone full of fire just like the ones my grandma used to collect.

Gabriel taps me on the shoulder from the back of the car and prompts, "Mom, you're supposed to say something here. It's sort of crucial that you answer him. Put the poor man out of his misery."

Jaxson looks back at Gabriel. "Thanks for being my wingman. I've got it from here." He turns back toward me and asks solemnly, "Donda Kristen Whitaker, I love you more than I ever thought possible. Will you marry me?"

I nod as tears stream uncontrollably down my face, "Of course I will."

Suddenly, Gabriel rolls down the window and shouts, "My mom said, 'Yes!'" as he gives a fist pump.

Immediately, the cars surrounding us honk their horns and flash their lights.

As the last train car is passing by, Jaxson is placing the ring on my finger and sealing our promise with a kiss. I look up just in time to see the train engineer release a bunch of pink and red balloons into the air. "Oh, it's too bad we didn't catch any of that on film, it would've been so pretty to include in our wedding video," I lament sadly.

I hear Gabriel choke back a guffaw of laughter. "Mom... Really? Am I not in this car with you? Do I not own virtually every type of camera known to mankind? What makes you think I would help Doc plan the most romantic moment of your entire life and not document it on video from several different angles?"

I swing my head around to look at my techno-gadget-genius son as I confirm, "Please tell me you're not kidding. You really have all this on video? Even the big sign on the train? Your grandma would get such a kick out of that — although come to think of it, Denny might enjoy it even more."

"Mom, I've got it covered. There's a high-speed camera and a wide-angle camera on the roof of Doc's car and there are two more cameras in here."

"What if you run out of bits or bytes or whatever?" I fret.

"Mom, these are the cameras I use for my webcast, they all back up wirelessly to the cloud. It's all good. I will even make you a movie quality presentation of the day so you can show everyone what happened. If you guys want me to, I'll make you a website for your wedding."

"Thanks. That sounds cool if it's not too much

work for you," Jaxson replies.

"It's no big deal, this kind of stuff is fun for me, I'd rather do it then have you guys pay somebody to do a bad job," Gabriel responds with a self-deprecating shrug.

━━━●◆●━━━

There are some sensory memories you never forget. One of them is the feeling of the gel they use for ultrasound exams being squirted on your belly. I'm instantly transported back seventeen years to the first time they checked for Gabriel's heartbeat. Even though I'm still not technically married for this pregnancy, the circumstances feel different. I remember feeling so isolated and alone the last time I almost felt suicidal. I distinctly remember sitting in a room very much like this one and having a conversation with Gabriel before I even knew whether he was a boy or girl and promising him I would do the best I could to stay strong for him and telling him I understood that it would probably be him and me against the whole world for the rest of our lives. I remember an overwhelming sense of dread and fear about what was coming in the future.

As the ultrasound technician is calibrating her machine, I watch Jaxson explain the diagrams on the wall to Gabriel. Gabriel is absorbing the information like a sponge asking increasingly complex questions with each explanation. The technician glances over at me. "I'd be polishing off the scholarship applications if I were you; that kid is going places." She swivels her chair around and faces Jaxson. "Are you ready to meet your little one, Dad?"

Jaxson absorbs the word as if it's a physical blow to his body. He walks over, stands beside me and grips my hand tightly. "You okay?" I whisper.

He nods curtly. "It's just been a really long time since anyone has called me that. I guess I better get used to it."

The technician asks Jaxson, "How far along do you think she is?"

"Based on fundal height, my guess is somewhere between fifteen and seventeen weeks —"

I interrupt him as I practically screech, "What? Are you telling me you think I'm four months pregnant?"

Jaxson nods. "That's my best guess — it might be a little more, it's hard to tell because you're so tall. The tech will be able to tell more precisely with the sonogram."

I feel my face grow hot as I sputter, "Jax, if I'm that far along, I probably got pregnant one of the first times we were together."

Jaxson scrubs his hand over his face as he softly chuckles. "Babe, I'm pretty positive your teenage son didn't need to know that about his sibling."

Gabriel pretends to stick his fingers in his ears as he quips, "I'll just add it to the pile of things I know about the two of you I really wish I didn't. You two are worse than watching my friends in high school. Think about that for a minute. Wait, I take that back, don't bother. You'll probably get bad ideas."

Just then, I feel a cascade of movement underneath the ultrasound wand. It feels like a cascade of butterfly wings. The technician grins widely. "Wow! She's an active one. Sometimes that can make it easier to get measurements, but sometimes it can make it a little tricky too."

Jaxson looks teary. "Are you using the word she in a generic sense or are you relatively certain it's a girl?"

"Well, you know better than most the song and dance we're supposed to do here. But you can see from the image here that she's giving us a clear view and although she doesn't look quite twenty weeks, it's pretty evident there is nothing developing in that area. It's safe to say you're going to have a daughter."

"When will the baby be here?" Gabriel asks.

"I need to go in and do a lot of little technical measurements of the bones and the size of the skull to tell you more precisely, but most people like to get the big looming question out of the way first."

"I actually have a more important question than whether she's a boy or a girl," Gabriel asks tentatively.

The technician grins at Gabriel. "Shoot. That's what I'm here for."

I smile to myself at her comment because I wonder if she knows what she got herself into. I'm not sure it's ever a good idea to give Gabriel unlimited access to questions — Especially when there's science and computers involved. It could be a very long appointment.

Gabriel glances at me and then at the ultrasound technician. "Mom, don't take this the wrong way or anything, but I've been doing some Internet research about pregnancy, and they say that at your age, you're considered high risk." Gabriel looks at the ultrasound technician. "You can look for different things like those special folds on the neck, right?"

"Gabriel, I'm well aware of the fact that I'm pushing the edge of old age here. You're not giving me a newsflash I don't already know. They always do a basic set of measurements and if anything is off, then they'll send me back for a much more intensive ultrasound. I'm sure I'll be in the best set of hands ever. Between my OB/GYN and Jaxson watching out for me, they've got the bases covered for worrying, you don't have to. I promise."

"You know I'm going to anyway, because it's just who I am."

"Yeah, I know. That's what's gonna make you a phenomenal big brother too," I praise.

The ultrasound technician is silently measuring and clicking and measuring and clicking. It seems to go on forever until she smiles and shifts in her seat as she pulls something off of her printer. "I don't get shots like this very often, in fact it's probably the most unique one I've captured in a while. I have a feeling this little one will have some personality." She holds up the printout and against all the swirls and bubbles is my daughter's beautiful face and right next to it she has her hand formed in a little baby version of the ASL sign for 'I love you'.

Gabriel's face lights up when he sees the picture. "Uncle Aidan and Aunt Tara will love it." He turns to the technician and asks, "Can I download that onto a flash drive?"

She shrugs. "I don't see why not, if you've got one with you."

Gabriel fishes his car keys out of his pants pocket and pulls his flash drive off his key ring and hands it to the technician. "I was thinking about starting a website for her so I can save all her pictures into it as she grows up. I think this would make an epic cover page."

Epilogue

Jaxson

My soon-to-be brother-in-law just smirks at me as he takes in my outfit for the day. "I'm assuming somebody told you where we're throwing this little party today?"

I tilt my head in acknowledgment as I respond, "I'm aware, but your nephew clued me in on a few things too. I happen to know my beautiful blushing bride is a sucker for big romantic traditions even though she claims they don't matter much to her. So, if she has her heart set on sweet and sentimental with all the bells and whistles of a southern mansion, I'm going to do my best to give it to her — even if it means wearing a monkey suit in a park."

As Gabriel comes around the corner, he is fiddling with his tie with a frustrated expression on his face. "With as many times as I've done this before, you'd think I would have it figured out. I hate these stupid things. Dad, can you help me here?"

His words stop me in my tracks. I think this is the first time he's actually called me 'Dad' — he usually prefers to stick to Doc. When I don't speak for a few seconds, he addresses the stunned expression on my face. Gabriel rolls his shoulder nonchalantly as he explains, "I was talking to Justice Gardner and he says the adoption stuff is pretty much a done deal. I figure I should probably get used to calling you 'Dad' before Kennadie gets here. I don't want to confuse her."

"Kennadie?" I repeat, baffled by his name choice. Donda and I were touched by his offer to choose the name. After Gabriel got a chance to see her on the ultrasound studies, he became invested in everything about her and insisted as her big brother, it was his duty to christen her.

"I settled on Kennadie Michaela Shepherd. It was Mindy's idea to add the change in the ending to ie on Kennadie to make it sound more girly. I like Michaela because it means from angels and I'd like to think your daughter is helping me watch over her. My grandma tells me stories about Mom's dad, the one who drowned. She told me Grandpa Don thought President Kennedy was the smartest man who ever lived and if he had lived through his presidency, America would've been a much better place. I thought Mom would appreciate it if I remembered her dad — besides, I think it's dank. If she decides to become an artist like Mom it totally works; and if she becomes a professional like Uncle Jeff, it's still sounds distinguished."

I reach forward to fix his tie as I try to formulate the words to convey what all this means. "I can't think of anything more perfect, your mom will love it." I swallow hard. "You can call me whatever feels most natural to you, but I have to admit 'Dad' feels pretty great."

Denny comes into the room and rubs his hands together. "Fine day for a wedding. I don't think you could've custom built a better day. This park is almost as pretty as where Gwendolyn and I tied the knot." He turns to Gabriel and asks, "Are you ready to walk your mom down the aisle?"

Gabriel nods. "I am, but Mindy's a little bummed out. She thinks I should walk her up the aisle as the bridesmaid like I always do. She thinks it's bad luck for me to break the tradition. I tried to explain to her I can't be in two places at once. She's not thrilled to substitute her baby brother for me."

Denny chuckles. "That granddaughter of mine has always been really picky about how a wedding should go. I feel sorry for whatever fella she picks. If you thought Donda had stars in her eyes, that's nothing compared to Mindy. Speaking of your beautiful bride, let's go make a few of her wishes come true."

Up until this very moment, I haven't had much of a chance to get nervous. My schedule at work has been beyond insane and Donda's hasn't been much better. She's been handling all sorts of media inquiries about her show. Her network sent out a bunch of preview tapes to agents who handle syndication and apparently her edgy, in-your-face commentary together with her solid design aesthetic is appealing to a lot of people. Originally, the station wasn't terribly optimistic her show would get more than a cursory look but I guess their email boxes have been overflowing with people asking about her abilities.

As Denny and Gabriel go off to collect Donda, I'm

glad Jeff and Tyler are up here with me. Tyler hands me a breath mint and whispers, "Whatever you do, don't lock your knees. It won't look good on video if you pass out." It's true, Gabriel has worked hard to turn a little corner of the park into a world-class wedding venue and he would be disappointed if we messed up his work.

Aidan, Mindy and Aidan's new touring partner, Tasha start to play the wedding march on their acoustic guitars. I can't think of a more perfect setting. Donda and I have walked along these trails so many times over the last few months and now this picturesque place is playing a central part in launching our future. I suppose it's considered unmanly, but I have to wipe tears from my face as I see her come down the path toward me. She looks like some Greek goddess in her light peach colored gauzy gown. I know she thinks she's unbearably fat, but that's not what I see at all. To me, she looks perfect. She is my claim on love. She is the life I always dreamed of and never thought I would find. I know she'll never understand her true value, but to me she is everything.

Jeff hands me a handkerchief as he comments, "Don't worry, brother, I get it. I still feel that way every time I see Kiera. It's a very good thing. It'll help things in perspective when the baby comes."

I nod as I watch Gabriel and Denny help Donda with her veil as they kiss her on the cheek before placing her hand in mine. Gabriel whispers to Donda, "Thanks for trusting me that day, Mom. I think he's a great dad."

We are jarred out of emotion of the moment when a woman with a twin stroller loudly busts through the middle of our ceremony. "Oh for God's sake! You shouldn't be using a park for your wedding; this is government property. Go pay for someplace to get married like everybody else does. By the looks of things, you should have been married a while ago anyway, now I have to explain this fornication to my kids. You should've kept your nasty business to yourself."

I place my hands around Donda's waist to keep her from falling down from the venom in the woman's words, but all of us are too stunned to say much of anything — everyone except Jordan.

Jordan hands her bouquet of succulents and purple tulips to Heather and walks up to the offensive woman and draws herself up to her full height as she demands, "Do we know you?"

The woman backs away a couple steps and shakes her head no.

"Then, I have to wonder why my brother's wedding is any of your darn business. You don't know anything about what brought us to this point. Yet, somehow you feel like you're entitled to ruin the happiest day of his life. You know what? I'm not okay with that. There are more of us than you and I've got some tough military officers and lawyers on my side. I suggest you choose a different path to walk on."

The woman with the stroller puffs herself up and mutters under her breath as she turns her stroller around and takes off, "You skanks are all alike, sticking together."

As Jordan lunges forward to follow her, Tara rushes over and places her hand on Jordan's arm to hold her back. "I know it doesn't seem like it right now, but trust me when I say this really isn't your fight. Things will change for you as soon as you can let go."

Donda releases my hand and walks over to Jordan and envelops her in a tight hug. "Don't tell my brother, but I always wanted a little sister and you are exactly who I envisioned. You're pretty fierce."

Jordan shoots her a teary grin. "You know, I was thinking the same thing, Sis. The world better watch out for the two of us."

After Donda returns to her place beside me, William remarks, "After that little drama, I might just skip the part where I ask if anyone objects to the wedding —"

I shrug as I respond, "Sounds reasonable. Just don't skip the crucial parts, like where I promise to love her until the day I die."

William chuckles softly. "I've been performing wedding ceremonies almost as long as you've been alive and I promise you I've never forgotten that part. I think you're safe. If I did manage to leave out something so important, Mindy would bring me right back in line, wouldn't you?"

When William turns to look at Mindy, she blushes bright red, as she stammers, "Yes, Your Honor, I would — but so far so good with this one."

EPILOGUE

DONDA

As I glance down at my bare ring finger, it still makes me sad. I had to take my wedding ring off because the swelling in my hands is absolutely ridiculous and I haven't seen my ankles in I can't remember when. Forget cankles — my ankles are as big as my thighs. I am so ready to be not pregnant. Don't get me wrong, the men in my life have taken excellent care of me, I am the most pampered pregnant woman on the planet. I've never eaten so well in my whole life. But I am so bored I could scream. I want to be out painting, running and functioning. Unfortunately, the baby is not cooperating with me. There are enough worrying signs my OB put me on bed rest for the last three weeks. I've discovered there's a lot of really bad TV on during the day.

I'm so bored I'm actually cleaning out my email box — that's how tedious my life has become. Among my spam mail, I spot a new email from my attorney and it's marked URGENT. Honestly, I'm not sure I even want to open it. I've decided Jaxson is right. Whatever happens with Kevin Buckhold and his filth is so far behind me he can't touch my joy anymore. I have an amazing husband, a baby on the way and a son who defies all odds. My husband loves me despite all the crap I've been through my whole life. In the end, I have won the battle and I can claim love. I am me and that's enough. Kevin Buckhold can rot in hell for all I care. My finger twitches over the delete button as I try to decide whether or not to open it, but in the end my curiosity wins out.

I quickly scan the email. Usually when I get these things I have to forward them to Jeff to make sure I understand everything, but my lawyer leaves absolutely no doubt this time. Her opening line simply reads. "You can breathe. It's over." She goes on to explain some complicated legalese like standing and harm and the nature of the conflict. It boils down to those two words. It's over.

Holy cow! I've waited a lifetime to hear that. I sit in stunned silence as waves of shock roll over me. It's true. I'm free. I'm not sure who to tell first. My mom needs to know, but so does Jaxson. My mom's probably at work and this is something I should probably tell her privately in case she has a meltdown like I'm having at this moment. So, I'll start with my husband.

Jaxson is down in the kitchen making me chili dogs, of all things, because it's what I'm craving. We finally reached a compromise. One day a week he indulges my craving for junk food and today is my day. I set my laptop down and roll out of bed — which these days is quite a feat. As I stand up I feel a gush of liquid down my leg. *You've got to be kidding me! I'm never early for anything.*

"Jaxson!" I bellow.

He must've heard the panic in my voice because he runs up the stairs and almost collides with Gabriel.

Gabriel takes one look at me and announces, "I'll go get your bag for the hospital."

Jaxson calls after him, "You might want to grab some towels too."

"Anything else?" Gabriel asks as he pauses at the door.

"I need my phone charger," I respond as a contraction hits and I gasp.

Jaxson studies me intently. "How often is that happening?"

"They just started. I was getting up to tell you we won the case against the Jerk-Wad and this happened. It's been years since I've done this, but don't we have hours before anything serious happens?" I question, trying to disguise my panic behind a smile.

"Normally that's the case, but your non stress tests have been a little dicey and your fluid levels are low so I'd really like to get you to the birthing center so we can get monitors on you."

I roll my eyes at Jaxson as I quip, "You're *such* a doctor. This was much easier when no one around me knew what was going on. Between you, Denny, Gabriel, Mindy and Madison I know far too much about what's about to happen to me. I'm freaked out, to be honest. I miss the good old days when I was completely in the dark."

"It's true, the Internet has changed the world of

medicine. Sometimes for the better and sometimes not," Jaxson agrees with a smirk.

"Can I clean up first?" I suddenly feel sticky and gross.

Jaxson walks over to the closet and gets my robe. "Somehow I knew you would ask me that. All I ask is that you carefully hurry."

"I thought we were going to take the other route. Wasn't it shorter?" I question as I try to breathe through another contraction.

Jaxson grips the steering wheel tighter. "That was Plan A, we've had to move on."

"What? What do you even mean by that?" I demand, hysteria changing my voice to a near squeal.

"Mom, it's not his fault. They're doing bridge construction and the whole road is closed. According to Google, this is the fastest way," Gabriel answers from the backseat. "We are about nineteen minutes out."

I dig my fingers into Jaxson's thigh and he grimaces. "I take it that one was a tough one?"

"You have no idea!" I snarl. "I don't know if I'll make it for twenty more minutes. I feel like I need to push. It didn't go this fast when I had Gabriel, I remember I pushed for hours and hours. Something must be wrong!"

"Donda, I need you to try to focus here. Listen, okay? If you can, just breathe."

"Whoever came up with all that breathing crap is full of it. It doesn't help."

"You might be right, but for now let's pretend the

breathing thing works. Try to pant through the contractions for me," Jaxson instructs. He turns to Gabriel and asks, "You got any MJ on your playlist?"

"Dad, you know what happens to her when she hears this stuff, are we sure we want her to start dancing right now?" Gabriel responds incredulously.

"As far as distractions go, I've seen worse." Jaxson explains.

Gabriel syncs his phone to the stereo and my favorite song plays. "I will never figure out how you do all that stuff. I still can't figure out how to get the clock on the microwave to stop blinking," I muse.

I lay my seat back and close my eyes as *Billie Jean* starts to play. My little musical break is quickly interrupted when the car comes to a stop and I hear Jaxson cuss under his breath. I struggle to bring the back of my seat up so I can figure out what's going on.

Jaxson lets out a huge sigh of frustration and announces, "You might as well lie back down. We might be here a bit."

I look out the car window and realize we are at the train crossing. *Our* train crossing. However, the train on the tracks is not moving. As in, standing still. Completely still. It takes a couple of moments for the full impact of that to hit but when it does my brain practically explodes, "I have to get to the hospital! What are we going to do? They have to move the freaking train! They can't do this!"

"I'm sure they'll get it moving pretty soon," Gabriel adds. "This is a busy road, they won't want to tie up traffic."

Just then a huge contraction overtakes me and I'm suddenly massively nauseous. "Help me please," I plead as I start to gag. I throw the car door open and puke on the pavement. As my stomach muscles clench involuntarily, I feel a familiar tearing sensation and I can feel warm blood running down my legs. "Jaxson, she's coming and I can't stop her!" I exclaim before I vomit again.

Jaxson throws the car into park and points to Gabriel. "I need you in the drivers seat, son. Call 911 and tell them where we're at. Tell them there's a doctor on scene, but this isn't my specialty. The baby is thirty-seven weeks gestation. No other known complications."

Gabriel is remarkably composed. He walks around the car and gets my bag out of the trunk, puts it in the front seat next to us and calls 911 as Jaxson scoops me out of the front seat and carries me to the back. Jaxson doesn't even bother to remove my underwear, he just takes out his pocket knife and cuts them off.

Jaxson looks so serious as he examines me that I'm frightened about what he sees. Finally, I can't stand the silence any longer and I ask, "What's going on?"

"Well, the good news is that you won't be one of those women who labors for hours and hours," Jaxson responds vaguely.

"What's the bad news?" I ask as another contraction starts to hit.

"I don't think our deposit on the birthing suite is refundable, and it doesn't look like you'll need it today because you're going to be giving birth right now."

"Right now? In your grandpa's car? Waiting for the

stupid train the pass?" I ask, blurting questions like a rapid-fire machine gun.

"Our daughter didn't give us much choice. It looks like she's arriving on her own schedule. Okay, here we go … On the next contraction, I want you to bear down as hard as you can, she's already crowning, it won't be long."

"I don't think I'm ready to do this, I'm *not* ready," I protest as a strong contraction hits me. Fortunately, my body seems to remember what to do and I get a second wind. All of my energy becomes focused on delivering my precious baby girl into the world. I feel all my muscles cooperate and squeeze with one purpose.

Jaxson and Gabriel start to cheer. "Come on, Mom! You can do it!"

I feel more burning but finally the contraction passes and I can breathe again. I'm trying not to focus on my surroundings. It's hard not to as the sun shines into the car window and reflects off of the gleaming surfaces in Jaxson's car. I can't believe I'm giving birth in a car in public. All of our carefully laid plans gone. Jaxson has been so meticulous about making sure everything was organized and planned, yet here we are. My whole body is trembling with adrenaline and I am drenched in sweat. I wish I could get up and walk. I feel like I need to move, but I know it's not possible. My body is telling me to do something, but I just can't tell what.

"Gabriel, hand me one of those burp cloths," Jax briskly instructs.

"She's got one of those nose suckers. Would that help?" Gabriel asks as he digs through my overnight bag.

"That would be even better. Is there a string of

some sort? I'll need some clean blankets too."

Gabriel hands Jaxson some stuff and continues to dig through the bag. "I don't see any strings in here, but will the cord of my sweatshirt work? It's clean."

"It'll do in a pinch. I'll try not to use it if I don't have to. If the paramedics don't get here in time, it's an option." Jaxson briefly looks up from what he's doing as he provides a disjointed play-by-play, "You are a rock star. Her head is out and I'm just cleaning out her mouth and nose so she can breathe. The next big hurdle is her shoulders. It will probably sting a bit because you've progressed so quickly you've torn. After you get through this part, the rest of it's pretty easy. You are amazing! I think you can do this in one or two more contractions."

"I hope it's only one," I whimper. "I'm exhausted. I forgot how much work this is!"

"Donda, she's so beautiful. Trust me, you'll forget all about how hard it is when you see her. On the next contraction push as hard as you can, for as long as you can."

"Jax, it's not fair for you to tease me that way, I can't see anything; my dress is in the way," I protest. "Does she look like her ultrasound pictures?"

"They didn't even begin to do her justice. You did so good, Baby. She's gorgeous. My colleagues at the hospital are going to be sick of me. I'm going to spend all day showing off pictures of my beautiful family."

My lip starts to sweat as another contraction gathers. Jaxson can tell by the tension in my body another one is coming. "Okay, Ms. Bold, do your thing in the biggest, boldest way you know how."

I take a deep breath and push harder than I have ever pushed in my whole life. It feels like my entire pelvic bone is breaking. I can feel the baby's shoulder pop out. Jaxson steadies her and eases her the rest of the way out. He grabs one of the towels that Gabriel brought to the car and starts to vigorously dry her off. It's frightening I've never seen someone treat a baby so roughly before.

"Doc, take it easy! She's just little. You're going to break her ribs or somethin'," warns Gabriel with wide eyes.

A breathy cry erupts from her and I can see Jaxson slump with relief. "Ahh, there she goes. Maybe she was a little sleepy from her big adventure." Just as he says that, our daughter takes a big lungful of air and lets out a large wail.

Gabriel chuckles softly. "Kennadie Michaela Shepherd, I don't think Dad meant that as an invitation to turn up your volume. I think he just meant he's happy you're around."

Jaxson fumbles around a little more with the blanket Gabriel handed him. He quickly pulls open the snaps of the shirtdress I'm wearing as he deposits Kennadie on my chest. "Kangaroo care will help keep her warmer," Jaxson explains as I get my first look at our daughter.

I gaze at her face in wonderment while Jackson tucks a blanket around both of us. "My mom will be so shocked — she's the spitting image of my mom's childhood friend, Althea. My mom used to have pictures of her everywhere. She was one of my mom's favorite people."

"Genetics can be funny that way," Jaxson comments. "Whoever she resembles, Kennadie Michaela Shepard is about as perfect as they come. Thank you for creating her and working so hard to get her here safely. I know it wasn't easy under these circumstances. I love you. You are one tough mama."

My eyes mist up as I fully process her name. Much to my dismay, everyone around me has been keeping it a big secret until today. I glance over at my oldest child and my heart almost bursts with pride. "Gabriel did you really name her Kennadie? That's more perfect than you know. I'm so happy right now. I can't even be mad at the train. If it wasn't for that train, I would've never found this much love to claim."

THE END

The next book in the Hidden Beauty Series is Jude's Song. Discover the journey of Tasha Keely as she deals with the consequences of fame.

NOTE FROM THE AUTHOR

Dear Reader,

Thank you so much for reading *Love Claimed*. I hope you enjoyed it.

It is so much fun to write about characters who are underdogs. In *Jude's Song*, you'll meet and then usual cast of characters with incredible inner strength.

What if the way the world sees you is not the way you see yourself?

Once former competitors, Aidan O'Brien offered Tasha Keeley the record deal of a lifetime.

There's only one problem. Tasha isn't sure she wants it.

She has different plans.

For as long as she can remember, Tasha has been on stage performing. Now she wants to leave and become the person she always dreamed of being.

Jude Hernandez thinks Tasha is crazy.

He'd give anything to trade places. He's worked his whole life for an opportunity like that.

Can Jude and Tasha see eye to eye and conquer challenges together while making beautiful music?

You'll love this sweet interracial romance with a hint of danger.

Get *Jude's Song* in paperback, e-book, or read for free with Kindle Unlimited now.

~Mary

Because love matters, differences don't.

RESOURCES

If you need help immediately, call 911.

National Sexual Assault Hotline:
1-800-656-HOPE (4673)

National Domestic Violence Hotline:
800-799-SAFE (7233) or 800-787-3224 (TDD)

National Eating Disorder Association Helpline:
1-800-931-2237

Domestic Shelters.org— A tool that enables you to find a domestic violence shelter in your area by ZIP Code or address. You can search by the specific service you need. There are also informative articles about how to help someone who may be a victim of domestic violence or sexual abuse.

RAINN (Rape, Abuse, Incest National Network) — The nation's largest anti-sexual-assault organization. RAINN operates the National Sexual Assault Hotline at 1.800.656.HOPE and the National Sexual Assault Online Hotline at rainn.org, and publicizes the hotline's free, confidential services; educates the public about sexual assault; and leads national efforts to prevent sexual assault, improve services to victims and ensure that rapists are brought to justice.

<u>National Eating Disorder Association</u> — this organization serves as a clearinghouse and a resource guide regarding eating disorders for individuals suffering from eating disorders and the families that support them. They also offer a hotline available from Monday-Thursday from 9:00 am - 9:00 pm and Friday from 9:00 am - 5:00 pm (EST) by calling 1-800-931-2237.

<u>When Georgia Smiled</u> — A Foundation created by Robin McGraw to create and advance programs that help victims of domestic violence and sexual assault live healthy, safe and joy-filled lives. Initiatives include a phone app that helps create a safety plan for use in domestic violence date rape situations, education initiatives for use in high school and college settings and support programs for women.

<u>Afterthesilence.org</u> — an online community and messaging board designed to support victims of sexual assault and childhood sexual abuse while giving them a safe anonymous place to share their stories.

<u>Alcoholics Anonymous</u> — a twelve step recovery program designed to encourage recovery from alcoholism. The website has several resources available including publications and links to local meetings. There is an app for your phone to allow you to find local meetings in your community. This is a worldwide

organization and the oldest of its type.

<u>Narcotics Anonymous</u> — The sister organization to Alcoholics Anonymous focused on treating other substance abuse issues. The website includes a link to an app to find meanings in your local community.

Acknowledgments

I'll be honest with you, this book has been rumbling around in my head since I wrote Until the Stars Fall from the Sky. Every time I would talk about Donda's story with someone, they would look at me with pity in their eyes and shake their head sadly while they muttered quietly to themselves about what a messy, chaotic place my brain must be. The ironic thing is that I don't disagree with them. This was a very messy story to write. That was precisely the point. Incest is ugly and messy. Eating disorders are destructive and can tear families apart. Drug and alcohol addiction can change who you are. The lucky ones find their way out of the mess — and for those victories we cheer. Yet, we can never forget the messes left behind.

I want to thank some people who bravely shared their stories with me and whose influence is sprinkled throughout this book. First, I want to thank Dave for an inspirational conversation we had several years ago about choices you made that almost cost you everything and how you began to make different choices with the help of a twelve-step program. I appreciate your honesty, candor and your fight to make a difference every day. Secondly, I want to thank Richard for all of his advice and attention to detail. I appreciate the touches of realism you enabled me to add.

I want to thank Kathern Watts for being a great sounding board and phenomenal proofreader. I love sending you my chapters because you always get outraged at exactly the correct moment. Thank you Lacie Redding for keeping me honest as a writer and making me better with each and every book. Thank you to my friends on the NaNoWriMo board who kept me company during CampNaNo and who sprinted with me when I was too ill to breathe properly. You helped me power through. I will be forever grateful. A huge cyber-hug to my dedicated beta readers. You make things clearer and sharper along the way. Thanks.

Lastly, I would not be able to do this without the support of my family. It takes something extra special to be the spouse of a writer. My husband, Leonard, is amazing. He can shift from the real world to my book world in a fraction of a second without batting an eyelash and he is my biggest supporter. I'd also like to thank my son, Brandon, for all of his unofficial fictional diagnoses of my characters. I barely even have to preface my conversations with the phrase, "Don't worry, there's nothing new wrong with me this is just for a book…"

ABOUT THE AUTHOR

I have been lucky enough to live my own version of a romance novel. I married the guy who kissed me at summer camp. He told me on the night we met that he was going to marry me and be the father of my children.

Eventually, I stopped giggling when he said it, and we've been married for over thirty years. We have two children. The oldest is a Doctor of Osteopathy. He is across the United States completing his residency, but when he's done, he is going to come back to Oregon and practice Family Medicine. Our youngest son is now tackling high school, where he is an honor student. He is interested in becoming an EMT.

I write full time now. I have published more than thirty books and have several more underway. I volunteer my time to a variety of causes. I have worked as a Civil Rights Attorney and diversity advocate. I spent several years working for various social service agencies before becoming an attorney.

In my spare time, I love to cook, decorate cakes and, of course, I obsessively, compulsively read.

I would be honored if you would take a few moments out of your busy day to check out my website,

MaryCrawfordAuthor.com. While you're there, you can sign up for my newsletter and get a free book. I will be announcing my upcoming books and giving sneak peeks as well as sponsoring giveaways and giving you information about other interesting events.

If you have questions or comments, please E-mail me at Mary@MaryCrawfordAuthor.com or find me on the following social networks:

Facebook: www.facebook.com/authormarycrawford

Website: MaryCrawfordAuthor.com

Twitter: www.twitter.com/MaryCrawfordAut